A TRAITOR AMONG US

A CAPE MAY HISTORICAL MYSTERY

A. M. READE

D0868989

PAU HANA PUBLISHING

Pau Hana Publishing

Print ISBN: 978-1-7355221-7-3

Ebook ISBN: 978-1-7355221-6-6

Printed in the United States of America

ALSO BY AMY M. READE

STANDALONE BOOKS

Secrets of Hallstead House
The Ghosts of Peppernell Manor
House of the Hanging Jade

THE MALICE SERIES
The House on Candlewick Lane
Highland Peril
Murder in Thistlecross

THE JUNIPER JUNCTION COZY HOLIDAY MYSTERY SERIES
The Worst Noel
Dead, White, and Blue
Be My Valencrime
Ghouls' Night Out
MayDay!

THE CAPE MAY HISTORICAL MYSTERY COLLECTION
Cape Menace
A Traitor Among Us

THE LIBRARIES OF THE WORLD MYSTERY SERIES
Trudy's Diary

ACKNOWLEDGMENTS

I would like to thank my editor, Jeni Chappelle, whose guidance has been indispensable in making this a better book. If you're looking for a professional and prompt editor who is easy to work with and a great person, visit Jeni at https://www. jenichappelleeditorial.com. With that being said, any and all errors in this book are mine and mine alone.

I would also like to thank my husband, John, who is always my first reader, as well as Patti Linder and Holly Bolicki, who have provided valuable assistance in the final draft of the book.

GLOSSARY

Cleverly: in good health

Cobbler: a person seeking to imitate those of superior social standing or wealth; snob

Dinner: a meal eaten at midday

Fewmet: (vulgar) droppings of animals hunted for prey

Filcher: thief

Midden: rubbish heap

Pottage: stew

Ruffler: man

Rum dubber: a thief who preys upon taverns and their guests

Sturdy beggar: an able-bodied person who is capable of work but begs for alms instead

Supper: a meal eaten in the evening

PREFACE

In the year 1777 the Revolutionary War was raging in the American colonies, and particularly in New Jersey, New York, and Pennsylvania. The county of Cape May only saw one battle during the Revolutionary War; however, British aggression, foraging parties, and the possibility of military campaigns originating across the Delaware Bay and traveling through the county and on to Philadelphia were common threats.

The residents of Cape May County were, in general, fierce patriots. There were British sympathizers in New Jersey, of course, but although some counties had large populations of Loyalists (those who opposed independence), Cape May County's Loyalists were few and far between. Those who remained vocally loyal to the English crown were often targets of anger and retribution by Cape May County officials.

Many counties in colonial America set up revolutionary committees to provide a network that would organize activities, enforce the laws made by provincial assemblies, and communicate with citizens. Cape May County was no exception. The Committee of Safety was one such committee, and it was tasked with providing executive authority in the county and organizing the local militia. To be asked to join the Committee of Safety was a prestigious honor.

Women played an important role in Cape May County during the American Revolution, as they did in every other county, in every other colony. The women of Cape May County organized a relief society, part of the New Jersey Women's Relief Society, that provided clothing and other assistance to the men in the Continental Army and corresponded with other such societies in the New Jersey colony.

The Cape May County of the eighteenth century was divided into three main precincts: Upper, Middle, and Lower. Each precinct was comprised of a handful of settlements and villages. As a general rule, Upper Precinct was largely Quaker (Society of Friends), Middle Precinct was largely Baptist, and Lower Precinct was largely Presbyterian. It was not until 1798 that the Precincts were referred to as "Townships." The family in the story you are about to read are Quaker, and as such they subscribe to the tenets of simplicity, peace and nonviolence, truth, humility, and integrity, among others. It was common for Quakers to refer to a stranger as "Friend," to avoid most honorifics (such as "Madam" or "Mister"), and to refer to elders, friends, teachers, and others by their first names. (If one was not on familiar terms, the first and last names were typically used, but for the sake of reading ease, I have used first names as a form of address in this novel.)

At the northern tip of Cape May County, on the shore of Great Egg Harbor Bay, was a tiny hamlet known as Stites Point (also known at various times throughout its history as Goldin's Point, Willet's Point, and now Beesley's Point). A ferry would transport travelers across the bay between Somers Point and Stites Point, and there was a way station, or hostelry, adjacent to the ferry crossing in Stites Point as early as 1736; interestingly, there has been an inn or tavern on that spot ever since.

A Traitor Among Us is a work of fiction that takes place in and around that hostelry at a crucial and volatile time in American history.

CHAPTER 1

SEPTEMBER 24, 1777

*I*t was long before dawn and I had not yet slept. There were so many thoughts tumbling through my anxious mind. I did not want to wake my sister with my tossing and turning, so I rose to start my chores for the day. I dressed quickly without the aid of the oil lamp, closed the bedroom door behind me with a soft *thud*, and hurried to the kitchen. I reached for my apron where it hung on a hook next to the back door and tied it over my skirts as I slipped outside.

I stood near the door for several moments, listening. The only sound was the occasional far-above rustling of bird wings as they flew toward the south in great flocks. Cold weather would be here soon. The bird songs I enjoyed in the daylight were absent, lending an unsettling hush to the darkness.

It was not unusual for me to be out-of-doors in the early morning, but this time was different. This time, not far away, I knew a stranger shared the darkness with me. A stranger who did not belong here. I hoped he was still asleep and that I could retrieve my washing tub without waking him. Something in my abdomen flipped over and twisted, reminding me to be quick and silent.

Fog swirled low above the ground. I hurried past the storehouse, which we were filling every day now with more bounty from the late summer's crop of fruits and vegetables, and on toward the barn. The fog shifted, its wisps pulling apart and forming again as my shoes padded along the damp ground. I held my lantern aloft to dispel both the darkness and my relentless worries as I approached the barn that stood nestled against the woods that separated our home from the waters of the bay.

I set my lantern down to retrieve the heavy iron key from my pocket, before realizing with a start that the door was slightly ajar. I whirled around and peered into the darkness that had crept behind and surrounded me, but I heard nothing. Saw nothing.

I shook my head, chiding myself for my silly fears. Of course my brother, Jesse, had forgotten to lock the door.

It was Jesse's job to take the animals out every morning and return them to the barn every evening. It was also his job to make sure the door was locked when the animals were inside the barn. I would not tell Mother or Father of this carelessness, but I would have to mention it to Jesse. For all we knew, a party of British soldiers might come foraging for supplies and livestock in the barn. I wondered if the stranger—Oliver Doolittle was his name, though speaking it left a sour taste in my mouth —was inside. I presumed he was. He was lazy, so he was unlikely to be awake and moving about at such an early hour.

I placed the key back into my pocket and stooped to pick up the lantern again. I stepped gingerly into the gloom of the barn, taking care to be as quiet as possible. I listened for the snufflings and snortings of the animals and was relieved to hear their comforting murmurings. I approached the stalls and small pens, trying to count the animals in the darkness to make sure they were all there, but I abandoned my task after just a few moments. The animals, annoyed that I had awakened them, were making known their displeasure with a series of loud grunts, clucking, and lowing. I moved away as quickly as I dared, hoping their sounds had not awakened Oliver, whom I suspected—I hoped—was still asleep toward the rear of the barn.

I did not relish being alone in the barn in daylight, let alone in the grim darkness of predawn and with the knowledge that Oliver slept nearby, so I made haste, as quietly as possible, to retrieve the washtub I had come for. It hung on the back wall. As I made my way toward it my skirts swished against rough-hewn boards, tendrils of hay that protruded from wooden mangers, and the large crates of corn husks that Prissy and I would soon use to make floor mats and stuff the mattresses in the guest rooms of the inn.

I stumbled as I reached the back wall. My lantern swung wildly in my hand and cast long, grotesque shadows on everything the dim light touched. I very nearly exclaimed aloud, but I caught myself in time and pressed my lips closed.

I reached for the washtub and set it down on the ground with a hushed *thump* as the lantern flame stabilized. I knew there was no hope that Oliver would remain asleep now.

Whatever had tripped me needed to be put away, since I knew I would be blamed if Mother came out and tripped, too. I picked up my skirts and looked down, then gasped.

A man lay at my feet.

When I saw his head cocked at a strange angle, his shirt front slashed in several places, and his eyes staring at me with a glassy emptiness, my horrified scream broke the morning stillness, reaching through the woods and echoing over the waters of Great Egg Harbor Bay.

CHAPTER 2

I could hear Mother muttering to herself even before she stormed into the kitchen. She stood inside the doorway, her hands on her hips and a dour look on her face. "Etta, I thought I told you to put the extra pewter candlestick in the cupboard in the front hall."

"That's where I put it."

"It isn't there."

"I put it there early this morning, just as you asked."

Mother clenched her jaw and I pondered what it would be like to be in a constant state of vexation. Quaker families like mine believed the light of God was in every person, but Mother seemed to forget that on occasion.

"Prissy, did you take it?" she asked, wheeling on my sister.

Prissy shook her head. The blond curls which had escaped her cap swung gently around her face.

Mother let out an exasperated sigh and turned around, exclaiming behind her as she moved toward the front of the inn, "Etta, you will have some explaining to do when I find it. That candlestick was costly."

Prissy looked at me, her eyes round with anxiety. "Don't

worry, Pris," I said. "She'll find the candlestick. And Father's missing shirt, and the utensils, and everything else that she cannot find right now." Prissy looked doubtful.

Jesse, who was only two years older than I, sauntered into the kitchen as I was speaking to Prissy. He took up an apple from the sack on the floor near the back door.

"What's the matter?" he asked, seeing our faces.

"Mother is angry because she cannot find the candlestick she bought in Romney Marsh."

"Where is it?"

I faced Jesse with my hands on my hips, looking, I supposed with a frown, rather like Mother. "If I knew where it was, do you think I would not tell her?"

Jesse shrugged and grinned. "It might be amusing to keep it a secret for a little while. Anyway, I'm off to help Father with the oats. He'll already have been out there for an hour."

"Be off with you, then." I shooed him away with my apron. He smiled at us again and left, the door closing with a loud *thwack* behind him. Prissy hunched her shoulders at the sound.

Mother came back into the kitchen several minutes later. "I cannot find the thing. Perhaps one of the guests took it upstairs before leaving this morning."

There were currently three guests in residence at our family's inn. I had found them to be unobtrusive, quiet, and little trouble. If any of the men had taken the candlestick upstairs, each would surely have returned it before leaving for the day on his personal business. I suggested as much to Mother.

"Just the same, go look in the rooms."

I bustled up the steep, narrow stairs to the second floor, where all the guests' rooms were located.

I knocked on the first door just in case the guest was still inside. Hearing no voice, I used my key to open the door. Glancing around, I didn't see the missing pewter candlestick.

I did the same thing with the other rooms. None of the

guests had left a candlestick behind in his room, and it was not in any of the unoccupied rooms. I returned to the parlor. "The candlestick is not upstairs, Mother."

"Upon my word, Antoinetta, you and your sister have done nothing but provoke me this morning. I will find the candlestick myself. Go help Priscilla prepare the noonday meal. Heaven knows she won't have finished the soup yet."

I hurried to the kitchen, where Prissy was slicing potatoes. She gave me a sidelong glance, her cheeks flushed from the fire's heat. I hoped she had not heard Mother's words, but if she had, she gave no sign of it. Despite her being eighteen, only a year younger than I, I felt the need to shield her from such biting comments.

"I can't imagine where that candlestick has got to," I said in a whisper. I wiped my hands on my apron and took up a potato. "Would you like me to help you with the potatoes?"

Prissy shook her head and smiled. I set the potato down on the wooden board she was using and fetched a large measure of salted beef which I had brought in from the storehouse earlier. I placed it on another wooden board and sliced it into small chunks. When I had finished that tedious task, I placed the pieces of meat into the large kettle of soup already bubbling gently over the fire.

"It will smell good in here before long. Have you cut the squash yet, Prissy?" My sister shook her head and pointed to the squash lying on the floor near the back door. I hefted the large fruits onto the board and began slicing them next.

Prissy and I worked in silence until all the ingredients for the hearty soup were in the kettle. "Pris, would you go out to the storehouse and bring back an armload of madder root? We need to start preparing it for the rose dye today." Prissy nodded, untied her apron, and hastened out the back door in the direction of the storehouse.

When Prissy returned, I was not surprised to see Sylvanus,

our eldest brother and Prissy's favorite sibling, following her with an armload of madder. "Sylvanus, Prissy is perfectly capable of carrying the madder."

"I know." He winked at Prissy. "I was passing near the storehouse and saw her, so I thought I would help. I've finished chopping the wood and I need something to eat before I go help Father and Jesse with the oats."

He set the madder down next to the door and helped himself to a large apple from the sack on the floor.

"I'll be back for dinner. Smells good." Sylvanus waved goodbye and hurried away. I shook my head and Prissy grinned.

"He and Jesse are insufferable," I said, though I well understood their desire to coddle our youngest sibling. She had been frail from infancy, and even all these years later, the boys still did not seem to understand that physical work helped to strengthen her. She never asked for help—in fact, she could not ask for help verbally, as she had never in her life spoken a word. Sylvanus and Jesse merely took it upon themselves to help her whenever possible, except, of course, when it came to the womanly tasks of cooking, cleaning, sewing, and mending.

There could be no doubt that Prissy was the most handsome of the Rutledge children. Everyone thought so. How many times had I wished my hair, thick and unruly and the color of coffee, were as long and soft and golden as hers? How often had I wished my skin, fair and covered with freckles, was as fresh and glowing as hers? It did not help that Prissy was the type of girl who simply looked like she needed a man's help with anything difficult. And the way Jesse and Sylvanus doted on her—well, one would be forgiven for thinking she was helpless.

I shook my head, displeased with myself. One could also be forgiven for thinking I was vain and petty with such musings.

Prissy and I divided the madder roots and got to work grinding them into a clumpy paste. It was hot, arduous work and because we toiled in silence, I spent the time wondering if

Mother would allow me to help the Women's Relief Society with the countywide effort to provide Continental soldiers with socks and gloves for the coming winter. I was a passable seamstress and I wanted to help. Quakers might not be permitted to take up arms, but they were allowed to support the army in other ways. Thus far, Mother had not permitted me to help, saying instead that my time was better spent doing chores around the inn and farm.

By the time we had finished with the madder, the first of the guests had arrived for the noonday meal. Prissy and I cleaned our faces and arms of the dark pink droplets that had splashed from the madder paste, donned our aprons, and spooned large ladlefuls of steaming soup into a ceramic tureen. While Prissy placed bread into a large basket, I carried the soup into the dining room. Two men were already there, waiting for their food, and by the time I had carefully set the tureen down on the wooden table in the corner, Father, Jesse, and Sylvanus had also come into the room, hungry and ready to eat. Father smiled at Prissy and me; he was a tall man, but thin and slight, so one would be surprised to learn how much food he consumed.

Mother came into the dining room and sat down at our family's table. Prissy and I sat across from her.

"Have you finished preparing the roots?" Mother asked.

"No, but we started it this morning."

She sighed. "Make haste. We need to prepare the dye solution and dye the cloth as soon as possible."

After dinner, the diners left and Father and the boys went back outside. Prissy and I spent the next hour cleaning up after them and returning the uneaten soup to the pot for the evening meal. There would be more people for that meal, since the inn guests would be there, too. They had all been returning to the inn every day in time for supper.

Prissy and I continued to prepare the madder dye that afternoon. As soon as that was done we took two large baskets and went into the woods in search of black walnuts. We would use the meat from the shells in a pie for our guests the following day; we would use the shells to prepare the brown dye for cloth.

Prissy didn't often venture into the woods by herself, so I stayed close to her while we looked for walnuts. She had gone behind a tree to relieve herself when I heard a shout.

"Etta!"

I turned around to see Sylvanus making his way toward me.

"Where's Prissy?" The alarm in his voice was unmistakable.

I pointed farther into the woods behind me. "Don't fret. She just needs a moment of privacy."

His shoulders relaxed and he nodded. "I was worried when I didn't see her."

"You know I wouldn't send her into the woods alone."

"I know. I can't help it, Etta." He was speaking in a whisper, but as soon as Prissy came back into view, his voice grew louder. "Mother sent me to tell you that she needs both of you to come back to help her with the pigs."

I turned to Prissy. "Let's go, Prissy. I don't want to keep Mother waiting."

Prissy nodded and hoisted her basket of walnuts onto her hip.

"I'll carry that, Pris." Though she had shown nary a sign of distress or discomfort, Sylvanus reached for the basket and carried it the rest of the way through the woods and back to the storehouse. I could only shake my head in amusement.

CHAPTER 3

*A*fter we deposited our walnuts in the storehouse, we went to the pig yard in search of Mother. She was there, shooing one of the sows away with her skirts. The sow was trying to eat the fabric. I barely managed to suppress a grin as I hurried to help.

"Get away from her, you," I scolded the enormous animal. She didn't even look in my direction. I grabbed a thin wooden board that was leaning against the fence and hurried toward her. Pigs could be tricked into thinking they were walking beside a solid wall—I held the board down by my side and used it to guide the sow away from Mother's skirts and into another enclosed pen.

"Thank you," Mother said. She looked down at her skirt in disgust. "Now this will have to laundered again on the next washing day." She frowned. "Etta, Priscilla, please finish feeding the pigs while I feed the chickens. She left, closing the gate tightly behind her so no pigs would escape, and walked off in the direction of the chicken coop.

We were, of course, lucky to have so many pigs on our farm. There were many families in Upper Precinct and in Stites Point who could not enjoy the luxury of pork as often as we did. But it was easy to forget our good fortune when it came time to feed the gigantic, dirty things, as neither Prissy nor I relished the task.

Neither did Mother, of course, which was why she was feeding the chickens.

Sylvanus had disappeared after leaving the walnuts in the storehouse. He probably would have preferred to feed the pigs so Prissy didn't have to do it, but I knew he would be expected to return to the fields to help Father. He did not have time to do both and Father would be angry if Sylvanus didn't help him.

After a short while we finished feeding and watering the pigs. Prissy and I had to clean up so we could start preparing supper for the inn guests and any travelers who might be hungry.

It was nearly time to serve the meal when a man appeared in the kitchen doorway. He held himself up against the wooden door frame with one hand and made a croaking sound.

I hurried over to him, noticing with alarm how pale he was. His lips were pinched and white from being pressed together so hard.

"Friend, are you ill?"

He nodded and Prissy ran around me to get a chair from the dining room. She pushed it to where he was standing and he slumped into it.

"Pris, run and get Mother."

Prissy ran across the dining room and was gone in an instant. She returned just a few moments later, with Mother in tow.

"Upon my word! What has happened, Etta? Who is this?" Mother bent down to look closely at the man's face. "Are you ill?" she asked.

I hadn't wanted to leave the man alone while Prissy fetched

Mother, but now I left to pour a mug of cider for him. I carried it to him and he was able to lift his hand to accept it.

With shaking hands he lifted the mug to his lips. He took a long draught and leaned his head against the ladder back of the chair, breathing heavily.

Mother and Prissy and I looked at each other and back at the man. "Friend?" Mother asked.

After several seconds the man opened his eyes. "Thank you," he said with a cough. "I am feeling quite uncleverly."

"Where are you from?" Mother asked.

The man was silent for a moment, then replied in a raspy voice, "I have just left Cape May. I am traveling to Philadelphia, but I suddenly fell ill a ways down the road. It has taken me some time to get here." He stopped and steadied his breath. "I was to take the ferry from this side to the other side of Great Egg Harbor Bay, but I fear I am in no condition to travel."

"I will send a message to your family in Cape May so they may fetch you and take you home," Mother said.

The man shook his head weakly. "I have no family in Cape May. I was visiting the town on business. Do you have a room here where I may stay?"

Mother cast a wary look in my direction. I knew what she was thinking: if the man were to stay in our inn, we would be responsible for taking care of him and nursing him back to health.

But if the man had no family nearby, how could we possibly refuse him lodging? It was clear he could travel no further. Before Mother could object, I answered him. "Yes, we have a room available. You may stay here." I didn't need to look at Mother to know she was glaring at me.

The man addressed himself to Mother, not me. "Thank you, good woman. I can assure you I will recompense you well."

"Can you climb the stairs?" I asked him.

"I shall attempt it." The man stood up shakily and put his

hand on the wall to steady himself. He moved slowly toward the staircase in the center hall of the inn. I followed him closely and Mother followed both of us. She asked Prissy to tether the man's horse to the railing in front of the tavern and fetch his traveling sack. Prissy disappeared through the front door.

The man made excruciatingly slow progress up the stairs, while I followed with my arms ready to support him if necessary. Mother moved around us at the top of the stairs and opened the door to one of the empty rooms. She pushed the door inward and stood in the hallway as the man made his way to the bedstead. He lay down with a loud sigh and closed his eyes, as if they pained him to remain open.

"What is your name?" Mother asked, stepping into the room.

"My name is Isaac Taylor."

"Etta, please fetch Isaac another mug of cider and leave it with him. I shall need you to keep watch over him while he is here." Mother left the room a moment before Prissy entered with two large, heavy-looking sacks in her arms.

"Prissy, you can place the sacks there on the floor," I directed her. I turned to Isaac. "I will return shortly with cider. Do you need anything else?" He shook his head in response.

Prissy and I left the room and I closed the door quietly.

"Mother told me it will be my job to take care of him," I whispered. Prissy's eyes widened. "No matter," I assured her. "I will make sure he has plenty of food and cider and I am sure that will help him feel better." In truth, I rather fancied the thought of nursing one of our inn guests. It would help break the monotony of chores and household tasks.

After I took the cider to Isaac I hurried to help Prissy serve supper to our guests. There was soup, of course, and bread. There was also a meat pie I had made with salted pork and nutmeats and Pippin apples.

I checked on Isaac again soon after supper was over and found him sleeping fitfully. I decided against waking him.

It was growing late and quite dark when Prissy and I finished cleaning the kitchen that evening. Mother, Father, Jesse, and Sylvanus had gone into the tavern directly after eating. The tavern was attached to the inn, but had a separate entrance. I always thought it a bit funny that neither Jesse nor Sylvanus thought cleaning up from a meal would be too taxing for Prissy. They, of course, were interested in the news of the day, and particularly now that fighting that had been predicted as near as Philadelphia. They always hurried into the tavern as soon as they were done with supper.

Mother and Father usually served up ale and cider as the guests requested, though Prissy and I helped, too. Men from neighboring farms would visit the tavern of an evening to discuss the news and talk among themselves. I rather liked the atmosphere, but I knew Prissy oftentimes found it intimidating. She and I went to the tavern together after our kitchen chores were complete.

The tavern was full of men that night. A good number of the neighboring farmers and their sons had come and the talk was noisy and boisterous.

I stood behind the counter helping Mother and Father serve while Jesse and Sylvanus spoke to the men in attendance. Prissy stayed behind Father and Mother and I, helping only when asked, not keen to take part in the din.

Even Thomas, our new farm hand, was there. Father had taken him on a week previously, but Thomas had only visited the tavern on one other occasion since then. The poor man walked with a pronounced limp and preferred to remain in his cabin when he finished work for the day.

Thomas stood by the counter as Mother poured him a measure of rum, his beverage of choice. Ben Drake, one of our closest neighbors, walked up to Thomas and introduced himself.

"The name is Benjamin Drake," he said, holding out his hand to Thomas. Thomas shook his hand heartily.

"It is good to know you," he replied.

Father noticed the exchange and joined the two men. "Ben, this is Thomas Blackwell. I have just hired him to help on the farm. The oat and rye harvest will be bigger than usual, so the boys and I decided we needed an extra hand."

"Is this your first day on the farm?" Ben asked.

"No, sir. I have been here for a week," Thomas said.

Ben's bushy eyebrows arched. "I am surprised that I have not seen you in here before now."

"My leg is lame, sir. The Rutledges were kind enough to give me a cabin to live in, so I cook my own meals mostly and I rest my leg in the evening so I can work the next day."

"You know the cabin, Ben," Father said. "The one just to the southwest of here."

Ben nodded and his eyes dropped to Thomas's leg. He very likely had not meant to be inquisitive, but Thomas noticed the glance and spoke calmly.

"I was injured in a fall from a horse."

Jesse came up behind Thomas and patted his shoulder. Thomas turned and smiled at him.

"Thomas here is a hard worker, Ben. We were lucky he came calling," Jesse said. Thomas smiled at the compliment.

"Come over here, Thomas. I'll introduce you to the other men here tonight," Ben offered. He led Thomas to a group of rowdy men, all neighbors of ours, and pulled a stool from a nearby table so Thomas could sit down. He seemed to be enjoying the company and was soon caught up in the conversation.

CHAPTER 4

I was bending down to lift another jug of cider from the floor when Prissy tapped my shoulder. I straightened up and looked at her. Her eyes were alight and smiling. She nodded her head toward the center of the room, where one of the men, Thaddeus Marshall, was leaning down and opening a case next to him on the floor. He had brought his fiddle, and soon the tavern would be filled with music and singing voices. He played a few notes, then launched into "Planxty Browne," accompanied by the enthusiastic clapping of many of the men in the tavern. Next he played "Flowers of Edinburgh" and it wasn't long before Jesse grabbed Prissy's arm and whirled her around the tavern floor, laughing and enjoying the wild claps of everyone watching, with the exception of Mother and Father. Prissy seemed to be enjoying herself, despite her profound shyness.

Father allowed music in the tavern because he knew that some of our patrons loved music and were fond of singing and dancing, but as strict Quakers, we were supposed to frown upon music and other forms of lively entertainment. I suspected Jesse and Prissy would be subjected to one of Father's stern lectures about hedonism and sin before the evening's end. I wished we could enjoy music freely, since it was so much fun listening to Thaddeus play. Oftentimes one of the other men would join him with a fife or a cittern. The honeyed woods of the instruments were as beautiful to look at as they were to hear.

But I was right about Father. After the music ended and the tavern emptied of patrons and neighbors, he kept us all in the large room to discuss with us the sins of merry-making and music. It seemed we were all to be required to hear the lecture, even though only Jesse and Prissy had joined in the dancing.

"It is a frivolous and undignified pursuit," Father told us. Mother stood behind him, stony faced. "Dancing and listening to music like that which Thaddeus Marshall plays on his fiddle are useless and indiscreet amusements. I know we must listen to the music because that is an enjoyment some of our patrons indulge, but we do not need to encourage the behavior with ridiculous and silly activities which are displeasing to God."

We all nodded solemnly at Father's words. Jesse's lips were pressed together in a tight line, as if he were trying to keep words from escaping his mouth, but Father did not seem to notice.

Jesse and I were the last ones in the tavern after Mother, Father, Prissy, and Sylvanus had made their way back into the inn and to our family's small rooms behind our private parlor. Jesse extinguished the last candle and I hung back in the large room to wait for him.

"Are you angry about something?" I asked him in a low voice.

He made a soft scoffing noise with his nose. "The rules Father sets for us, the rules we're required to follow as Friends, they make no sense to me. I do not understand why dancing is wrong and why such joyful sounds like cittern and fiddle music are wrong."

"Well, I suppose for the reasons Father stated," I said. "They're undignified and frivolous."

"But *why* are they undignified and frivolous? Do you think Thaddeus looks undignified when he plays the fiddle? I don't think so. He looks happy. He looks like he's intent on playing well. Do you think Prissy and I look undignified when we take a turn around the tavern?"

I wanted to say *yes*, but I knew that would only serve to provoke Jesse. "The music is very pretty, I agree."

But Jesse knew me too well to ignore my remark. "So you do think we look undignified?" he asked with a sudden grin. "Is that so bad? Is it so bad that Prissy be happy for a few minutes of her day?"

"I think Prissy is happy more often than you realize," I said. We had stopped walking, but I touched his arm to get him to continue toward the front door of the inn with me, lest our parents wonder what was taking us so long. "She and I both enjoy being outdoors and I know she enjoys feeding some of the animals. She is certainly more content when she cleans than I am, and I know she likes to bake."

"Very well. I take your point. But I ask again, is it so bad for one to enjoy oneself sometimes? I just don't agree with Father that dancing is wrong."

I said nothing in response, knowing it would be futile to continue the discussion. But what Jesse said next took me by surprise.

"Etta, I don't want to be a Quaker anymore."

I had been walking in front of Jesse, but at hearing his words I wheeled around to face him.

"Jesse, you can't say such a thing! What if Father hears you?" I kept my voice as low as I could.

"I think the time may be coming when Father and I have to have a discussion about me continuing to be a member of the Society of Friends."

"You can't do that, Jesse. He'll disown you! You won't be allowed to live here anymore." My voice was becoming more urgent. The sudden thought of life without Jesse was too sad to contemplate.

"I'm not sure I want to live here anymore, Etta."

"But...but..." I was spluttering, but I could not form words. Jesse's announcement had shocked me into confusion and distress.

"It's time, Etta."

"Can't you—"

The door opened and Mother stuck her head out onto the porch, holding a lantern above her head. "What are you two doing out here? Come inside. It's time I locked the door."

Jesse and I did as we were told. I followed him into the house under Mother's suspicious gaze. "What's going on out there?" She addressed herself to Jesse.

"Nothing, Mother. Etta and I were just talking."

Mother grimaced and asked no more questions. She locked the door behind us and made a motion to shoo us through the family parlor and into our rooms. I didn't get another chance to talk to Jesse that evening.

CHAPTER 5

The next morning I took a tray of porridge, a bit of salt pork, and a mug of cider to Isaac. I knocked on his door and heard a strangled sound from inside the room. I stepped through the doorway and was met with a grim sight: his skin was white against the homespun bedding and he was shivering. There was a bright sheen of sweat on his forehead and his eyes wore an empty look. I hurried to his bedside.

"Isaac, what can I do to help you?"

He managed to lift his hand slightly from where it lay on the bed, though I did not know what he was trying to tell me. I placed the tray on the floor, pulled a small table from its spot against the wall, and placed the tray on the table within his reach. He made no move to touch the food or drink, so I held the mug to his lips while he took a small sip of the cider, then lay back against the bed as if the effort had exhausted him.

"Shall I send for the doctor?"

He nodded weakly.

"I'll do that immediately. Can you eat some porridge? I can help you if you wish." The shrunken man before me shook his head from side to side almost imperceptibly.

"I'll send for the doctor now." I left the food behind in case he was able to eat, though I suspected he would have a difficult time trying to hold the mug or eat the porridge without assistance.

I found Mother cleaning the floor in the dining room. "Mother, Isaac is very ill. He wants me to send for the doctor."

Mother scowled. "I will write a note to my friend Eugenia in Cape May and ask her if she knows anything about this Isaac Taylor. Perhaps she knows someone who could come fetch him and care for him so we do not have to do it. You are falling behind on your chores."

We *are not caring for the sick man*, I thought. I *am caring for him*. I knew I could do a good job and help Isaac to become well. If Mother would not allow me to take part in the efforts of the Women's Relief Society, perhaps I could help in other ways, such as nursing the sick. If I could help Isaac recover, it would prove that I could help other people recover from illness or injury, too. More than anything, I wanted to be of use to others. What I wanted was the opportunity to help someone simply for the sake of doing good.

I supposed Mother's concern was not entirely misplaced. If I spent my time nursing a guest of the inn, I would fall even farther behind in my other chores—or at least I would if Mother would allow it. But she would simply make Prissy take on more of my duties. I did not want to burden Prissy with more work to do.

Mother sighed and straightened up from where she had been kneeling. "Take the horse and go to Doctor Wheeler's house. Tell him we have a traveler who is ill and ask him to come quickly. I want that Isaac Taylor out of this inn as soon as possible. While you are away I shall write to Eugenia and the doctor can take the note when he leaves here."

I set off for the paddock at a run. Isaac looked so sickly and pale that I was afraid for his life. I took our dark chestnut horse and spurred him down the dusty road toward the doctor's house.

When I had delivered my message and Doctor Wheeler had promised to come as quickly as he could, I returned to the inn. I checked on Isaac and found him in a disturbed sleep. I helped Prissy prepare dinner and hurried through my normal morning chores as best I could. Prissy watched me, blinking, her mouth drawn. I knew what she wanted to say: that she would happily do my chores in addition to her own.

"I know you don't mind taking on my chores, Pris, but I'll do as many of them as I can by myself." Prissy smiled and nodded.

The afternoon was a blur as I hurried from one task to the next, all the while checking in on Isaac whenever I had an opportunity. The doctor thankfully arrived as the sun was beginning to set. Mother and I met him in the front hall as he came downstairs from examining our guest.

"He's got the ague. It comes on quickly. You'll need to keep a close eye on him and hope the fever breaks." I could feel Mother's eyes on me, but I did not look at her and instead nodded at the doctor.

"Give him plenty to drink and keep him cool with wet cloths," the doctor instructed. "I'll be back in a couple days to see how he's doing. Try not to get too close to him or you might fall ill, too."

Mother handed him a piece of paper. "Doctor Wheeler, could you please take this note? I've written to a friend in Cape May to learn whether she knows of any family or friends of the man upstairs who could care for him better than we can here."

The doctor reached for the note and placed it in the pocket of his jacket. "I surely will, Davinia. I know how busy you all are now that fall is coming, and I know you have other guests in the inn, too. I'll make sure your letter gets to Cape May. I likely won't deliver it myself, but I know someone who is headed in that direction tomorrow morning."

"Thank you, Doctor Wheeler." My mother offered him a rare smile. It softened her face and she was pretty. I wished she would show it to us more often.

Suppertime was fast approaching and Prissy and I hurried to finish preparing the meal and get the dining room ready for our guests. I set a small amount of food aside for Isaac.

The light outside was growing dim when the guests arrived for supper and Father and Sylvanus came in from the fields. Thomas, as usual, did not accompany them but had chosen to take supper in his cabin.

Only one person was missing when Prissy and I finally sat down and joined the other diners.

"Where is Jesse?" Mother asked, looking around the room.

"I thought he was here," Father replied. Mother shook her head.

"I'm sure he'll be here soon," I said. Prissy nodded her head in agreement. I stood up, but Mother stopped me.

"Etta, sit down. I know what you are doing, and you are not to set aside food for your brother. If he cannot be here in time to have supper with the rest of the family and our guests without so much as a word as to his own whereabouts, he will wait until the morn to eat."

I glanced at Prissy out of the corner of my eye and sat down slowly. The guests were staring openly at Mother and me and I was embarrassed on Jesse's behalf.

There was little conversation that evening at the table, though Father and Sylvanus spoke quietly between themselves about the harvest. I spent most of the meal wondering where Jesse had gone, and judging from the creases between her eyebrows, Prissy was wondering the same thing.

Thinking Isaac might be able to eat some supper, I took a tray to him. Unfortunately, I found him thrashing about, an acrid sheen of perspiration on his forehead. I ran for more cool compresses and opened the window a bit to allow cold air into the room. I do not believe Isaac was at all aware of my presence.

I helped Prissy finish cleaning the kitchen after tending to Isaac. Everyone else had retired to the tavern. I saw Prissy looking at me out of the corner of her eye.

"Are you worried about Jesse?" I asked. She nodded. "He cannot have gone far. He probably called on a friend and lost track of the hour," I said. I think I was speaking more to calm myself than her, but she did not look convinced, either.

I was carrying a heavy wooden bucket filled with dirty water to the small garden behind the kitchen when a twig snapped nearby. I froze, the water sloshing down the front of my frock. I peered into the darkness, wishing Prissy or someone else had come out-of-doors with me.

"Etta?" The loud whisper came from the stand of trees not far away.

"Jesse? Is that you?"

"Yes." He stepped into the clearing behind the kitchen and I heaved a sigh of relief. "Where have you been?" I hissed.

"I was calling on a friend." He stepped closer "Are Father and Mother angry with me?"

"I don't know about Father, but Mother is. You should have told someone where you were going, or at least told Mother you would be late for supper."

"I know. I did not expect to be gone so long. Is there any supper left?"

"Yes. I saved you some. Mother told me not to, though, so don't let her see you eating it." I beckoned to him and he followed me through the back door. Prissy's eyes lit up when she saw him, and he grinned at her.

"Don't worry about me, Pris. I can take care of myself."

I bent down low and reached under one of the kitchen shelves that were not easily visible to anyone coming into the room. I pulled out the basket I had filled with Jesse's supper.

"Remember what I said. Don't let Mother see you."

He winked. "I won't. I'll eat this outside right now. Thanks, Etta."

He left, closing the back door softly behind him. Prissy gave me a knowing smile and I held my finger to my lips in mock seriousness.

I was hanging my apron on its hook, having finally finished cleaning the kitchen, when Jesse came back inside. "Thank you again for saving me some supper, Etta. Is there any more? I'm powerful hungry tonight, and Father asked me to go nighttime fishing with Daniel and David Hughes. I need nourishment." He smiled.

I smirked at him. "It's bad enough you don't come home for supper, Jesse, and now you want me to get out more food?" I sighed. "All right." I took the basket he held out to me and bustled about, slicing more bread and giving him a small crock of butter. There was still stew hanging in the pot over the low fire, so I scooped some of that into a trencher for him and bade him be quiet when he went back outside. He pecked my cheek as he left.

"Thanks, Etta."

I shook my head as his form was swallowed by the darkness outside.

CHAPTER 6

*A*las, no one had brought an instrument to the tavern that evening. The talk revolved around the movement of troops near Philadelphia.

"It looks like Howe is about to take Philadelphia," Ben Drake said. There were murmurs of both concern and agreement. Philadelphia was not even two days away.

"I've heard—" one man began.

The door opened with a loud bang and all eyes turned to see who was coming in. It was a young man, grizzled and covered with grime and dirt. He looked around the room with eyes that appeared wary and untrusting.

"Good evening, Friend," Father said.

The man nodded and clumped toward the counter. I glanced at Father and he seemed to understand that I did not want to talk to the man. He stepped up in front of me.

"What can I get for you?" he asked.

"Ale. A large tankard of it, and cold," the man said.

Father nodded toward me and I busied myself pouring the stranger's drink. Prissy was watching the man with uncertainty.

I handed him the ale and he nodded toward me in a manner, I supposed, of thanks.

The man went to the corner of the tavern where it was darkest and sat down with his back to the wall. The tavern was warm and cozy, with firelight flickering in the huge hearth along one side of the room, but the atmosphere seemed cold suddenly. Talk among the other patrons had ceased, and everyone was quiet for several moments.

Father beckoned to me. "Etta, I want you to go outside to the storehouse and fetch more ale, please."

"Yes, Father." I walked into the back room behind the counter and Prissy followed me. "It's all right, Pris. I'll be right back. I'm just going for more ale." She nodded, but made no move to go back to the front of the tavern. "That man is frightening, isn't he?" I asked. She grimaced. "There is no need to worry. The other men in here are all our friends and they will keep that man in his place." She gave me a quicksilver smile and sat down on a stool. She was obviously going to wait for me to return before going back into the tavern.

I was only gone for a few moments, since I ran to and from the storehouse, but much had transpired in my absence. Prissy met me at the door, her eyes wide with fear, and pointed toward the front of the tavern. I hurried to see what was happening.

The stranger in the corner and three other men were arguing loudly. Father was watching them warily, as was Sylvanus. Mother stood with her hands on her hips, looking like she was about to stop the ruckus with a few sharp words, but I knew she was waiting for a sign from Father. Prissy and I watched the scene unfold from the safety of the back room.

"I tell you, traitors are not welcome in this part of New Jersey. Take yourself off and go to the Brandywine where the British have use for the likes of you!" Richard Miller said in a loud voice. The stranger stood up, his eyes blazing. He held his tankard above his head and some of the ale sloshed over the side and onto the wooden floor.

"To hell with you and I'll drink to the health of King George!" he roared in a slurred voice.

Chairs scraped and two of them toppled over as men leapt up and made toward the stranger.

"Enough!" The word sounded like the boom of a cannon and had come from my father. Even Mother's eyes widened as she turned to look at him. The men halted their movements and turned around as if to confirm that it had been my father speaking. He continued.

"I'll not have unruly behavior in my establishment." His voice had quieted already. He nodded toward the men from Upper Precinct. "Let him alone. He'll find out soon enough he's in unfriendly territory." The men shuffled back to their seats and the stranger sat down.

"Davinia, please fetch some bread and stew from the kitchen. We need to get some food in this man if he's to be taking the drink." My father took his eyes off the stranger long enough to talk to my mother, who left immediately. Prissy and I ducked further into the back room so Mother would not see us lurking about, but she didn't even glance in our direction. She went directly out the front door of the tavern and into the house.

She returned presently with the stew and bread Father had requested, and Prissy and I returned to the counter. Mother set the food on the table before the stranger. The man scowled and gnawed the crust off the bread. The room had quieted and everyone was looking around, as if waiting for another outburst from the man. But as he continued to eat, the patrons at the other tables eventually began talking again, this time in lower voices.

That night in the tavern there were more men than usual, so Father asked me to fetch several additional mugs from the dining room. He instructed Sylvanus to tend to the fire in the hearth while he and Mother continued pouring ale and cider at the counter.

I was returning to the tavern, my arms laden with additional mugs, when the stranger lifted his mug in the air and waved it, presumably demanding more. Prissy was the only one of us who was idle, so the task was left to her. She hurried over to where the man sat in the semi-darkness and reached for the mug, but he brought it close to his person so she had to move closer to him to grasp it. As I set the mugs down on the counter, I noticed Sylvanus straightening up from his position by the hearth. We both chanced to look at Prissy, who was taking the mug from the stranger's hand. As she turned to walk away, I saw, to my great horror, the stranger place his hand on Prissy's bottom. He pinched it! I glanced quickly at Sylvanus, who had also seen the odious movement, and he crossed the room in four long strides as Prissy's face darkened to a deep pink and her eyes searched out Father with a frantic look.

"See here, you cad!" Sylvanus' voice boomed. The stranger looked up at him with a smirk, almost daring my brother to continue speaking. Every eye in the tavern was trained on Sylvanus.

"I'll not condone that behavior in this tavern, man. You need to leave the premises straight away."

Everyone seemed to understand immediately that the stranger's behavior had involved Prissy somehow, though only Sylvanus and I appeared to have seen it. All the men present turned toward Prissy. It looked to me like she might faint away from the sudden and unwanted attention. Father noticed her unease, too, and left his spot behind the counter to intervene between Sylvanus and the stranger. I had set down the mugs and inched closer to Prissy, grasping her cold and trembling hand in mine when I reached her. I daresay she was as upset by all the attention paid to her as by the stranger's outrageous behavior.

"Sylvanus, allow me to handle this." Father gently pushed Sylvanus aside and faced the stranger, who rose to his feet unsteadily and leaned on the table for support.

"He pinched Prissy's bottom, Father!" Sylvanus said. I glanced at Prissy, who gasped and closed her eyes. I know she had not wished Sylvanus to reveal to everyone in the tavern what had happened.

"What?" the man asked in a querulous voice.

"I'll not allow despicable and ill-bred behavior in this tavern, sir. You will leave the premises at once or you will sit in this chair until you have sobered."

The man sat down heavily and waved Father and Sylvanus away. He muttered something to himself and stared at the table, his shoulders hunched and his dirty hair falling around his face.

"Father, you're not going to send him out?" I asked. I did not mean to sound accusing, but Father stared at me.

"Would you have him succumb to an accident in the woods or on the road because he is too taken with drink?"

I wanted to scream *Yes!* but I knew better than to do that. Father would rebuke me for being sinful. Instead, I turned to Prissy, who was still shaking. "Do not worry about that man, Prissy. Sylvanus and Father and the other men will not let him anywhere near you again." I put my arm around her thin shoulders and held her close to me. She was as a young child, small and frightened.

Sylvanus stepped close to Prissy and me. "Prissy, that good-for-nothing scoundrel will not come near you again. I will make sure of it." Pris gave him a tremulous smile.

CHAPTER 7

It was still quite early in the evening, though the darkness outside was almost complete and it felt like we had been in the tavern for hours. I was not surprised when Elijah Webber came in.

"Welcome, Elijah," Father said with a warm smile. "It has been what, a week, since we've seen you here?"

"That it has, Nathaniel," Elijah replied. Elijah was just a year older than Jesse. He knew Father and my brothers from their mutual membership in the Committee of Safety for Cape May County. His father was a magistrate in Romney Marsh, a village to the south of the Upper Precinct, and his mother was the leader of the county's Women's Relief Society.

Elijah had the soft hands, pearl-white skin, and polite bearing of someone not accustomed to working out-of-doors or in rough conditions. He was haughty, too, in my opinion, though his appearance gave him no excuse for pride. His mouth was too wide and a lock of his molasses-colored hair always fell into his eyes. His eyes were too green. He took care to avoid looking in my direction, but instead looked at Prissy, who smiled shyly at him.

"May I have a mug of cider, please?" he asked her. She nodded and complied, pouring him a large measure and handing it to him. "Thank you, Priscilla," he said, placing a coin on the counter.

"Any news, Elijah?" Sylvanus asked.

Elijah nodded and leaned in close to Father and Sylvanus. I stepped a bit closer. I wanted to hear what Elijah had to say, despite his attempts to ignore me. His eyes flicked in my direction, then back to Father and the boys. He did not seem to care that I was listening.

"There's been trouble in Romney Marsh," he said in a low voice.

Father frowned. "What sort of trouble?"

"The master list of locations where munitions are hidden in the county has gone missing."

Sylvanus' eyes narrowed as he drew back in surprise. "And you have no idea who took it?" he asked.

Elijah shook his head. "This means we are going to have to move the munitions to new locations before anyone in a position to use the information against us has an opportunity to make good."

Father and Sylvanus nodded. "When will that happen?" Father asked.

"As quickly as possible. Can you come to Romney Marsh two days hence, before dawn? A few of us, myself included, know the locations without having to consult the list, so we have a small group of trusted men who are going to travel to the locations where the weapons are held and move them."

"We will be there on the morn, and we'll bring Jesse," Father said. Sylvanus nodded. It was strange to think that our family would assist in the movement of weapons and ammunition given that we were members of the Society of Friends, but Father had told us that we were responsible for helping when necessary, as long as it did not require us to use the weapons.

Elijah seemed to relax after he had spoken his piece. He leaned on the counter and took a long look around the room as he raised his mug to his lips. Most of the other men in the tavern knew Elijah, so they raised their hands in greeting and he returned the waves.

But his body stiffened when his eyes came to rest on the stranger in the corner.

"Who is that?" He turned to look at Father.

"I do not know the man. But he has caused a fair share of trouble in here tonight. I've told him he has to leave immediately or sober up." Father paused. "Do you know him, Elijah?"

"I do not know his name or where he hails from, but I know him to be a scoundrel. I am quite sure he is the one I saw running from the general store in Romney Marsh, having escaped with the contents of the money box." Elijah scowled.

He set his mug on the counter and pushed back his stool slowly. "I'm going to see what he has to say, Nathaniel, with your permission."

Father nodded gravely and Elijah made his way to the stranger in the corner. Once again, all talk ceased so the other men in the tavern could hear Elijah speak.

"You there. Were you in Romney Marsh several days ago?" The man turned a sullen stare on Elijah. "I am speaking to you, man."

The stranger's lip curled and his eyes glittered. "And if I was?" he asked in a loud voice.

"You stole all the coin and paper money from the general store. I saw you running away with it. Do you deny it?"

The stranger laughed, a loud, hacking noise punctuated with a fit of coughing and an unseemly snort.

"Where is the money you stole?" Elijah asked.

"I'll not tell."

"I do not doubt that you're a rum dubber, too!" Elijah cried.

"Are you planning to steal the money from this tavern, too, and the good family that runs it? Are you?"

The man stood up too quickly, knocking his chair to the ground. He lowered his head and rushed toward Elijah, who was not quick enough to realize what was happening and was knocked to the floor. All the men in the tavern leapt to their feet, bellowing and charging after the stranger, who had darted out the door with surprising speed for a drunken man.

Elijah was back on his feet almost instantly. He caught the eye of Sylvanus, who ran toward the door and reached it before anyone else.

"Gentlemen! Your attention! Elijah and I will go. It is best if only two of us go so we can use stealth to find the filcher." Sylvanus held the door open and Elijah ran through it. Sylvanus followed and they had disappeared into the darkness within seconds.

It took some time for the men in the tavern to quiet themselves. Every few moments someone would look toward the tavern door, as if expecting Sylvanus or Elijah to burst through holding the stranger by the scruff of his neck.

But no one came in, save for Jesse, who entered an hour later wearing a wide smile.

"Congratulate me, Father! I caught six flounder and just as many striped bass." He looked around the tavern and sobered immediately when he saw the men's tense faces. "What has happened?" He turned toward the counter as if to satisfy himself that Prissy and I were there. "Where is Sylvanus?"

"He and Elijah Webber left to give chase to a sot who stole money from the general store in Romney Marsh."

"Where have they gone? I'll help them."

Father shook his head. "No, Jesse. You'll never find them in the dark. They've been gone over an hour. The best thing to do now is to wait for them to return. With luck they will have caught the man."

"Who is the man?" Jesse asked.

"No one seems to know his name," Father said. The other men nodded in agreement.

It was then I remembered Isaac Taylor. I hadn't checked on him since before supper, so I hastily poured a mug of cider.

"What are you doing?" Mother asked.

"I'm taking this to Isaac. Hopefully he is feeling well enough tonight to take a drink."

Mother grimaced. "I hope to receive an answer to my letter soon so someone else can take care of him."

I hurried to the inn and up the stairs to Isaac's room. To my surprise, he answered my knock, though his voice was very weak.

"How are you feeling, Isaac? I have brought you a bit of drink. Would you like some?"

He managed to prop himself up on one elbow in his bed and grasp the mug I handed him. He took a small sip, then another one, then lay his head back again. "Thank you."

"Would you like more?"

He shook his head. "I heard shouting earlier."

"There was a commotion in the tavern."

He opened his eyes. "What caused the commotion?"

"There was a man, a stranger, who took to drink and then was accused by another patron of stealing the contents of the general store money box in Romney Marsh. The man who accused him saw the stranger running away from the store but was not able to catch him."

Isaac shook his head. "These are perilous times. I have heard stories of ill doings in this vicinity."

Certainly he is going to tell me what he means by that.

But Isaac did not continue. His breath rattled in his throat as he lay back and sighed heavily. I did not want him to tire himself with talking, but I could not bear to wait for him to tell me the stories he had heard.

"What stories, if you please, Isaac?"

He swallowed and opened his eyes again. "Stories about the Tories in Cape May County, and in the Upper Precinct, in particular," he said with a wheeze, then paused for a long moment and spoke again. "The few Tories around hereabouts are planning, so I have heard rumors, to ally with the British and to ransack sites in this area."

My blood ran cold.

The act of speaking had exhausted Isaac. He took several shallow breaths and closed his eyes again. "Would you bring me more cider on the morrow?"

"Certainly. Can I get you anything else this evening?"

He gave a slight shake of his head and seemed to sink further into his bed. I blew out the candle on his bedside table and left the room.

When I returned to the tavern, my face must have betrayed my grim thoughts. Jesse looked at me with concern. "Etta, you're very pale. What happened?"

I shook my head, not wishing to discuss Isaac's words with him in the tavern. He opened his mouth, probably to insist that I tell him what I had heard, when the door opened and Sylvanus and Elijah entered the room. Everyone started talking at once, wondering where the stranger was and whether they had caught him.

Sylvanus held out his hands and said, "May I have your attention?"

The men in the tavern quieted at once to listen to Sylvanus.

"We were not able to locate the man once he escaped into the darkness. You all got a good look at him, and you know that he not only burgled the general store in Romney Marsh, but he also made his true character known to all of us here with his despicable actions. Remain vigilant and if you see him, notify someone and try to apprehend him. He has caused enough trouble."

There were murmurs of agreement all around the tavern, and men began to leave shortly after that. Many of them had stayed later than usual to see what came of Sylvanus and Elijah's search. Elijah was the last to leave, so he stood finishing the ale Father had given him while they and my brothers discussed the stranger's whereabouts.

"We need to be especially careful since that louse is very likely angry now and seeking revenge for the embarrassment we brought upon him," Elijah said. "From what I have been able to gather, he is allied with the British and will not stop his activities because a handful of men from a country tavern are looking for him. Be watchful, gentlemen, and send word to me if you catch sight of him."

He took his hat from where it hung by the front door and left after bidding Father and the boys a good night. He ignored me, as usual, but nodded to Prissy and Mother. I could feel my cheeks flame with anger and humiliation. What was wrong with me that he wouldn't wish me a good evening, too?

CHAPTER 8

"Etta, come here." Jesse was locking the tavern door after Elijah had left and the rest of the family had returned to the inn to go to bed. Only Jesse and I remained on the porch. I stopped with my hand on the inn doorknob.

"What is it?" I asked.

"What happened earlier to make your face go white?"

I sighed and spoke in a low voice. "The sick man upstairs, Isaac, told me that there are a small number of King's Men in Upper Precinct working closely with the British to cause trouble in this area. I'm afraid for the war to come any closer. The fighting is less than a two-day ride as it is. What will happen if the British come closer?" I shivered.

"I do not believe the fighting will come to Cape May County. But if it does, preparations must be made on both sides, Etta. You must understand that. Not everyone believes the colonists are right in their beliefs. Not everyone believes the British deserve what they have received at the hands of the people on these shores. Not everyone believes that the best course is to shun the protection of the British Empire."

"Pray do not talk like that, Jesse. What if someone hears you?

They could be forgiven for thinking you yourself are in league with the King's Men." I was practically hissing, such was my concern at being overheard.

Jesse looked away, into the darkness beyond the porch of the inn.

"Jesse?" He turned around and I could see pain in his eyes. "What is it?" I asked.

"Etta, I must ask you not to reveal to anyone what I'm going to tell you."

For the second time that evening, my blood turned to ice. Somehow I knew what Jesse was going to say.

"I may be leaving Stites Point, Etta. I do not agree with those who believe fighting the British is an honorable pursuit."

"Don't say foolish things, Jesse." The words came out half-heartedly because I had a sudden suspicion about what was to come next.

"What I am trying to tell you is that I *am* one of the King's Men. I do not believe in the movement for independence from Britain. I may leave to fight for the King, Etta."

Such was my alarm, if not my surprise, at hearing these words spoken aloud that I swayed forward and caught the railing with both hands. Jesse reached for my arm, but I pulled it toward me.

I swallowed and looked away from him. I didn't want him to see the tears threatening to fall. "We should go inside before Mother comes out wondering what we're talking about." I composed myself and turned to him. "Jesse, please, think carefully before making any decisions. You know what will happen if you denounce the Society of Friends, leave Stites Point, and take up arms for the King. Father will never allow you to come home. Please, Jesse, please don't go."

I left him standing on the porch in the darkness. I could not bear to talk about it any longer.

I did not sleep that night.

Early the next morning, Prissy and I were in the kitchen preparing the noon meal when Jesse came in. I glanced at him out of the corner of my eye, but pretended not to have seen him. I had not thought about what I would say to him, so I ignored him and continued chopping the vegetables for the pottage.

But Prissy looked up at him and smiled, so he addressed himself to her.

"I'm starving, Pris. I did not have enough to eat at breakfast. Could I have a little more to take with me?"

Prissy began to gather some food and place it in a small basket. Jesse whistled while he waited for her, seemingly content to pretend he hadn't scared me witless the night before.

Prissy finally finished packing the basket and handed it to him. He thanked her and left through the back door. I lifted my head and watched him go, and quite suddenly I had the urge to run after him, to try again to dissuade him from leaving Stites Point. I let my knife clatter to the cutting board and hastened toward the back door. Prissy looked up in alarm.

"Prissy, I just thought of something I have to tell Jesse. I'll be right back. If Mother comes in, don't let her know where I went."

Prissy nodded, though her eyes betrayed her confusion. I hated to ask her to lie to Mother, but hopefully Mother was busy somewhere else.

Jesse was hurrying through the thicket of trees behind the house.

"Jesse!" I called, running after him. He turned around in surprise.

"What is it, Etta?"

"I didn't want to say anything in front of Prissy. I have thought of nothing else since you told me you were thinking about leaving Stites Point and I—"

I stopped when I realized Jesse was headed the wrong way.

He should have been going to meet Father, Sylvanus, and Thomas to bring in the crops, but he was headed in the opposite direction.

"Where are you going?" I asked, cocking my head.

"Nowhere. I mean, nowhere important. I'm going down to the water."

"You're going to eat a second breakfast down by the water, when Father and Sylvanus and Thomas are waiting for you in the field? You expect me to believe that?" I stared at him through narrowed eyes.

Jesse nodded.

"I do not believe you, Jesse." Then a horrible thought occurred to me. "Are you leaving, Jesse? Are you leaving Stites Point right now?" I covered my mouth with my hands and swallowed hard.

"No, Etta. No. I'm not leaving. Not right now, anyway. I am merely—" He stopped, closed his mouth, and blew a long breath out his nostrils. When he spoke again, his voice was very low. "I am taking this food to a man in need of it. I apologize for misleading you and Prissy."

My brow furrowed in confusion. "Who is it? If someone is hungry, we would be happy to give him food. Even Mother would not mind giving food to someone in need, Jesse. Why not tell the man to come up to the kitchen? We'll give him a meal and then send him with more food, too."

"I would, Etta, but this particular man..." His voice trailed off and his eyes took on a pained look.

The tone of Jesse's voice held a warning.

"Who is this man, Jesse, and where is he from?" I was becoming suspicious.

My brother clenched his jaw. "I believe it is the man who was in the tavern last night. I did not see him, but he fits the description I heard of the man who was in there."

"Elijah? He has plenty to eat, Jesse. His family is wealthy."

"No, not Elijah. The other man. The one who caused the trouble."

I stared at him in disbelief. "Jesse, you are taking breakfast to that man—that, that *cad*—right now? How could you do such a thing?"

"He is hungry, Etta. He is starving."

"He cannot be. We served him a large meal last night in the tavern to dull the effects of all the ale he drank."

"He may not be exactly starving at this moment, but he has nowhere to go. He will be hungry by tonight. I thought I could help him by giving him food."

"He is not a good man, Jesse. Do you know what he did to Prissy? You were not there when it happened."

Jesse's face darkened. "I do know. Sylvanus told me."

"And that does not convince you that he is not to be trusted?"

"I spoke to him in very strong terms early this morning, Etta. I have told him I will not help him if he so much as looks at Prissy again. And he is a supporter of the British, as he made clear, and I fear he will travel long and far before he finds anyone else who will help him."

"I am more concerned about his behavior than his beliefs. You think that merely rebuking him will stop his lecherous behavior?"

"I believe it will."

"I fear your belief is misplaced."

"I need to take this to him in the barn now, or else Father will wonder where I am." Jesse lifted the basket of food. He set off along the edge of the grove of trees. I watched him go and said a fervent prayer that Jesse's belief in the stranger was deserved. Then I realized what he had said.

"Wait, Jesse. That man is in our barn? Is he sleeping there? How long has that been going on?"

Jesse turned and for a moment I thought he would not answer me, but at length he spoke. "His name is Oliver Doolittle. He has been here several days."

Now I knew where Mother's missing candlestick had gone.

CHAPTER 9

I turned on my heel and stalked to the house.

Back in the kitchen, I found I could not look at Prissy directly. She knew I was keeping something from her. I knew she wanted to know what Jesse and I had spoken about, but I couldn't tell her. I could not tell her the truth—that I was colluding with Jesse to feed and protect the sot who had leered at her and pinched her bottom—but neither could I lie to her. So I said nothing and she remained curious.

Isaac was no better that morning when I took food to him after breakfast. He was awake, though hardly alert. I daresay I was able to make him a bit more comfortable in his suffering by smoothing the sheets around his torso and by plumping his pillow, but it was a hollow improvement. I was afraid for him.

Mother met me as I was descending the stairs after looking in on him. She stood with her hands on her hips.

"Etta, you are spending too much time attending to Isaac. You have a good deal of other work to do."

"He is very ill, Mother. I cannot just leave him up there to suffer alone. If I can help him, I should do that. Do you not agree?"

Mother did not answer. I knew why—because she could not disagree with me.

I dared not wait for Jesse outside the tavern that night, though I had questions for him, because if Mother saw us she would become suspicious about our whispered conversation. And as worried as I was about Oliver's presence on our property, I was also worried about what Mother and Father would do to Jesse if they discovered he was hiding that cad in our barn. Would they send him away? I could not bear the thought. I was forced to keep his secret.

The next day Thomas was left to do as much of the harvest as he could with help from a few neighbors while Father and the boys hastened off to Romney Marsh before daybreak, as they had promised Elijah they would.

Knowing of Jesse's sympathy for the British soldiers, I now wondered if he should be among the group of men hiding munitions from the British. But I knew Jesse, and I knew he would not betray the new locations of the weapons. Jesse did not even have time to take food to Oliver that morning, and I did not do so, either. It would do Oliver some good to feel hunger, I thought. Maybe it would spur him to leave this place and find a job far away.

Isaac took a turn for the worse that day. Doctor Wheeler returned to examine him and told Mother and me that all we could do was wait to see if the poor man was able to conquer the fever. Meanwhile, I was to continue offering him food and cider regularly in case he was able to eat or drink. He would need to restore his strength with good food if he was to recover —indeed, if he were to survive at all. Doctor Wheeler praised my attempts to nurse Isaac back to health and out of the corner of my eye I could see Mother grimace.

The next morning Father and the boys would go back into the fields, and I knew Jesse would come into the kitchen again pretending to be hungry. So I prepared a basket for him—I provided less food than Prissy had, since I knew who was eating it—and told Prissy I needed to speak to Jesse. I waited for him outside, near the back door.

When he appeared I fell into step with him as he walked toward the barn. I handed him the basket with a frown.

"Thank you, Etta."

"How did you meet him? Oliver, I mean."

"Last week I had to go to Romney Marsh. As I approached the southernmost part of Upper Precinct where the woods are thickest beside the road, I came upon a man who had clearly been asleep only moments before. The sound of the horse's hooves must have awakened him."

I nodded impatiently. I did not care what had awakened the man.

Jesse continued. "He approached me and I slowed to speak to him. He was respectful and sincere. He asked if I had any food I could spare. I told him I was not carrying any food, but offered to take him to Romney Marsh, where I would procure some for him."

"Is the man always hungry?" I mumbled. Jesse frowned at me.

"He said he had been in Romney Marsh and no one gave him food, so—"

"And why should they?" I interrupted. "He robbed the general store! Why should anyone feed him after that?"

"He only took the money from the general store so that he has enough to survive after he leaves here and continues on his journey. Do you want to know how I met him or not?" Jesse was becoming exasperated. I gestured for him to continue.

"I took pity on him. I promised to get food in Romney Marsh and to deliver it to him upon my return home. He said he would wait there for me to pass by again, and he was in exactly the same spot when I returned home just two hours later."

"So you gave him food. You also had to provide a roof over his head?"

"While Oliver ate the food I had brought for him, he told me about himself. He had been traveling and was looking for a place to stay. I told him our family has an inn, but he allowed as how he had no money."

"Except for what he can steal." I could not help myself.

Jesse ignored my comment. "I knew Mother would not allow him to stay in the inn, so I resolved to let him to stay in the barn. I asked where his money had gone and whether he is a tradesman. I thought perhaps he could find work."

"And is he a tradesman?" I doubted so.

"He did not answer me except to say he had been involved in transporting certain goods. I know that to be a euphemism for smuggling, and that led me to believe he is a supporter of the British cause. Someone in this area would not use that phrase if they were assisting the Continental army. I realized he and I are not so very different."

"You're quite different, Jesse. You are an honorable man and he is not. Just because you both support King George does not make you similar."

"Being a fellow supporter of the British cause, I felt a kinship with him, Etta. I felt it was my patriotic duty to help him."

I scoffed. "How long must he stay?"

"I do not know."

"He cannot stay forever. Neither you nor I can keep his presence from Mother and Father and everyone else indefinitely." My voice was becoming urgent. We had stopped walking and were facing each other.

"I am sure he will wish to move on 'ere long. A man cannot provide for himself merely by begging food and shelter from strangers. He will need to leave in order to find work.

"And speaking of work, I need to get this food to him and help Father with the work in the fields."

I returned to the kitchen, where Prissy was again waiting for me with a question in her blue eyes.

I could not answer her unspoken question, so I told her I needed to clean the parlor. I left her in the kitchen by herself.

Later that afternoon I was sweeping the porch of the inn and the tavern when Mother stuck her head outside. "Where is Priscilla?" she asked.

"She was in the kitchen after dinner."

Mother went back indoors. I continued sweeping for a moment, then wondered, with increasing unease, what Mother needed Prissy for. I dropped the broom and hurried to the kitchen in time to hear Mother instruct Prissy to go to the barn to fetch the washtub.

"I'll go," I offered.

Mother turned around. "You're sweeping the porch."

"I'm done, so I'll run out to the barn. That way Prissy can continue getting supper ready and preparing the corn to put up for the winter."

Mother raised an eyebrow and gave me a look that said *Do not countermand my orders again*, but she said nothing. I breathed a quiet sigh of relief as Prissy returned to the corn she was preparing and Mother went back to the parlor.

I could not let Prissy go out to the barn by herself. What would happen if Oliver was in there? I suppressed a shudder and tried not to think about my younger sister alone with that lech.

When I reached the barn, I announced myself in a loud voice as I pulled the heavy door open.

I stepped into the gloom and stood in silence, straining my ears for any sound from Oliver. I wondered where he was, or if he might be asleep somewhere in the barn.

I made my way to the back of the barn, where the washtub hung on the wall. Looking left and right, I did not see anyone. I did, however, see a small bundle of something, probably clothing, on the floor. There was also a trencher and a knife, ones I recognized as coming from our kitchen, and the basket Jesse had given to Oliver that morning. But there was no Oliver. I think it was then that I finally allowed myself to breathe normally.

I lifted the washtub from the hook on the wall and noticed, as I turned to leave, a candlestick on the floor next to the bundle of clothes. Looking around, as if I were about to be caught stealing, I nipped the candlestick, placed it in the washtub, and left the barn.

Back in the kitchen, I quietly slipped the candlestick under one of the low shelves. Out of the corner of my eye I could see Prissy watching me, but before I could say anything Mother came into the room. She gave me a sharp look.

"What did you just put under that shelf?"

I didn't answer right away. I was startled to know she had seen me. Without waiting for an answer, Mother continued.

"Is that what I think it is? Is that the candlestick I have been searching for? Etta? Answer me this instant."

"Yes, Mother." She would ask more questions and I needed to think of answers.

"What is it doing in the kitchen? It belongs in the front hall —you know that."

"I ... I just found it, Mother. I was going to return it to the cupboard in the front hall, but I remembered something I forgot to do."

I was fortunate Mother did not ask what I had forgotten to do, because I would have had to lie to her again. Instead, she rebuked me for my forgetfulness and carelessness in storing the candlestick.

"Upon my word, Antoinetta, I do not know how you can be so inattentive. I have enough to do around this inn without having to wonder if you are putting objects where they belong."

I looked at the ground in the proper manner of remorse. "I'm sorry, Mother. It will not happen again."

"See that it does not."

Mother left the room and I glanced over at Prissy, who was frowning at me. I could practically hear the words that were in her mind: *Why did you lie to Mother? Why did you accept blame for something you did not do? Why are you acting so strangely? And where did you find the candlestick?*

I could not answer those questions without betraying Jesse's secret. "Prissy, I have a good reason for accepting the blame for the missing candlestick, but right now I cannot tell you what the reason is. I am sorry. I will tell you sometime, but for now I ask that you trust me."

Prissy gave me a frown, but she nodded, her mouth in a worried grimace.

The next day was a storm of activity as Father and Thomas and the boys brought in more of the oat crop and Mother was busy preparing to host a meeting later in the afternoon of the Women's Relief Society members. They were organizing a sock and mitten drive for the soldiers in Pennsylvania. I had asked Mother if I could attend the meeting to be given an assignment to help, but she had declined, saying my time would be better spent preparing apples and cream for the other women attending, helping Prissy make supper, and preparing the rose madder solution and dyeing the cloth. I tried to be thankful for the opportunity to serve my family by doing as Mother asked, but I was unsuccessful. I wanted to do more. I was finding my nursing duties agreeable, but I also wanted to do something that would help the soldiers.

It was early in the afternoon when I heard Mother calling to Prissy.

"Priscilla, please come and help me with this!"

I had no idea what Mother needed help with, but I could not leave the dye to find out. It was some time later when I finally began to pull the large swathes of cloth out of the dye and drape them over nearby bushes to allow them to dry. After that task was done, I dried off my arms and hands and went into the house to offer to help Prissy with the meal and other preparations.

I found Prissy in the kitchen, as I had suspected, chopping onions for the fragrant pottage which hung from a hob over the fire. Tears were streaming down her face, and I chuckled at the sight. I knew how uncomfortable it could be chopping onions.

"I may have had to prepare dye and the cloth this afternoon, but at least I got out of chopping onions," I said with a smile. I expected Prissy to roll her eyes and grin, but instead she put her head down and her shoulders shook.

This was not crying brought on by the chopping of onions. I hurried to her side.

"Prissy, what happened? Can you explain? Can you show me? Are you ill?"

Prissy shook her head, her face turning a deep shade of pink.

"Something went wrong, didn't it, Pris? Did Mother say something to upset you?" I could feel my chest constrict at the thought. But Prissy shook her head.

"Did you burn yourself? Cut yourself with the knife? Show me." But Prissy shook her head again, running a sleeve across her eyes and nose to wipe the tears away.

"Did something happen to Father or one of the boys?" My blood ran cold. I didn't even want to entertain the thought of anything happening to one of them. Prissy continued to shake her head.

"Was it—"

But I was interrupted by Mother, who came into the kitchen and asked Prissy to follow her to the parlor. She had a task she needed Prissy to do, she said. I took over chopping the onions and the other vegetables that would go into the pottage while I watched them leave. Mother didn't even seem to notice Prissy's distress.

The afternoon only became busier after that. The members of the Women's Relief Society arrived just two short hours later and Prissy and I were kept running between serving them and readying the dining room for supper guests. I supposed it was a good thing Mother had not allowed me to attend the meeting— Prissy would not have been able to complete all the chores by herself—but I would have loved to listen in on their plans and preparations.

After the women left and supper was over, Father asked Prissy to serve in the tavern while I cleaned the kitchen and dining room. When I trudged into the tavern, it was late in the evening and I was exhausted. To my surprise, Elijah was there. He was deep in conversation with Father and the boys and though he looked up when I entered the room, he quickly looked away, ignoring me as usual. He ordered ale from Father or Prissy. *He is so superior,* I thought peevishly. But part of me wondered why the rest of my family seemed not to be below his notice.

From the intense looks on the faces of those gathered, I knew the men were discussing something of great importance. I sidled closer to them, busying myself with cleaning the floor, the shelves where we kept the mugs, and the counter. They lowered their voices, but I was still able to make out some of their words.

"I have heard that the Tories intend to create havoc here in Cape May County, and particularly in Upper Precinct," Elijah said, his head drawing ever closer to Father's. Sylvanus and Jesse looked on, frowning. I wondered if Jesse was frowning because he was expected to or because he did not want other people to know what the Tories had planned.

"What sort of havoc?" Father asked.

Elijah shook his head. "I wish I knew more. We must be diligent and watchful, Nathaniel. I know you have no intention of fighting, but we can count on you to help our cause as much as possible, am I correct?"

Father nodded. "We will help you in any way we can, short of taking up arms."

The thoughts running through my mind were staggering. I had already heard this information from Isaac, and the more people who knew about possible troublemaking by the British supporters in the southern part of New Jersey, the more likely it was to be true. This made me especially nervous about Jesse. Was he part of the plan to wreak havoc where we lived? It didn't seem possible that he would go to such lengths to support the troops under the command of King George.

But he was undoubtedly a supporter of the British soldiers. I had to admit that it certainly was possible.

I needed to talk to Jesse, alone and quickly.

CHAPTER 10

That night after Jesse locked the tavern, I waited for him on the porch. Mother and Father had gone ahead to bed, so no one would be watching us or wondering what we were talking about.

Jesse smiled when he saw me. "Were you waiting for me?" he asked.

"Yes. I have some questions for you."

"What are they?"

I took his arm and drew him away from the front door of the inn. "Jesse, are the rumors true that British supporters are intent on causing trouble hereabouts?"

"You do not need to worry about anything like that, Etta."

"You did not answer my question, Jesse, and I will not be put off that easily."

"I do not know anything specific. The other British supporters in this part of New Jersey know that I am a Quaker and that my family owns the inn and the tavern along Great Egg Harbor Bay. They do not wish me to renounce my religion, even though I have told them I am willing to do that. They are

careful what they tell me because they know I am in an uncomfortable situation."

I looked away, searching the darkness for reassurance and
answers I knew were not out there.

"Etta? They have assured me they have no plans to cause any
trouble near us or our property."

"That is not good enough, Jesse. They cannot do anything. It
will draw us closer to the war. Are you not afraid of that?"

"No. I want the war to end, and if bringing it close to home
is the way to do that, then so shall it be."

I balled my hands in frustration with my brother. How could
he not see that the war encroaching on our shores could bring
only sorrow and pain? I wanted the war to end, too, but I
wanted it to stay as far away from Upper Precinct as possible.

"Etta, I'm glad you waited for me tonight. I have a favor to
ask of you."

I suspected what Jesse was going to ask me. Though he had said
nothing about Oliver, I knew the man was still staying in the barn. I
had seen evidence of his presence. Someone, likely Jesse, had fash-
ioned another candlestick for Oliver out of wood, and I had found
it in the barn while there to deposit corn cobs and husks into the
cribs where they would be left to dry. I also found remnants of
small meals that had, no doubt, been provided by Jesse.

I had a hunch Jesse was going to ask me to do something
that benefitted Oliver in some way. And I was correct.

"I cannot let the animals out or take breakfast to Oliver
tomorrow morning, Etta. I have promised to go to the fields
early with Father and Sylvanus. The nights are getting colder
and Father wants the oats completely harvested as soon as
possible. Can you take Oliver breakfast in the morning?"

I gritted my teeth as I faced my brother. "You know how I
feel about Oliver. I do not want to take anything to him. Can he
not miss one meal?"

"Please do this for me. I have been speaking to him about leaving for Philadelphia, and I think he will go there to find work soon. He may only be here for a few more days."

"What is preventing him from going to Philadelphia now?"

"He was quite weak from hunger when I found him on the road all those days ago, and I think he is trying to regain his strength before making the trip to Philadelphia."

He had not looked weak from hunger to me. I sighed. "Very well. If it will make him leave sooner, I will take breakfast to him in the morning. Mind you, I will only do it this one time."

"That is all I ask. Thank you. I appreciate it."

Jesse and I went into the inn and retired to our bedrooms. As I brought the coverlet up to my chin, I thought I heard a noise coming from Prissy's side of the bed. I listened closely, but heard nothing.

"Pris?" I spoke in the lowest whisper I could manage. But she did not answer, so I closed my eyes. It was a long time before I slept, because my mind was filled with possible excuses I could offer her in the morning to explain why I had to go out to the barn so early.

I finally determined to simply tell her the truth, or at least part of it: Jesse asked me to let the animals out since he had to accompany Father and Sylvanus to the field so early.

I was able to sleep after that.

When Prissy and I went to the kitchen the next morning, we found Father and the boys filling their pockets with bread and apples for their breakfast. I hurried to provide mugs of steaming coffee, too, but Father said they did not have time to wait.

They hurried outside into the black morning and I left shortly after they did, telling Prissy that I had to let the animals out of the barn early so Jesse could go with Father. Her eyes grew wide and she grabbed my sleeve, shaking her head.

"I have to go, Prissy. The animals need to be let out."

She shook her head again, her eyes grave, and stood in front of the door.

"Prissy, you have to let me go. Is something bothering you?" She nodded solemnly.

It was at that moment I realized, with a sudden sick clenching of my stomach, exactly what was wrong with Prissy.

CHAPTER 11

"**You** know about the man in the barn, don't you?" I asked in a gentle voice. She nodded again. A single tear rolled down her cheek, and I finally understood her crying and her reluctance to let me go outside alone.

"Don't worry about me, Pris. I can take care of myself. He won't dare bother me. And we'll make sure he doesn't bother you, either. But this is important: do not let Mother or Father or anyone else, even Sylvanus, know that Oliver is in the barn. Heaven only knows what will happen to Jesse if anyone else finds out." Prissy took a deep breath and let it out slowly. We could hear footsteps approaching, and we turned toward the sound.

Mother stood in the doorway to the kitchen. "Good. I'm glad you're both in here early. You need to get started changing out the mattress husks this morning." Every fall we took the worn corn husks out of the mattresses upstairs and replaced them with fresh ones, and though the job was tedious, it was not difficult.

It was fortunate Mother came into the kitchen when she did, because it afforded me the opportunity to go to the barn without Prissy joining me, as I was sure she would insist upon doing.

"Mother, I have to let the animals out of the barn this morning. Jesse and Sylvanus have already left with Father."

Mother sighed. "Very well. Priscilla, you get started on the mattress in the empty guest room. Antoinetta will join you when she returns from the barn. I will prepare breakfast myself today. I would like some strawberries with my porridge, so this will give me an excuse to fetch some berries from the storehouse." Her eyes took on a wistful look. "Our cook used to serve strawberries every day for breakfast when I was young." She bestowed one of her rare smiles upon us. "Would you girls care for strawberries?"

We nodded and I thanked her enthusiastically, then I wheeled around and left through the back door before anyone could stop me. I picked up the basket I had left outside and walked at a fast clip toward the barn. As much as I would have liked to take my time so Oliver would have to wait for his breakfast, I dared not take too long. Mother's benign mood would not last; she would be angry if I did not return to the inn very soon to help refresh the mattresses. Besides that, I did not like to linger in the woods alone.

When I reached the barn, I let the animals out before venturing further inside to find Oliver. At length I took up the basket and, holding my lamp in front of me, I walked slowly toward the back of the barn.

"What took so long?" came a deep, raspy voice. My heart thumped in my chest and I swallowed before answering.

"I had to let the animals out first. I've brought your breakfast because Jesse had to go out to the fields early this morning." Why was I explaining myself to this man?

There was a shuffling noise and a moment later Oliver appeared in the dim circle of light cast by my lamp. I tried not to gasp, but I was taken aback by his appearance. He was unshaven and the hair on his face gave him an unnatural, bestial look. I took a step backward, and his face split into a leering grin.

"Ah, the older sister. What have you brought me to eat?"

"Bread and butter and two apples."

"Nothing else?"

"No. If you want to eat more, I'm afraid you'll have to go elsewhere."

Oliver clenched his jaw and I took another step backward. But I was too slow, and he grabbed my arm in a swift and sudden move.

"Let go of me," I demanded.

"Why don't you come back here with me?" His breath reeked of rot and uncleanliness. He gripped my arm tighter. "I've got a nice bed set up on the ground. Nice and soft. Come on."

"I most certainly will not. Jesse will hear of this, you can be sure."

Oliver laughed, a harsh, menacing sound, as he threw my arm away from him. "Get out of here, girl. I like your sister better. She's easier on the eyes than you are."

I whirled around and fled. How dare he treat me in such a way? My heart pounded so hard I feared I would faint before getting far enough away from him, but eventually I was able to slow down and catch my breath. It would not do to allow Mother to see me in such a state, so I calmed myself before going back inside. I avoided the kitchen door, knowing Mother would be in there. I went through the front door of the inn instead.

I seethed with anger every time my mind repeated the words Oliver had spoken: *I like your sister better. She's easier on the eyes than you are.*

Part of me was ashamed and embarrassed by my own vanity. Was I that homely? Was I so unattractive that a man, starved for attention from any female, would discard me?

A much larger part of me, however, was terrified at the thought of what Oliver might do if he got hold of Prissy. I would have to keep her in my sight at all times until the odious beast left our property for good.

After breakfast, which included some of the sweet, deep red strawberries we had preserved over the summer, Prissy and I went upstairs to the unused guest room. She turned to look at me as I walked into the room, her eyes full of questions and concern. She had not stopped thinking about me going to the barn where Oliver stayed, I was sure.

"It's all right, Pris. I'm fine. But I do not want you going anywhere by yourself until that man is gone. I will speak to Jesse and make sure he sends Oliver away as quickly as possible."

Prissy lowered her eyes and nodded. I sat down on the floor next to her and together we worked in silence, removing the corn husks from the muslin cover and placing them in large piles on the floor. It was a thankless task because the piles would have to be taken out of the room to burn and then the small debris from the husks would have to be swept up, but the next person to sleep in the bed would be pleased with the fresh mattress fill. It would have been a good time for me to ask her why she had been crying the other night and to try to figure out what had upset her, but my thoughts were preoccupied with wondering when Oliver might leave.

After we had worked for a while I went to check on Isaac. His eyelids fluttered at the sound of me entering the room, but he did not stir. I had brought a small dish of strawberries with me, hoping their heady scent would rouse him from his spasmodic sleep, but even they did not work to waken him. I crept softly out of the room, went downstairs to refill a pitcher with cider, and returned to his room, where I placed the drink on the bedside table. I wished he would open his eyes and talk. It would be a welcome indication that he was feeling better, but perhaps the fever could be conquered by sleep.

After the midday meal, Prissy and I completed our work in the empty guest room and moved on to the mattresses in our family's quarters behind the parlor. We started with Mother and Father's bed, of course. I had to leave to answer a traveler's query and was only gone for a few minutes. When I returned to the bedroom, I was dismayed to see Prissy wiping tears from her cheeks.

"Prissy? Are you ill?" This time I could hear her swallow hard.

"Prissy, are you all right? Answer me." My whispered words were gaining urgency.

There was a loud sniffle and she turned to face me.

"Pris, why are you crying? What happened?"

She sniffled and shook her head.

"Can you show me what happened to make you cry?"

Over the years, Prissy had grown to be adept at using her hands and facial expressions to communicate with our family. We almost always understood her meaning. But this time she shook her head again.

"You can tell me."

She stared at me for a long moment, then pointed toward the bay.

"Is it something outside?"

She nodded.

"In the bay?"

No.

"Is it Father or the boys?"

No.

"The fields?"

No.

"The barn?"

At the mention of the barn, Prissy's body stiffened. I felt a sudden drop in my stomach, as if I could sense an impending doom. She closed her eyes.

"Are you upset about Oliver?"

She nodded ever so slightly.

"Are you crying because of something Oliver did?"

Another nod.

"To you?"

Yes.

"Was it the lecherous thing he did to you in the tavern?"

No.

The tiniest hint of nausea began to make itself felt in the very bottom of my stomach.

"It was something else?"

No response.

"Prissy, did Oliver do something else to you, after what happened in the tavern?"

A fat tear snaked down her cheek.

The nausea made its way into my throat.

"What did he do?"

Prissy put her hands over her ears, then shook her head. Her eyes were squeezed shut.

I touched her arm gently. When had Oliver had an opportunity to do anything to Prissy? I had made sure she stayed away from the barn after his disturbing behavior toward her in the tavern.

Then realization began to dawn. Images of me, my arms in madder dye up to my elbows, Mother demanding that Prissy do some chore or other.

She had sent Prissy to the barn.

I inhaled sharply. "Were you ever alone in the barn with him?"

She made a choking sound in assent. My breath came faster. "Did he lay a hand on you?"

The choking sound became a quiet sob and I knew what had happened.

"Did he hurt you?"

She nodded. Her hair fell around her face and she made no move to push it out of her eyes. I tried to do it so I could see her clearly, but she shook her head with great force and buried her face in her knees, which she had drawn up to her chest. She was hiding. She was embarrassed.

"Prissy, I'm so sorry. This is all my fault. I should have insisted that you not be sent out-of-doors by yourself as long as I knew that monster was in the barn. Please forgive me."

I started to cry then, and before I knew what was happening Prissy had wrapped her arms around my shoulders and we were crying together, as quietly as we could so the other people in the house would not hear us. I knew Prissy would forgive me, but I doubted I would ever forgive myself.

I had no choice but to try to figure out what had happened. It was the only way I could help her.

As far as I could gather from questioning Prissy, Oliver had scared her and attempted to force himself upon her. Before he could know her carnally, though, it seemed a noise outside the barn had stopped him. I couldn't bear to think what would have happened if Oliver hadn't been scared by the noise, fearing someone would discover him committing a foul deed against my sister.

I was sick. I hated to leave Prissy, but I fled the room and barely made it to the privy in time to disgorge the contents of my stomach. When I could stand up without feeling dizzy, I ran back to Prissy.

She was dutifully filling the mattress cover with the corn husks. Her eyes had finally dried.

"Prissy, let me finish that. You go lie down. I'll tell Mother you're ill."

She shook her head vehemently. She clearly wanted to stay busy, so we worked until it was time to prepare supper.

"I will have to tell Father about this," I said. Prissy let go of the husks she was holding and gripped my hands in hers. She shook her head violently.

"You do not want me to tell Father?"

She indicated *no* with a shake of her head.

"All right. I will not tell him."

Prissy let out a sigh of relief and went back to stuffing the mattress.

Very well. I wouldn't tell Father. But she hadn't asked me not to tell anyone else, and I had every intention of telling Jesse what had happened. I was determined to tell him to send Oliver away that very night.

CHAPTER 12

*T*hat evening the dining room was full of people. Jesse and Sylvanus were talking excitedly about the Court Day coming up in October, when families from all over the county would visit Romney Marsh for a day filled with food, games, and visiting—once the court business had concluded, of course. Spectators had even been treated to an exciting display of military cannons at the last two Court Days. I was relieved to hear Jesse talking about it, because that meant he might be planning to stay in Upper Precinct instead of leaving to take up arms with the British. Given what had happened to Prissy, it was even more important now for Jesse to stay.

I kicked him under the table as we ate. He looked up at me in surprise, but thankfully didn't say anything. I nodded slightly and glanced toward the front hall. I hoped he understood what I wanted.

He understood. I met him in the front hall several minutes later, after the diners had all left to their own pursuits. I took Jesse's arm and led him into the guest parlor, which was empty of people.

"What is so important and secretive, Etta?"

"Oliver did something awful to Prissy."

"I know that, the rotter. I spoke to him about it. I told you that."

"I mean, he did something awful a second time. He tried defiling her."

My brother's eyes widened with understanding and a flush began to rise from his neck until his entire face was the color of madder dye. He clenched and unclenched his fists.

"Jesse, you have to send him away tonight."

"I will. I swear it."

"Send who away?" Sylvanus stood in the doorway. Jesse and I exchanged looks.

"I asked, who is being sent away?"

"I'll take care of this, Etta. I'll tell him everything." Jesse nodded toward Sylvanus.

"Tell me what?"

"I have something disturbing to discuss with you," Jesse said.

I returned to the kitchen and several minutes later I heard the front door slam. I peeked into the guest parlor and it was empty again.

The next morning I found Oliver's body.

CHAPTER 13

SEPTEMBER 24, 1777

I do not remember getting back to the inn after finding Oliver's body. The next thing I remember is being handed a cup of something that made my throat burn. The coughing fit it caused was enough to bring me back to alertness. I was startled to find Mother and Prissy leaning in close over the chair I was sitting on.

"Etta, what could possibly have happened to cause you to act in such a way?" Mother was frowning, as I should have expected. Prissy stood behind her, blinking rapidly. Her hands trembled.

"There's a dead man in the barn." I could hardly believe it, even though I had seen Oliver with my own eyes.

"Etta, I do not have time for such foolishness. You should be ashamed of yourself. Trying to attract attention like that is very unladylike. Why, when I was a young girl in Philadelphia, if I had done something so imprudent, I would have been sent to my bedroom without tea or cakes."

I could feel my face redden, whether in embarrassment or anger, I did not know. "I'm not trying to attract attention, Mother. There is a dead man in the barn. I tripped over him."

Mother's eyes narrowed as she regarded me in silence for a moment.

"Please, send someone to fetch the sheriff. Have Father and the boys come back from the field." I took another sip of the amber liquid in the mug I was holding and winced. It steadied my nerves, though, and I stood up on shaky legs. Mother made no move to do as I was pleading.

"Very well, I'll get Father and Jesse and Sylvanus myself," I announced. My voice sounded stronger than it felt. Prissy grabbed my arm. She shook her head with a force I did not usually see from her. I gently took her fingers from my forearm.

"Prissy, I have to go. The only other person in the inn is Isaac, and he is too weak to sit up in his own bed, let alone go outside."

Her arms fell to her sides. She was resigned to my leaving.

"You and Mother stay here. As soon as I reach Father, he will send Jesse or Sylvanus to get the sheriff."

Mother opened the front door and glanced outside, then looked around at me. "I don't see anyone or anything out of the ordinary. You very likely tripped over something left on the ground carelessly and have convinced yourself it was a man's body." She shook her head and sighed.

I answered her without even thinking about it. "Mother, I know what I saw and what's more, I know who it is." I closed my eyes in chagrin, realizing I had just put Jesse in jeopardy, but there was no point in attempting to hide Oliver's presence any longer.

At this revelation, Mother's eyes became round and white, like the full moon in winter. "Who is it?"

"A man named Oliver Doolittle." In a very short time, everyone in the entire county would know who he was and that he died in our barn.

"Who is he? How do you know a dead man?" Mother asked. Her voice had risen and the color was draining from her cheeks.

"Please, Mother. Let me go get Father and the boys and I will explain everything as soon as I can." I did not wait for her to answer, but brushed past her out the front door and ran in the direction of the field. I stopped short as soon as I was out of sight of the house. What was I doing out here by myself? Someone had killed a man and here I was, alone without any way of protecting myself. I took a shaky breath and turned around to run back to the inn and safety.

But something stopped me. I could not let Oliver's death go unreported. Who else was going to do it? Certainly not Prissy. Not Isaac. And Mother seemed an unlikely choice. It was left to me. I whimpered a little in fear as my heart raced. I couldn't very well stand like this for the rest of the day. I determined to run as fast as I could to Father and the boys. I only hoped no one was lurking about.

I ran as fast as a rabbit. When I was close enough to see Father and Thomas and the boys, I yelled for them. I yelled as if the very devil was chasing me. They all stopped what they were doing at once and started toward me—even Thomas was hurrying despite his lame leg. When we reached each other, I had to bend over and put my hands on my knees to catch my breath. While I was doing that, Father and the boys peppered me with questions.

"What is it, Etta?"

"Is someone hurt?"

"Is Mother ill?"

"Is Prissy all right?"

Finally I was able to slow my breathing and straighten up. I swallowed hard. "There is a dead man in the barn." I looked at Jesse, whose face had paled. "It's Oliver."

Father and Sylvanus paled, too. Father looked from me to Jesse and back to me, his mouth hanging agape. "Who is Oliver? Why is he dead? Why is he in our barn?"

"I can explain, Father," Jesse said. "But first I'll get the sheriff." Without waiting for a reply, he fled.

His departure seemed to spur Father to action. "Let's go. Thomas, you stay here and keep working. We'll be back to join you if we can." He and Sylvanus started running. Though my chest hurt as if my lungs were on fire, I kept up with them. I had no intention of staying behind by myself. When we reached the inn, Father stopped and turned to me. "Etta, you tell Mother Jesse is getting the sheriff. Sylvanus and I will go to the barn to see what we can learn." He and Sylvanus left at a quick clip. Before he left with Father, Sylvanus caught my eye. The look he shared with me was one of fear mixed with trepidation and disbelief. The truth would have to come out now.

I found Mother and Prissy in the parlor. Prissy was staring at her hands folded in her lap while Mother paced the floor, muttering to herself. I told them breathlessly where Father and the boys were. Mother turned to look at me with an expression of confusion and disquiet.

"Etta, are you sure of what you saw?"

"Absolutely sure, Mother."

"How do you know the identity of the man in the barn?"

I paused. How much to reveal? "He had been staying in the barn for several days."

Mother gasped. "And you were aware of this?" I nodded. "Why was he staying in the barn?"

"He had no money and nowhere else to go."

"How did you come to meet this man?"

"Jesse found him on the road between here and Romney Marsh."

"So it was Jesse who brought him here?"

I nodded again. I despised myself for telling her about Jesse's involvement with Oliver, but there was no way to hide it now.

"And you helped Jesse hide the man?"

"No. I merely took the man food two or three times."

"Was he feeble?"

"No."

"Upon my word, Antoinetta. You were foolhardy to allow him to stay in our barn."

"But I—" I started to protest, but Mother held up her hand for silence.

"You knew there was a sturdy beggar staying in our barn and you allowed him to remain. Not only that, but you took food to him. Am I correct?"

"Yes, but—"

Mother held up her hand again.

"You will face severe punishment for this, Antoinetta. To think that you allowed this family to be placed in danger because of—"

Father and Sylvanus came into the parlor. Father wiped a hand across his eyes. "I suppose you know what happened?" he asked Mother.

"All I know is that there is a dead beggar in the barn, he has been living in there for days, and his name is Oliver."

"Then you know more than I do." Father turned to me. "You found him, Etta?"

"Yes, Father."

"I have seen him someplace before," Father said, his eyes narrowed in concentration.

Sylvanus spoke up. "He is the man who toasted the health of King George in the tavern." Father nodded with the realization as he and Mother exchanged glances with eyes wide as saucers. "Who invited that man into the barn?"

All eyes turned to me. I could feel myself withering under their stares. "It was Jesse, Father," I said in a small voice. I was spared having to respond to angry replies by arrival of Jesse, who burst into the inn with the sheriff close behind him.

"I met the sheriff on the road not far from here." Jesse was breathless from riding so fast.

"Nathaniel, Davinia." The sheriff nodded at my parents. He looked grim. "It's true, then? There is a body in the barn? Who is it?"

Father stepped forward. "It is a beggar who has been in the tavern on at least one occasion."

"Why was he in the barn?"

Father glanced at Jesse. "My son allowed him to stay there without my knowledge."

Jesse added, "He is a man I met on the road to Romney Marsh. He had no place to stay and no money, so I offered him the barn to lay his head. He was to leave last night."

Father gave Jesse a suspicious look. "Where was he going?"

Jesse shook his head. "I do not know. I told him he had to leave."

The sheriff looked from Father to Jesse. "I have more questions, but I'd like you to take me to the barn right now." He pointed at Sylvanus. "My deputy was taken ill this morning, so I need you to fetch the coroner." Sylvanus nodded and departed.

Father led the way, followed by the sheriff and Jesse. Mother and Prissy and I remained in the house, looking warily at each other.

It was two hours later when we saw the sheriff, followed by Father and Jesse, coming from the barn toward the front of the house. The sheriff was carrying a large sack. When they got to the inn, the sheriff led the way into our family parlor. Father followed him and beckoned Mother to accompany them, then closed the door. Prissy and I could hear Mother's voice inside, so we crept near the door so we could hear what was being said without fear of being caught eavesdropping.

"I've taken the personal belongings I found in the barn," the sheriff said.

"Does anything belong to us?" Mother asked.

"I don't know." We heard a rustling sound, then the sheriff spoke again. "Do these look like yours?"

"Yes!" Mother cried. "Those belong in the kitchen. What else is in there?"

We heard more rustling, and finally Mother spoke again. "I'm relieved to have the trenchers and utensils again. And the baskets, too. Upon my word, had that man no shame?"

"There is something even more important," the sheriff said. "I found the paper listing the locations of the hidden munitions in Cape May County—the one that had been stolen from Romney Marsh. The man in your barn must have known the importance of the list. I wonder if he shared the information with anyone."

Father replied in a grave voice. "I wish there were a way to ask him."

A noise at the front door startled us, and Prissy and I jumped away from the parlor door. Sylvanus came inside and frowned when he saw our sheepish faces.

"The sheriff is in there," I whispered, pointing to the parlor. "We wanted to know what he found."

Sylvanus nodded and gestured over his shoulder with his thumb. "I've brought the coroner. He's on the porch." He knocked on the door and opened it after Father instructed him to enter.

Presently the sheriff came out to greet the coroner. The two men climbed into the coroner's wagon and directed his horse toward the barn. Their heads were bent close together in conversation and I wondered what would happen to Oliver's body.

Before long, the coroner emerged from the woods in his wagon. A long object wrapped in burlap was laid out on top of the box behind the coroner's seat. Oliver's body. I was thankful I didn't have to see it again. I shuddered as I watched the horse plod toward the road not far from the house. Prissy held my arm as the wagon passed by, her fingernails digging into my skin.

"He's gone, Prissy. There's nothing to worry about now."

But there *was* something to worry about. I had seen Oliver's body and he had not been alone when he died. Someone killed him.

CHAPTER 14

*E*arly the next morning the sheriff returned to our house to ask me more questions about the condition of Oliver's body when I stumbled over him.

"What time was it when you found him?" he asked.

"I did not look at a clock before I left the house, but it was still dark out and everyone else was asleep. At least, I assume they were."

"Did you notice any strange or unusual noises while you were in the barn? Or maybe outside the barn?"

I closed my eyes so I could think clearly without having to stare at the sheriff's face. "No, I don't recall hearing anything out of the ordinary."

"Did you notice any footprints in the dirt near the barn door?"

"No."

"Did you, by chance, remove anything from the area around Oliver's body?"

"Only the washtub."

"Can you think of anything that might have been of importance?"

"I do not believe so, Sheriff."

"So you did not see a weapon of any kind," he said with a frown.

"No, Sheriff."

Mother was vexed when the sheriff left.

"Does that man think you have nothing better to do?" she asked, shaking her head.

It did not seem the type of question that required an answer.

After checking on Isaac, I hurried to help Prissy prepare dinner, but she had finished most of the work by the time the sheriff left the house. I went into the parlor to work on a basket of mending when I heard the front door open. I set aside the mending and went into the foyer to see who was there.

A man I had never seen before stood inside the front door. He was disheveled, with crumpled clothing, a beard that needed trimming and washing, and a hat that needed mending. I fought the urge to take it right off his head and fix it for him.

"Might you have a room to spare in your establishment?" he asked.

"Yes, Friend. There is a room available upstairs."

"Would you be willing to rent it to me? I'll keep my comings and goings quiet."

"Yes. We will rent it to you."

"Thank you."

"May I have your name?" I moved to the desk where Mother kept the guest log and picked up a pencil.

"Abel Smith."

"And where are you from?"

"Boston."

I noted the information in our ledger. "And will you stay just the night?"

"No. I am a salesman and I need a place to stay while I travel around the area. I may be here for several nights. Is there a place I can tie my horse?"

"There is a hitching post by the biggest tree out front. One of my brothers can show you the paddock later." I handed him the key to an empty room. "You'll notice that the mattress is not stuffed. My sister and I will do that at once."

He nodded and went back outdoors, where I watched him lead a beautiful black horse to the hitching post. The horse was laden with boxes and sacks. I wondered what goods Abel sold. He began to take the parcels from the horse's back and flanks; I hurried to get Prissy so we could stuff the mattress quickly.

Mother was in the kitchen issuing instructions to Prissy about serving the noon meal when I found them.

"Excuse me, Mother. We have a new guest. Prissy and I need to stuff the mattress in the empty guest room."

Mother frowned. "What guest?"

"He just arrived. He's unloading his horse right now."

"Who is he?"

"His name is Abel Smith. He's a salesman."

Mother wrinkled her nose. "'Smith' is a very common name. What does he sell?"

It seemed uncharitable of Mother to comment on the commonness of Abel's surname, but I said nothing, as doing so would only have exasperated her. "I don't know what he sells. I only know that he has a large number of boxes and sacks hanging from his horse."

"Hmm. I will speak to him. We don't want any unsavory sorts renting rooms here."

I knew Mother would find Abel's appearance suspect. He was in clear need of a bath. I motioned for Prissy to follow me so we could finish the mattress before dinner.

We stuffed the corn husks into the mattress quickly. While we worked we could hear the front door of the inn open and close several times. I figured Abel was bringing his goods indoors before bringing them upstairs to give me and Prissy time to finish preparing his room. I could hear Mother tut-tutting every time he went back outside.

After we finished the mattress, we stretched a sheet and a coverlet across the bed. By the time we swept the floor of the extra corn husk pieces, Abel was bringing the first of what would be many loads of items up the stairs.

"Thank you, Miss Rutledge."

"You are welcome." I continued downstairs, followed by Prissy. People were already gathering in the dining room for dinner.

We found Mother, who was in a state of high excitement.

"Antoinetta, I do not want that man staying here. You should have consulted with me before allowing him to rent a room."

"I'm sorry, Mother. He seems polite, even if he is dirty."

"It's not just his odor. He is not merely a salesman, but a *peddler*, Antoinetta." She said the word *peddler* like it was shameful.

"What's wrong with being a peddler? We see them around here all the time."

"But one has never stayed here before. They have a reputation for being ill-bred and boisterous."

"Abel seems neither ill-bred nor boisterous."

"We shall see."

Shortly after the noon meal, I was about to walk into the parlor when I heard Father and Mother in earnest conversation. I stood listening at the door, hoping they would not notice my presence.

"Let the man stay for now, Davinia. We need the money that comes from renting the room. If he becomes a problem, we will ask him to leave."

Mother sighed loudly. "As you wish, Nathaniel. I will see to it that he is adequately comfortable. Between him and the sick man upstairs, I feel like we are running an almshouse. My parents would be horrified if they were still alive."

Father let out a low chuckle. "Your parents would be horrified if you were anything less than empress of the colonies."

I crept away from the parlor and instead went up to check on Isaac. He still lay in the bed, squirming in discomfort, but his eyes were open and he managed the words "thank you" when I refreshed the cool cloth on his head and hurried downstairs for more cider. He was even able to take the mug with both hands and raise it to his lips himself. It seemed he was finally beginning to improve, and I hoped it would continue.

Abel took supper with the rest of the guests and diners that evening, then repaired to the tavern with the other men afterward. Mother went too, with a look of distaste on her face as she watched Abel walk away from the dining room.

Later Thaddeus Marshall came into the tavern. Prissy looked disappointed that he had not brought his fiddle. Everyone greeted him fondly, as he was a favorite among the men present.

"Evening, Thaddeus," Father said.

"Evening, gentlemen," he replied, his eyes sweeping the room. "Nathaniel, how about a large measure of ale? I could use some after what I've read." He held up a newspaper in his hand.

"Eh, Thaddeus?" Ben Drake asked. "You'll read it aloud, won't you?"

Thaddeus nodded and sat down at a table with a couple other men. I took the ale to him and he thanked me with his kind smile. "There's a good girl, Etta."

He took a long draught of the ale and wiped his lips with his sleeve. "Ah, just what I needed. Your ale is always sure to settle my nerves, Nathaniel." Father smiled broadly at the compliment.

"Get to the newspaper, man," Ben said. "What have you learned?"

Thaddeus took another long draught and set the tankard aside. He adjusted his spectacles. Men talked among themselves quietly for a moment, but as soon as Thaddeus reached for his newspaper, all talk stopped. Everyone was interested in hearing the news.

All eyes were on Thaddeus as he cleared his throat and scanned the paper in front of him. My mother nodded at me and I carried a candlestick and a tall candle to his table.

"Thank you, Etta," he said.

I bowed my head in response and turned around as if to leave the room, but I lingered in the doorway so I could hear what he had to say. My hands were clammy and my throat felt like it was closing. I hoped the armies weren't moving toward the south and our little part of New Jersey. Prissy was watching me with wide eyes, as if she could sense how I was feeling. I knew it made her nervous, too, so I tried to give her a bright smile. I'm afraid it looked like more of a grimace.

Thaddeus cleared his throat again and commenced reading from one of the stories in the paper.

"Now, this newspaper is from the fourteenth day of September, just eleven days ago," he began. He stopped reading aloud and scanned the article quickly. He looked around at the gathered men.

"This says General Washington's troops suffered defeat at Brandywine Creek on the eleventh day of September."

A chorus of murmurs arose from the men.

"How bad was it?" Richard Miller asked.

Thaddeus didn't answer right away, but continued reading the article silently. The entire room was silent, waiting for him to answer the question.

"It says here over a thousand casualties on our side."

Several of the men muttered oaths, shaking their heads and frowning.

"What else does it say, Thaddeus?" one of the neighbors finally asked.

"There's a story here about the British prohibition of

weapons and munitions. It seems some places are trying to fight the Tories without enough reliable weaponry. Those damnable Britons—laws like that are the reason we need to be free of the King's yoke." Thaddeus's voice was rising.

"Any other stories of interest?" my father asked. I knew he was attempting to keep Thaddeus from becoming over-excited.

"It does not appear so." He folded the thin newspaper and offered it to Father, who thanked him and asked me to put it in the parlor. He would read it later. He often accepted newspapers from Thaddeus as payment for ale.

The men all left the tavern earlier than usual that evening. It was the busiest part of the harvest season and almost all of them had crops to bring in. No doubt they, like Father and the boys, would be working in the fields long before the sun rose the next day.

Father spent a mere ten minutes perusing the newspaper in the parlor before going to sleep that night. After he went into the room he shared with Mother, the inn was quiet. I lay on my side and fell asleep listening to Prissy's breathing and to the rustling of the dry leaves as they swirled along the ground outside my window.

I felt safe inside the inn with the doors locked, but I wondered where Oliver's murderer was. I hoped he was far away.

CHAPTER 15

When I awoke some hours later, I was covered in a thin sheen of cold sweat and my cheeks were wet from tears I did not recall shedding. My heart beat a rapid rhythm in my chest and I feared Prissy would be awakened by the sound of it. A rushing noise in my ears made it hard to hear the silence in the dark room.

I had been having a bad dream. In my dream, I had found Oliver's body again, but this time it wore a hideous grin and it mocked me, reminding me that Prissy was the prettier sister. When I tried running away, the barn door was locked and everywhere I ran inside the dark building, I stumbled over Oliver's body again and again.

I squeezed my eyes shut and shook my head to dislodge the thoughts reeling around inside. I tried calming myself by taking deep breaths. Alas, sleep eluded me for the rest of the night.

I was cross and irritable that day, snapping at Prissy for things that were not her fault and groaning inwardly when Isaac, who was feeling a bit better, asked me to smooth his bedding and stay to talk to him after I had already taken breakfast to him. Did the man not realize I had other things to do besides look after him? Then I felt ashamed of myself for thinking so poorly of the man in my charge. A woman whose duty it was to nurse others back to health should not be thinking ill of them, I thought ruefully.

Prissy did her best to stay out of my sight that morning, and I could not blame her for doing so; I was a miserable wretch. She joined me when it was time to serve dinner at noon, but avoided my eyes lest I reprimand her for something else. I realized with chagrin that I sounded just like Mother.

I was pleased to see Thomas at dinner. I felt sorry for him, preparing his meals alone in his cabin. It was always better to take a meal with other people. Even Isaac appreciated having me for company when he was able to eat anything.

Father and Thomas and the boys returned to the fields as soon as they had finished dinner and Prissy and I spent the rest of the day refreshing the mattresses that had not yet been done. It was important to finish the beds in the guest rooms while the guests were out, so we had to hurry.

Much to our misfortune, there were not enough corn husks to fill the last mattress. Prissy looked at me and I knew what she was thinking: someone had to go out to the barn to fetch more stuffing.

The dread in my chest was heavy and dark. I could never ask her to go with me to the place where Oliver had tried to take his advantage of her, nor would I ask Mother to do it. I knew she would decline and say my fears were foolish. I could not ask Father or the boys to accompany me, since they were in the fields. Isaac certainly could not go with me, Abel Smith had been out all day, and there were no other guests I could ask.

I would have to do it myself.

"I'll go, Prissy." I took a deep breath. The thought of being in the barn, in the woods, while Oliver's killer roamed free was horrifying. Prissy clutched my arm and gave me a pleading look.

"I do not want you to go with me, Pris. You should stay here. I'm not afraid." I said a quick prayer that God would forgive my lie because I lied to protect my sister.

But Prissy shook her head several times and followed me downstairs, close on my heels.

I turned around at the door. "Very well. You can go, but let us hurry. I do not want to be out-of-doors or in that barn any longer than necessary."

I truly did not wish her to go with me, but I had to admit there was a small part of me that felt great relief at having a companion.

We hurried through the woods and arrived at the barn out of breath. Prissy accompanied me into the barn, her hand gripping my elbow tightly.

Neither of us spoke as we crept toward the cribs where the corn husks were kept and I seized the closest wooden box. I set the box on the floor and both of us took armfuls of the corn husks and deposited them in the box. I was lifting one particularly heavy load when I lost my grip and several husks fell to the ground, landing with a metallic clang.

I immediately stopped what I was doing. Prissy's eyes grew wide. What had caused that sound?

I picked up one of the husks and saw something that caused me to draw my hand back as if I had touched fire.

It was a rope, tied into the shape of a noose, with a twisted iron bar at one end—an iron bar that would be used to squeeze the rope tighter. I gasped, then noticed Prissy's confused look. I stood up quickly and kicked the object out of our sight and back into the corn crib. She must have wondered what I was doing, but I made no explanation. I knew right away that she did not recognize the object for what it was. But I had seen Oliver's neck after he was killed, and I knew I was looking at the weapon that had killed him.

CHAPTER 16

"We have enough husks, Prissy. Let's get back to the house." I spoke so quickly I think she did not understand what I said. But when she touched my arm and pointed to the ground of the corn crib, I knew what she was asking me. "It's nothing, Pris. Just a piece of metal. The sound startled me, but it's nothing. We don't have time to take care of it right now because we have to finish up that mattress." She seemed to accept my statement, so I reached for the box without another word. She reached out quickly to help carry the box and we sped through the woods as quickly as we could go.

I spoke to Jesse quickly while I was helping to serve supper. "I need you to fetch the sheriff as soon as you can."

He looked at me in surprise. "Why?"

"Shush. Keep your voice low. I found the weapon that killed Oliver."

Jesse's mouth dropped open." Where?"

"In the barn."

"What were you doing in the barn?"

"Jesse, please keep your voice low. I had to go to the barn to get more corn husks for a mattress."

"How do you know it's the weapon that killed him?"

"I just know. It was in among the husks. Whoever killed Oliver must have thrown it there and then left."

"I can go get the sheriff right after I eat supper. Have you told anyone?"

"You're the only one. And Prissy was with me, but she did not seem to know what the object was."

"You took Prissy to the barn with you?" He looked aghast.

"Shh! She insisted!"

"Very well. I'll leave as soon as I can."

"Thank you."

Jesse ate quickly, much to Mother's chagrin and suspicion.

"Jesse, why must you shovel food into your mouth like a starving man? It is rude and unbecoming."

"Sorry, Mother. I am just ravenous tonight, I suppose." He did not meet my glance when she grimaced.

After supper Jesse went over to where Father was talking to one of the inn guests. "Father, I believe the horse needs to be reshod. I'm going to go take a look."

Father raised his eyebrows at Jesse, but said "very well" and turned his attention back to the guest. Jesse left before anyone else could speak to him.

That night Abel visited the tavern again, and he brought a newspaper with him. Mother stared at him, her mouth set in a white line. She turned to Father.

"Is that the same newspaper Thaddeus Marshall gave you last night? I wouldn't be surprised if he stole it right out of our parlor." Mother asked in a low hiss.

"I don't believe it is, Davinia. My copy of the newspaper is still there. Abel must have a different one."

"Hmm," was all Mother said.

"Say, I see you have your own newspaper tonight," Ben Drake said, nodding toward Abel.

"Indeed I do, sir," Abel responded. "I ventured down to Romney Marsh today and bought this in the store there."

"Well, are you going to read it aloud?" one of the men asked.

"I am willing to read it aloud, though I fear it is the same newspaper your good neighbor read aloud in this very place last night."

"He couldn't have read the whole thing," one man spoke up. "Is there nothing else of interest?"

Abel looked down at the newspaper and perused it for several moments, turned the page, then returned to the first page. "Here's a mention of a killing that took place in Boston on twenty-sixth August. It says here, 'Patriot killed by unknown assailant close to Long Wharfe.'" Abel read silently again and then summarized it for everyone. "A young man of good family and education was killed by a vile fewmet under cloak of darkness some weeks ago. The young man was apparently a soldier with a Massachusetts militia. It says here the authorities think two mule-brained rufflers colluded to attack the young man and leave him dying in the street."

"'Tis better to live far from the cities," Ben said, shaking his head.

"Is it?" Abel asked. All eyes turned toward him.

"Do things like that take place here? No!" roared Richard Miller.

"It is my understanding that a body was found on this very property recently," Abel said.

"That may well be true," Richard responded with a splutter. "But the stranger in the barn certainly was not educated or from a reputable family."

I saw a look flash between Father and Jesse. Father was imploring Jesse to remain silent about Oliver—if the men in the tavern knew Jesse had befriended Oliver, there would be no end to the malicious gossip about where Jesse's sympathies lay in the war.

"Does the newspaper say if the two maggots were caught?" one of the men asked.

"It says here they escaped into the night and have not been located."

"I hope someone catches the scoundrels and strings them up," Abel said. There was a murmur of agreement from the other men in the room.

Abel went on to read two other stories—one about a man who had gone missing from Philadelphia and a more concerning article about British troops that were advancing from Canada and other British troops that were advancing into New York from the south and the west. It was speculated in the article that the generals of the British forces were planning to meet and overwhelm the colonial forces somewhere in New York. Reinforcements were being urgently requested. Father shook his head at hearing the story and I could tell he was dismayed at hearing more news of battles, with the injuries and deaths that were sure to result.

I shuddered upon hearing the news of the possibility of more bloodshed and lives lost. I couldn't help looking at Jesse, who caught my gaze and looked away. Prissy was watching me, so I tried to hide my signs of upset. I did not want her to worry, so I bustled into the back room of the tavern so she couldn't see my tremulous breath or my shaking hands. And, of course, I could not let Mother or Father see me because I did not want them to know about Jesse and his sympathy for the King's cause. They would wonder why I was becoming so nervous and agitated.

When I had calmed my breathing and my hands no longer shook, I returned to the main room of the tavern. There I found the men engaged in conversation with Abel, which I smiled to see. I found the peddler to be mild and pleasant enough, and it pleased me that the men in the tavern had judged him to be of good character. At least, I hoped they had done so.

When I returned to the counter in the tavern, Jesse had arrived.

"Where have you been?" Father asked.

"I took a look at the horse's shoe and determined he doesn't need to be reshod yet. Just to be sure, I took him on a short ride. He's doing well."

Father nodded, but gave Jesse a look of ... what? Was it suspicion? But he said nothing, and I hoped he would let the matter drop.

After the neighbors and inn guests left the tavern that night, Prissy and I cleaned the tables while Mother swept the floor, and Father, Jesse, and Sylvanus brought more ale from the storehouse to the tavern for the next evening. They would store it in the back room, where piles of wood chips and dust from hewn wood kept the jugs cool.

There was a knock on the door and I hurried to open it, prepared to tell the person on the other side that the tavern was closed and would not reopen until the following evening. But Thomas stood there, his hat in his hands.

"Pardon me, Miss Etta. But I thought Nathaniel should know that the sheriff came to my cabin asking about your brothers." Thomas spoke in a low voice so the others could not hear him.

My shock must have showed in my face, because Thomas reached his hand out as if to steady me, but did not touch me. "Perhaps you sit down over there, Miss Etta." He inclined his head toward the nearest table.

"Thank you, Thomas. I think I will." I moved slowly toward the table and sat down heavily.

Mother set her broom aside and stood frowning at me with her hands on her hips. "Gracious me, Antoinetta, all of us should be so carefree as to sit down whenever the whim moves us."

"I'm sorry, Mother. I suddenly felt ill."

At my words, Father came into the main room of the tavern and saw Thomas standing near me. "Good evening, Thomas," he said. "You're abroad late tonight."

"May I speak to you, Nathaniel?" Thomas asked.

"Of course. Come back here. I sent the boys for more ale. What is it?"

Thomas followed Father into the back room while Mother resumed her sweeping and Prissy and I finished cleaning the tables. I could feel Prissy's eyes on me the entire time we worked, but I could not speak to her about what Thomas had said. Not yet.

When Father and Thomas returned from the back room, Father handed him a candle, opened the door for him, and I heard him say "thank you" into the darkness as Thomas went back to his cabin. Father turned and faced us.

"Let us finish this tomorrow. We'll find time during the day. It's late and we all need to get some sleep."

Mother put the broom away and she and Prissy followed Father out of the tavern and into the house. I waited for Jesse and Sylvanus to finish their tavern chores. When Sylvanus had retired to the inn, I followed Jesse onto the porch. He locked the tavern door. He knew I was eager to hear what the sheriff had said.

"He'll be here in the morning," Jesse said without preamble.

"I'm surprised he is not here already. I thought he would want to collect the weapon from our barn as quickly as possible."

"His wife told me he and his deputy were busy at someone's farm down south of Romney Marsh. She thought they would be occupied most of the night. She said she would relay the message when he returned home."

I nodded. "I suppose we have no choice but to wait for him, then." I shivered, though not from the cold. Jesse peered into the darkness and I followed his gaze. "Do you think Oliver's killer is out there?"

He turned to me with a shrug. "I don't know. I hope the scoundrel is far away from here."

The front door opened. Father stood there with a frown. "Jesse, Sylvanus and I are waiting for you in the parlor. There is something we need to discuss. What is taking you so long?"

I had almost forgotten what Thomas had come to the tavern to tell Father. I felt a stab of guilt for not warning Jesse about Thomas's words, but I had been so intent on learning what the sheriff had said that it slipped my mind. I hurried through the parlor and into the bedroom.

I did not listen at the bedroom door to try to hear what Father was saying to Jesse and Sylvanus—I already knew. After we had our nightclothes on, Prissy touched my arm and raised her eyebrows. She wanted to know what Thomas had said. I was too tired to tell her anything but the truth.

"He came to say that the sheriff visited him in his cabin tonight. He was there to ask questions about Jesse and Sylvanus." Prissy's eyes grew wide and her lips parted in dismay. "Don't fret. I'm sure the sheriff is just doing his job by asking all kinds of questions about everyone who might have known Oliver. And Jesse knew Oliver—you know that already. I'm sure the sheriff was merely making sure that Jesse had nothing to do with Oliver's death. But of course he didn't. Oliver owed Jesse a debt of honor for allowing him to stay in our barn when he had nowhere to go, and Jesse felt the need to protect Oliver." I did not mention that the need to protect Oliver arose from their mutual sympathy for the King of England and his armies of soldiers.

Prissy frowned, marring her pretty features.

"Oliver is gone now, Pris. You need not worry about him any longer."

Prissy nodded and climbed into her side of the bed. I blew out the lamp and got under the coverlet, too. I hoped for a night of sleep that was free from dreams about finding Oliver's body.

CHAPTER 17

I was pleased and relieved the next day to find Isaac slightly less feverish. He managed a smile as I entered his room early in the morning carrying a mug of fresh cider and a trencher of porridge, then beckoned me to sit in a chair while he took a few bites of food. I was ashamed of my peevishness the previous day.

"I hope I have beaten this fever," he said, reaching for the cider.

I smiled, nodding. "You have been quite ill. You still need to rest so you can recover fully."

"What did I miss while I lay here in my incoherent state?"

I shifted in my seat, uncomfortable at the thought of telling him about Oliver. "Perhaps you should rest now and I can share the news with you later."

"Very well." He settled back against the pillow and closed his eyes. I left the tray of porridge and the remainder of the cider next to him in case he should awaken hungry or thirsty. When I went downstairs Mother was waiting for me. She spoke to me in a low voice.

"I have not had any reply to the letter I sent to my friend in

Cape May," she said, glancing at the stairs as if Isaac might come down at any moment. "How is he today?"

"He seems a wee bit improved."

"Good. I want him to leave as soon as possible. He is taking up entirely too much of your time as you nurse him back to health. You have other duties to attend to."

"I know, Mother. But I do think my ministrations are helping him recover. I will get back to my chores right now."

There was a knock at the door, interrupting our conversation, and it swung open. The sheriff stepped into the front hall and removed his hat.

"Good morning," he said.

"Good morning," Mother and I said in unison. Mother gave him an expectant look. "I hope you've come to tell us you have caught the person who killed the beggar in our barn."

"Unfortunately, we do not have anyone in our custody yet. I am here to talk to Etta."

Mother turned to me, shock written on her face. "Why Etta?" she asked him.

"Because I found the weapon that I believe was used to kill Oliver. I'm sorry I didn't tell you earlier, Mother, but I did not want you to worry."

Mother gaped at me, but the sheriff began asking questions straightaway. He wanted to know where and when I had found the weapon, why I had gone into the barn, and what I had done with the rope after I found it.

"I was holding a pile of corn husks and, unbeknownst to me, it was in the pile. It fell to the ground and made a clanging sound, so I knew it wasn't corn. I knew what it was as soon as I saw it, but I kicked it back into the corn crib so Prissy wouldn't worry. She did not seem to know what it was."

"Can you take me out to the barn and show me where it is?" the sheriff asked.

"Certainly." I turned back to Mother. "Do you want to go with us, Mother?"

She had recovered from her surprise. "I will stay here. You can show him what you found."

I led the way to the barn. The sheriff did not talk to me while we walked, but I felt a great relief at having the lawman with me in the woods. I did not need to fear anyone accosting me with him so nearby.

When we reached the barn, I slid the door open and pointed toward the corn crib. "It was back here," I said. I led the way to the place where I had been standing when the weapon dropped from my arms.

The sheriff knelt on the floor and began scraping corn husks and debris from the crib. He was amassing quite a pile next to him. Finally he sat back on his heels and looked up at me.

"There is no weapon here."

CHAPTER 18

"It must be there. I just found it yesterday. It was a noose with a short iron bar tied onto it."

"I have been through everything in this crib and there is nothing but corn leavings. Is there another corn crib?"

I shook my head, struck dumb by the absence of the weapon. I hadn't dreamed it. I couldn't imagine why it wasn't there anymore.

"I promise you, it was there."

The sheriff stood and wiped flecks of dust and corn husks from his trousers. "In that case, it has been removed." He looked around and settled his gaze on me. "I would like you to wait outside while I look around in here."

I did as he bade me and waited immediately outside the barn door. I was not going to venture further away from the building when Oliver's killer had not been caught.

After a long while the sheriff emerged from the barn. "The weapon is not in there." He gave me a hard stare. "Are you sure of what you saw?"

"Yes. I am certain."

"And are you sure you did not touch it again?"

"I am sure." I resented his implication that I was either misleading him intentionally or that I was too feeble-minded to recall what I had done with the rope.

"Then someone removed the weapon in the hours since you found it. I am going to have to speak to everyone who might have gone into the barn since yesterday."

"That was only me, sheriff, as far as I know."

"I need to get back to the inn." He strode away and I had to hurry to keep up with him.

When we reached the inn, the sheriff asked me to fetch Father and the boys from the field while he questioned Mother and Prissy. I hesitated.

"I'd like to talk to them as soon as possible, please" he said.

"I prefer not to go by myself, Sheriff."

He didn't say anything for a moment, then nodded. "Then I'll go myself. I'll talk to you when I return." He indicated Mother and Prissy with a wave of his hand.

He returned with Father and the boys before a half hour had passed.

"Etta, what is this?" Father asked when he came into the inn. "The sheriff says you found the weapon that was used to kill Oliver."

"Yes, I found it."

"Where was it?" Sylvanus asked. "The sheriff didn't tell us anything else."

Before I could answer, the sheriff interrupted. "I need to talk to each of you separately. I would like everyone to stay in the front hall while I talk to Mister Rutledge. Please do not speak while I am in there." He motioned for Father to step into the family parlor ahead of him.

Mother, Prissy, the boys, and I stayed where we were, as the sheriff had asked. Anxious looks passed between us, but no one spoke. Presently Father emerged from the parlor. He indicated

Jesse with a nod of his head. "The sheriff wants to speak to you next."

I followed after Jesse, then it was Sylvanus's turn, then Mother's, and finally Prissy's. I worried that the sheriff would ask her questions she would be unable to answer, but she was only in the parlor for a moment. The sheriff came out with her. "I've only asked her yes or no questions.

"If anyone sees anything that looks like what Etta has described as the murder weapon, send for me immediately. The sooner we catch the person who did this, the better the entire county will be able to sleep at night."

He left after promising to keep us informed of any progress he might make. When he closed the door, everyone started asking me questions at once.

"Where did you find it?"

"When was this?"

"How did you know it was the murder weapon?"

I held up my hands for quiet. "I found it yesterday in among the corn husks in the corn crib. I knew it was the murder weapon because..." I hesitated because Prissy had not known it was a weapon, nor did she know how Oliver had died. "I just knew."

"Etta, you should have told me," Father scolded.

"I'm sorry. But I didn't want you to worry because Prissy and I had been in the barn."

"You and Prissy were in the barn, unescorted?" Sylvanus's eyes were like saucers.

"Yes. We had to get more mattress fill quickly." I was exasperated and did not wish to entertain any more questions. "Please let me tend to my chores now. I want to think of something other than Oliver and his death." I left them all standing there and went into the kitchen.

Everyone must have realized I wanted to be alone, because

no one followed me. I busied myself with the never-ending list of chores I needed to do and relished the silence.

I briefly checked on Isaac twice more before supper that night, and each time he was reading a tome he had brought with him. The second time I went into his room, he was even sitting in the chair where I had sat earlier that morning. I promised him I would return after supper to bring him more food.

After supper Mother beckoned me into the front hall.

"What is it, Mother?"

"I spoke to Isaac this afternoon. He tells me he is not yet cleverly enough to continue on his travels. Do you believe he is telling the truth?"

Isaac had said nothing about talking to Mother. I wondered if he had simply forgotten. "I do believe him, Mother. He has been extremely ill and even now is so weak he cannot easily move around. I think to continue on his journey would result in him becoming sick again."

Mother nodded. "The money he is paying us to remain in that room is barely enough to cover the attention you have been lavishing on him as your chores are neglected, but I suppose we have no choice but to let him stay until he is better."

I thought it uncharitable of Mother to imply that I had not been doing my chores. I also disagreed that I lavished attention upon the poor man, but I said nothing. I knew better than to further vex Mother when she was in this sort of mood.

When Mother and Father, Prissy, and the boys had left for the tavern after supper, I went up to Isaac's room. I had been trying to figure out the best way to tell him about Oliver, but every time I thought about it I became so agitated that I pushed the thoughts away. Nevertheless, he was bound to hear about Oliver sooner or later, and I felt it would be dishonest if he heard of the killing from someone other than me or my parents.

After he had eaten a bit or two of the pottage I took to him for supper, he leaned back in his bed and said, "Tell me, Etta. What is the news? How long have I been here?"

"You've been here ten days, Isaac. We have had quite a time since you arrived."

Isaac raised his eyebrows. "Tell me about it."

"My brother met a man on the road between here and Romney Marsh. The man was hungry and without a place to stay, so my brother offered him the use of our barn to stay for several days."

"That was kind of your brother," Isaac interrupted.

"It was," I admitted. "But the man was killed two days ago."

Isaac was dumbfounded. He stared at me for several seconds as if trying to comprehend what he had heard.

"How was he killed?" he finally asked.

"He was strangled."

"Who was he, that someone should want to kill him?"

I shook my head. "I do not know, sir. All I know is that his name was Oliver. He was a supporter of King George."

Isaac fell silent for several moments. "I wonder if his Tory sympathies had anything to do with his death," he mused.

"No one knows. Least of all, no one here. I do not know if we will ever find the reason."

"But if someone killed the man, surely the sheriff will be investigating the incident. He will not let anyone get away with committing murder."

"I expect not."

"Well, it seems I slept through some very interesting days. Was there anything else I missed? Though I daresay missing a murder is excitement enough."

"We have received word that the colonial army lost one thousand men at a battle in Pennsylvania."

Isaac's eyes took on an even more troubled look. "When was this battle?"

"On the eleventh of September, sir. We read about it in a newspaper someone brought to the tavern several nights ago."

"That is indeed distressing news. The loss of one man on your property is startling, certainly, but the loss of one thousand men is one thousand times more grievous."

I nodded, not knowing what to say next.

"Thank you, Etta. I think I have heard enough news for one evening. Will you bring me breakfast on the morn?" He looked suddenly exhausted and ashen. I felt guilty for sharing such dire news with him. Clearly it had all been too much for someone who had so recently been very ill.

"Certainly."

I left him and went to the tavern, where Abel Smith was regaling men at the tables with tales of his travels. The men seemed to have accepted him as an authority on traveling throughout the colonies. Mother and Father watched and listened from behind the counter. Father was smiling; Mother was frowning. The reason, one I had suspected, was confirmed to me after everyone had left the tavern that night. Jesse and Sylvanus were in the storehouse fetching more ale and Prissy and I were cleaning the back room. Mother and Father were in the front of the tavern, not bothering to keep their voices quiet.

"Nathaniel, I do not trust the man."

"What man?"

"The peddler, of course."

"Why do you not trust him?"

"He's too smart. He reads the newspapers. What kind of a peddler reads the newspapers?"

"Davinia, are you being a bit of a cobbler?"

"Do you disagree?"

Father sighed. "I do not much care what kind of a peddler he is, or whether he is possessed of great intelligence or little, or whether he reads newspapers or nothing at all. He seems harmless enough, and he is an entertaining teller of tales. Most importantly, the men who come to the tavern seem to like him and his stories, so I am content with that."

Mother's eyes narrowed, but she said nothing. Father had a sad look in his eyes.

I stared at Prissy, who was staring at me. It was highly unusual for Father to talk to Mother that way. He was generally mindful of her and strove to be gentle with her when he spoke. Mother stared at him for a moment and then nodded primly. But she was not finished talking.

"When I was a girl, we did not welcome peddlers into our home."

"Davinia," my father said, his voice lowering and becoming softer, "this is not Philadelphia. You left that life behind long ago, when we married. People are different here."

My mother looked up at him, her lips in a thin line. "I am quite well aware of that, Nathaniel."

Father's face darkened for a moment, then he turned away from her and busied himself with other tasks.

When I took food to Isaac the next morning, I found him improved a bit more. He smiled and thanked me for bringing meals to him and asked me to sit and talk with him while he ate. He was still pale and reedy, but I hoped with time and food he would be healthy enough to continue his travels.

That day he talked to me about the countryside around us. "I like it here," he said, taking a long draught of cider. "The clime suits me and I enjoy the stiff and abiding breeze off the ocean."

"Do you like it here better than in Philadelphia?"

He thought for a moment. "It is different here. Not better than Philadelphia, but not worse. This place and Philadelphia are complementary of each other. Philadelphia has all the comforts and activities associated with a city; this place has the comforts and activities associated with nature."

"Many travelers come to this inn on the way to or from Philadelphia," I said. "My mother hails from Philadelphia, too, though she has lived here in Stites Point for many years. You do not sound like many of the people from Philadelphia whom I have heard speak."

"You are quite perceptive, Etta." Isaac smiled. "I am not originally from Philadelphia. I have only been staying in that city for a year. I hail from the great city of Boston. In fact, I was in Boston for a visit before journeying to Cape May early in September."

"Really?" I asked excitedly. "I hope you will tell me what Boston is like. Did you know we have another guest here from Boston?"

Isaac's eyebrows went up in surprise. "I did not know that. Tell me, what is the guest's name?"

"Abel Smith."

Isaac looked past my shoulder, lost in thought. Finally he spoke. "I do not believe I know that name, though 'Smith' is not a unique surname. I would like to meet the fellow and talk to him about how the city has fared since I left."

"I will see to it that you and Abel are introduced," I promised him.

"Thank you, my dear. And now I think I have tired myself. I am going to rest."

I left with the empty porridge trencher and the empty mug. I was pleased that Isaac's appetite was returning.

That night the dining room was full of travelers and inn guests, as well as the six members of my family. Father had just shared the blessing when I heard the front door of the inn creak open. I froze for a moment, the thought of Oliver's killer flashing through my brain. I looked up and saw a man standing in the foyer, his hat in his hands. Surely the killer would not risk returning to our property?

"Etta, would you please see who is here?" Father asked.

Mother and I exchanged glances and Mother gave me a pointed look. I understood immediately her unspoken command: I was not to allow another person to stay in the inn without her permission. She did not want me renting a room to another peddler. I walked into the foyer and the man smiled at me. "I was hoping for a meal," he said. "Is there enough food and a chair for one more person?" He nodded toward the dining room while I sighed with relief.

"We have sufficient food, Friend, and there are two chairs in the corner of the room. We can slide one chair up to the table where my family eats and you may eat with us if you wish."

"I would hate to intrude."

"I insist. Have you traveled far? You must be hungry."

"I have come from Cape May and I am on my way to Philadelphia," he said, following me into the dining room. "I thought I might sup here and then catch the ferry across the bay to continue on my way." I pulled a chair to our table, the legs of the chair scraping loudly across the wooden floor, but most people in the room ignored the noise and continued eating and conversing with their fellow diners.

While I was moving the chair Prissy hurried into the kitchen to prepare a trencher of food for the man. He smiled at her when she set the food in front of him. She inclined her head in acknowledgement and sat down next to me.

"My name is Nathaniel Rutledge," Father said to the man. "You are traveling from Cape May?"

"Yes, sir. I have been doing business on the island and now I must return home."

"How long were you in Cape May?" Father asked.

"Just two weeks."

"No doubt much has taken place in Philadelphia in two weeks. We do read the newspapers, but they are usually one to two weeks in getting here."

"I'm sure much has transpired in my absence. And since we are speaking of news, is it true there was a man murdered here on this property of late?"

Father looked at Mother, who frowned. Jesse and Sylvanus exchanged glances. "It is true, Friend. A man was murdered on our property recently," Father said.

"What happened, if you do not mind my inquisitiveness?"

Father cleared his throat. It was fortunate the other diners were talking among themselves and had not heard the conversation at our table. "The man was killed in our barn. The sheriff has not yet apprehended the person who committed the crime."

The man leaned in toward the center of the table and spoke in a low voice. "What did the man look like?"

"The dead man?" Father asked.

"Yes."

"I only saw him alive one time. He seemed unkempt and prone to taking too much to drink. He had long brown hair and remarkably poor teeth."

Father did not add that the man was uncouth, boorish, and a cad.

"I wonder if he is the same man I witnessed in Cape May on several occasions," the man mused.

"Why do you suppose?"

"During my time in Cape May there was a man, he being a stranger from parts unknown, who was run out of town on the suspicion of thievery. He was a cur with the womenfolk. I suppose it could have been the very same man who found his way north to your inn. As I recall, he did have long brown hair, though I never got close enough to him to see his teeth. He was described by some people in Cape May as 'unkempt' and 'a sot.'"

"It might very well be the same person. You say he was from parts unknown?"

The man nodded, his mouth full of food.

"Do you know what the man was doing in Cape May?" Father asked.

"I do not. If he had found employment, I daresay that would have been common knowledge."

"Did he travel alone?"

"It is my understanding he traveled alone, though there were some who said he arrived in Cape May with a companion."

Father looked at Jesse, who shrugged. Jesse had not mentioned a traveling companion with Oliver. Apparently he had not been aware of one.

"When does the ferry make its last trip of the evening over to the other side of the bay?" the man asked.

Father looked out the window at the gathering darkness. "Very soon, if not already. You should go now."

The man placed several coins on the table, more than the cost of his meal, thanked us for the hospitality, and hurried out the front door. We all sat looking at each other.

"Jesse? What more do you know about Oliver?" Father asked.

"I have told you all I knew about Oliver. What with the harvest and the tavern and other responsibilities, I never did have an opportunity to learn much about him."

I wondered at the brashness of any man who had been run out of Cape May.

CHAPTER 19

$\mathcal{I}$t was two days later when a man arrived on horseback with a small sack. I was walking the short distance from the storehouse to the inn when I saw him dismount by the kitchen door. I stiffened, wondering for a moment if I were looking at Oliver's killer. Should I scream for help? It was such a short distance between the inn and the storehouse that I did not worry when I had to go fetch something, but perhaps I should have asked someone to watch me from the back door. I shivered and my heart started to beat faster as I stared at him.

The man walked around the horse with a jaunty spring in his step. He saw me and waved.

"Do you live here, miss?"

He sounded friendly enough. I recovered myself with a little shake. "Yes, I do. Can I help you?"

"I've brought a delivery of letters." He opened the sack and thrust a short stack of envelopes toward me. I was so relieved I laughed aloud. He laughed, too. "It's always good to have news from back home, isn't it? No matter where that is."

I agreed with him, though relief, not the mail, had been the reason for my laughter. I offered to provide him with a drink, but he declined, saying he had more letters to deliver in Upper Precinct. He rode away in a cloud of dust and I hurried indoors.

"Mother, letter delivery!" I called out.

She hastened from the parlor, her eyes alight with anticipation. Even Mother felt the thrill of receiving letters. She held out her hand and I handed her everything the man had given me. She rifled through them quickly. "There's one from an old friend of mine from Philadelphia, one from your father's uncle, and one from a friend of your father from Philadelphia, and oh, here's one from Margaret." She plucked that letter from the small stack and placed the other letters on the desk in the foyer. She returned to the parlor, her finger sliding under the flap of the envelope, and remembered to mumble "thank you, Etta," as she walked away.

I was eager to hear what the letter contained. It had been at least a month since Aunt Margaret's last letter. I hoped Mother would share its contents with us at supper.

Shortly thereafter I was stirring the pot of stew when some of the piping hot liquid sloshed onto my arm, causing my arm to burn and my frock to become drenched in hot liquid. I hurried to my bedroom, where I donned a new dress. As I was walking through our parlor to return to the kitchen, I caught a glimpse of a piece of paper lying on a small table under the window. I wondered if it was Mother's letter from Aunt Margaret. I looked around and, not seeing anyone, I picked up the paper and glanced over it quickly. Indeed, it was the letter from Aunt Margaret. I knew it was wrong to read Mother's letter, but I could not resist a peek.

Alas, as my eyes skittered over Aunt Margaret's words, the gnaw of guilt became bothersome. I was about to place the letter back on the table, unread, when I caught the words *Jesse* and *taking up arms* very near one other.

I let out an audible gasp. Did someone know about Jesse's leanings? Did anyone suspect how he felt?

I had to read the letter from beginning to end. I had to know if Jesse's secret was no longer safe.

I sat down in the chair nearest to me and smoothed the paper on my lap.

My dearest Davinia,

I hope this letter finds you well and I trust you and your family are safe from the sore reality of wartime violence. Here in Philadelphia the mood shifts dramatically from optimism to grief and despair and then again to optimism. One never knows upon waking every morn what one shall encounter throughout the long hours of the day. I have been relatively safe, and I am grateful to be living in the security of our childhood home. It is a fortress compared to some of the other lodgings I have had occasion to witness in my work on behalf of the Women's Committee on Nursing. Though of course I am not a nurse skilled in treating disease or injury, I have visited many homes in the company of nurses to ensure that the women and children in such homes are not in want of sufficient food and clothing. We who are privileged have a responsibility to provide for those who are not so fortunate by circumstances of birth.

Of course you are aware that Philadelphia teems with both Whigs and Tories, and I have had the opportunity to listen to arguments on both sides of the debate about independence in the lofty salon of Elizabeth Willing Powel, whom I am sure you remember from your days before moving to New Jersey. She hosts the most insightful discussions at her home, and is good friends with General Washington himself. She corresponds with him and with his wife Martha on a regular basis and has shared with me some of the stories she has heard about the fields of battle where our countrymen fight and die.

Her stories paint a despairing portrait of grim death and violence, Davinia, in the wake of every battle and of every meeting between troops on opposing sides of the debate over independence from Britain.

Upon reading in your most recent letter that you suspect Jesse of harboring sentiments that suggest he may be amenable to taking up arms, I must admit that I found myself in simultaneous states of shock and fright.

Jesse has within his power, even as a Friend, the ability to aid the effort of the war without bearing arms against any man. He is a young man of able body, and thus may act in the capacity of recruiting soldiers, providing strategic assistance to local authorities, and raising funds necessary for the efforts put forth by the Continental Army.

Now I come to the most important item which I shall share with you in this missive. You see, my dear sister, I have been abroad on the streets of Philadelphia, at times in my capacity as a volunteer with the Women's Committee on Nursing, and been unfortunate enough to lay eyes upon more than a few men who have returned from battle in abhorrent condition—men on both sides of the divide. Davinia, I have seen with my own eyes former soldiers missing arms, legs, hands, feet, and sometimes even an ear or a nose. But more than the physical wounds and scars they carry are the invisible weights of despair at being unable to provide for their families, of grief over the loss of friends, brothers, sons, and fathers, and of melancholy and despondency over the prisons of memory and nightmares inside their own minds. Davinia, I know the depth of feeling you have for your children, even when you yourself are loathe to express it in words and deeds, and you and Nathaniel must do everything in your power to prevent Jesse from going to war.

It is my deeply held and fervent prayer that you and Nathaniel will prevail upon Jesse to conduct himself in a manner consistent with membership in the Society of Friends, not only because I do not wish to see him take up arms, but, more importantly, because I do not want you to see in his face the haunting stares of the former soldiers I have seen in Philadelphia.

I remain,
Your loving sister,
Margaret

With trembling hands, I returned the letter from Aunt Margaret to the table on which I had found it. My mind was aswirl with images of maimed and suffering former soldiers. It was clear from the letter that Mother suspected Jesse of being willing to take up arms. It was also clear, however, that she did not realize Jesse's sympathies lay with the British army, not the Continental army.

I needed to speak to Jesse as quickly as possible.

CHAPTER 20

*P*rissy had served dinner and sat down at our family's table while I had been reading the letter.

Jesse was not in the dining room. Fear held me in an icy, breathless grip while I wondered, just for a moment, if he had already left to join the British fighters. But I forced myself to take a deep breath and try to think calmly. I was afraid simply because I had just read Aunt Margaret's letter, I told myself, not because there was any sudden and pressing reason for Jesse to leave. I avoided the temptation to look at Mother, lest she somehow know that I had read the letter meant for her.

I thanked Prissy for doing my share of the serving and explained that my arm had been slightly burned by the scalding soup. She looked at me with concern and I felt a twinge of guilt at misleading her as to the reason for my long absence. It would not do to let her know about Jesse or about our mother's concern for him.

I ate slowly. I was hungry, but could barely swallow my food. Finally I could bear the silence no longer. "Where is Jesse?" I asked.

"He's helping haul wood to Thomas's cabin," Father replied.

I did my best not to heave a huge sigh of relief. I should have known Jesse wouldn't leave without saying something, but my fear had gotten the better of me and I needed to make sure it did not happen again. I gave Father a quavering smile and nodded. I would wait until Jesse came back to the inn, then I would talk to him.

But there was no time to talk to him that night. He came back hungry from helping Thomas, and while he ate Prissy and I had to do our evening chores. By the time I was done, he had gone into the tavern. With the neighbors and friends in there that evening, I knew he would not want to leave to talk to me.

The next day at noon we had almost finished eating dinner when Jesse turned to Father. "Once the work is done for the day, would you mind if I went to Dennisville? I have plans to visit a friend. Perhaps Sylvanus could help with my chores in the tavern tonight?" He glanced at Sylvanus, who nodded.

"What friend is this?" Father asked.

"Gabriel Tillotson."

Father frowned. "I'll speak to you alone after we're done eating."

The rest of us remained silent. I vaguely remembered meeting Gabriel Tillotson and his family at a Court Day in the spring. He seemed a decent sort, but of course I did not know him well.

Once the meal was over and Mother, Sylvanus, and the guests had left for their afternoon diversions and chores, Prissy and I began to clear the tables. Father and Jesse stood in the corner of the dining room, talking in quiet voices.

I lingered over my chores in the dining room, straining my ears to hear their conversation but pretending to ignore them.

"But Gabriel Tillotson is known to be a belligerent British sympathizer," Father was saying.

"Father, he is my friend. I do not care how he feels about the

British. He has been ill and it would be discourteous of me if I did not call on him."

There was silence for several long moments, then I heard Father sigh. "You may go. Do not be very late getting home. One night you will have to return Sylvanus the favor of doing your chores."

"I will, Father. Thank you." Jesse hurried from the room.

Very well, if I couldn't talk to Jesse in the house, I would find a way to talk to him away from the house.

It was nearing time for supper when I finished my chores in the house. I took a mug of cider upstairs to Isaac and when I returned to the kitchen, Mother was in there. I had been planning my subterfuge all afternoon, and it was time to act. I bent over double and groaned, leaning my hand against the door frame.

"What is the problem, Antoinetta?" she asked in a tired voice.

"I don't know, Mother. My stomach is suddenly clenched and it's burning."

"Can you finish your chores?"

"I'm already done."

"In that case, you should lie down for a while. I'll have Prissy start preparing supper."

I was a bit surprised by her response to my apparent stomach ailment. I had expected her to be peevish and cross and was prepared to act dramatically to prove how much my stomach hurt. I was relieved that more histrionics would be needless.

"Thank you, Mother." Prissy had seen me bend over and her eyes were wide with concern. "I'll be all right, Prissy. Don't waste any worry on me." I gave her my best feeble smile. A pang of guilt tightened its grip around my abdomen for a brief moment, but I walked out of the kitchen and into our bedroom.

I lay there on the bed, looking at the ceiling for many minutes before getting up and going into the kitchen. Only

Prissy was in there, checking on the stew in the pot over the fire.

"Pris, I need some air. I'm going to go for a short walk. I won't be long."

She whirled around and stared at me, shaking her head.

"I won't go far, I promise. I'll stay near the house." She swallowed hard and nodded. I could feel her eyes on me as I left the kitchen through the back door and headed slowly toward the road. My goal was the field where I knew Father and Thomas and the boys were working. In truth, I was terrified of being outside alone and if I hadn't felt such a strong compulsion to talk to Jesse about Aunt Margaret's letter, I would have stayed indoors where it was safe. The more time passed without an arrest for Oliver's murder, the more nervous I was becoming.

Once I was out of sight of the inn, I broke into a run. The reason was twofold: I needed to get to the field and hide myself before anyone started for home, and the faster I ran, the less I panicked over being alone away from the inn. I spied my father and brothers in the distance and bent down closer to the ground so they would not see me. Then I waited for them to finish their work.

I did not have to wait long, as I had suspected. I had tried to time my need for "some air" with Father and the boys' stoppage of work for the day.

I watched as Father and Sylvanus moved away toward the inn and Thomas toward his cabin. Jesse waved to the others and started off down the road toward Dennisville.

I felt like a war scout as I followed Jesse down the dusty dirt road. I was trying to tread quietly and to hide behind trees and bushes so he wouldn't see me, and I imagined that was how soldiers in the war had to move when they were trying to understand the lay of the land in unfamiliar territory.

Jesse had not gone far when he turned around.

"Etta," he called. "I know you're there. Show yourself."

My sheepishness must have shown on my face when I stepped from the shelter of the trees onto the road, for Jesse chuckled.

"Why are you following me?"

"I wanted to know where you're going."

"I assumed as much. But why?"

"Are you going to visit Gabriel Tillotson because you're planning to leave us?" I could feel my face finally crumpling with tears I had so far managed not to shed.

Jesse gave me a sympathetic look and walked toward me. "Etta, please don't cry. It is true that Gabriel is a British supporter. But that is unconnected with the reason I am visiting him."

"Then why are you going to his house?"

He cocked his head and regarded me gravely for a moment. "I know I can trust you not to say anything to Father or Mother."

My chest tightened.

Jesse sighed. "Gabriel is teaching me how to play the fiddle."

If Jesse had told me he and Gabriel were off to join a pirate brigade, I could not have been more surprised. "The fiddle? You're learning to play the fiddle?" I laughed aloud with relief.

He grinned. "Yes. You should hear me, Etta. I've come quite a long way. I don't get lessons very often, but each time I do, I'm getting better."

I sobered. "What will Father and Mother say if they find out?"

He gave me an arch look. "They won't find out if you do not say anything. I tell Father I visit Gabriel to talk to him, but that is not the real reason. You and Gabriel are the only people who know that I'm learning to play. It's another reason I don't believe I can remain in the Society of Friends, Etta. I am never happier than when I am playing the fiddle. I do not understand how anyone can think it is wrong to enjoy something that brings so much happiness. There's nothing evil about it and it does not prevent me from doing my work or anything else. It is simply a joyful thing to experience."

I smiled. "I wish I could hear you play."

"You can. Come to Gabriel's house with me."

"I have to go back to the inn. I lied to Mother and Prissy about being ill today because I had to follow you to know why you were going to Gabriel's house. I told Prissy I needed some air, but she will be wondering where I've gone to."

"You had better hurry home, then. Someday I'll take you with me to Gabriel's house. Maybe I can even teach you to play." His eyes twinkled as he spoke and I realized it had been a long time since I had seen such joy in his face. I was happy for him. And it gave me reason, however small, to hope that his words meant that he would stay in Stites Point instead of heading off to join the British in the war for independence. He couldn't very well take me to Gabriel's house to hear him play the fiddle if he were off fighting a war.

I hesitated a moment before turning around. There were two reasons: first, I was afraid to go home alone. And second, I hadn't spoken to my brother about the real reason I followed him, which was Mother's suspicion of his willingness to take up arms. But I couldn't bring myself to talk about it just then. The joy he felt about playing the fiddle with Gabriel was so obvious that I hated to spoil it with talk of Mother and her letter from Aunt Margaret. I would have to wait for another time to discuss it with him.

"If you're afraid to go back to the house by yourself, I can go with you," he offered.

As much as I wanted Jesse to walk me back to the inn, I didn't want him to think I was being silly. If I stuck to the road, it would lead me almost to our house. There was nothing to fear.

"No," I said. "I'll go by myself. I'll be fine."

He cocked his head at me. "Come along. I'm walking you home."

My relief was palpable. I was grateful to him for going out of his way to make sure I felt safe. As soon as we drew near to the inn, I turned to face him. "You run along to Gabriel's house. Thank you for bringing me home." I paused. "And Jesse, are you afraid? I mean, to go to Gabriel's house by yourself and to come home alone in the dark?"

"I confess I am a little nervous, yes."

"Are you sure you want to go?"

"Yes, Etta. Do not worry about me. I'll be fine. I can borrow Gabriel's horse to come home if need be."

I went into the kitchen and found Mother and Prissy in there, working in silence to prepare supper. Mother turned to me with a frown. "Where have you been, Etta? If you are well enough to be roaming around Christendom, you are well enough to help with supper."

"Of course, Mother. I took a walk, thinking some fresh air would make me feel better, and it did. I feel much better. I'll help Prissy now, if you wish."

Mother gave me a suspicious look as she untied her apron and hung it next to the back door. "You were not fearful of being outside by yourself?"

"A little bit, yes. But I needed some air, and the best way to get air was to go outside."

She did not ask any more questions. After she left, Prissy, who had not looked up from slicing bread since I came into the kitchen, glanced at me with a doubtful look.

"It is amazing what a bit of fresh air will do," I said, ignoring the twinge of guilt. "If you've already boiled the salt pork, I'll fry it."

Prissy apparently decided not to insist on knowing where I had been or how I suddenly felt better, for she smiled at me and returned to slicing the bread.

It was quite crowded in the tavern that evening. Many of the neighbors were there, which indicated to me that they were nearing the end of the harvest, just as Father and the boys were. The mood in the large, warm room that night was jovial. Court Day was coming, too, so that added to the air of excitement.

I was serving one of the men when I noticed Father move toward the back room. Sylvanus looked up from where he was talking to one of our neighbors and Father caught his eye, nodding ever so slightly. A moment later Sylvanus followed Father. I, of course, wondered what they were doing. Whenever Father went to the back room, it was usually to take stock of the casks of ale on the shelves. He certainly did not need Sylvanus for that. I sidled closer to the doorway so I could hear what they were saying.

"Gabriel is quick to anger and slow to reason." It was Father's voice. "He is not a Quaker Friend, and he makes no secret of his support for the King."

"But we do not know what he and Jesse talk about. They could speak of harmless topics," Sylvanus said.

"Do you believe that?"

"No." Sylvanus's voice was quiet. After a pause, he spoke again. "Father, do you think Jesse was in cahoots with Oliver? Is it possible Oliver shared with him the location of the munitions?"

Father was silent for a moment. As I strained to hear what he would say next, someone summoned me for more ale. I had no choice but to serve the man and leave my listening post. By the time I had returned to the counter, Father and Sylvanus were back in the tavern and talking to other people.

It seemed Sylvanus and Father had suspicions about where Jesse's sympathies lay in the war for independence. Jesse was not doing a very good job of keeping his own secrets. I wondered if he knew how Sylvanus and Father felt.

I did not have time to wonder long, because a few moments

later the tavern door opened and Elijah walked in, bringing with him a draft of cold night air.

Father welcomed him from where he was talking to several men at a corner in the room and Elijah made his way to the counter, where Prissy now stood next to me. He nodded to Prissy and asked for a mug of ale. I ignored him, wondering briefly if he cared whether I ignored him or not, and noticed that Father and Sylvanus were excusing themselves from the patrons they were talking to. A minute later they had beckoned Elijah to the back room. I knew something was happening and I intended to find out what it was.

"Prissy, could you handle things in here for just a minute? I have to go outside." I nodded my head in the direction of the privy, but that was not where I intended to go. Prissy nodded and I slipped out the front door.

I hurried around to the rear of the tavern where the door to the back room stood ajar to allow some cool air inside. I crept as close as I dared toward the doorway and pressed my body against the tavern wall so no one would see me. From where I stood I could hear everything that Father, Sylvanus, and Elijah were saying.

"...Gabriel Tillotson's house," Elijah said.

"That is correct," Father said.

"You both know that Gabriel Tillotson has a reputation for being an agitator," Elijah continued. "I fear The Committee of Safety has advised me to tell you that we have no choice but to assume Jesse is in league with Tillotson, and may have been in league with the dead man, on the side of the British in this damnable war."

There was silence from Father and Sylvanus. My own rage threatened to make itself known, but I clenched my teeth until my head hurt to keep myself from expressing my thoughts aloud.

"Of course this means that he can no longer attend meetings

of the Committee," Elijah continued. "I am sorry to have to be the one to inform you both of the Committee's decision, but it fell to me as my responsibility."

"Certainly, Elijah. We understand," Father said. "I am sorry the Committee no longer trusts my son, but I can sympathize with their position."

Sylvanus had said nothing during the exchange and I wondered if he had been the one who had voiced his concerns about Jesse to Elijah. Had he even told Elijah of Jesse's visit to Gabriel Tillotson? My fingernails dug into the skin of my palms as I tried to calm my breathing. How dare he? How dare anyone reveal private information about one of our family?

Just then I heard a whoop from the front of the tavern. It sounded like someone was summoning my father and whoever it was had enjoyed a bit too much ale. The conversation in the back room came to an end and I scurried around to the front of the tavern and slipped inside. Hopefully anyone wondering where I had been would think I had visited the privy.

CHAPTER 21

*I*t was late the next morning when I heard Mother uttering an oath from upstairs. A moment later she called down to me.

"Etta, please bring one of the small looking glasses we keep in the cupboard in the front hall. I broke one up here."

"Yes, Mother. Do you need a bandage?"

"No. I am not hurt. But please bring a broom, too."

I hurried into the kitchen to fetch the broom, then I leaned down and grabbed one of the small handheld looking glasses out of the cupboard. As I was doing that, however, I knocked over one of the candlesticks in the cupboard. It was the wooden one that had been removed from the barn after Oliver's death. I had struck it with my elbow and as it hit the floor, the candle fell out of its base. Leaving it behind, I hastened up the stairs, handed Mother the glass, and helped her clean up the broken one. When I had discarded the shards on the midden behind the house, I went back to the cupboard and knelt down to replace the candle that had fallen out of its holder.

Reaching for the base, I noticed a small piece of paper in the round depression where the candle belonged. I removed the paper. It was white, folded into a quarter square, it's surface waxy and dimpled where it had been crushed under the candle. I unfolded it; upon examination, I recognized it immediately as having come from a newspaper. I took the paper over to the door so I could see the writing more clearly in the light coming through the windowpane.

I gasped. It was an article, but not just any article. It was entitled "Patriot killed by unknown assailant close to Long Wharfe."

I scanned the paper quickly, thankful that Mother had schooled the boys and me so we could read skillfully. Indeed, it told of the death of a man in Boston on August twenty-sixth at the hands of two people. It was the selfsame article Abel Smith, the peddler, had talked of in the tavern.

But why had the article been hidden under a candle used by Oliver Doolittle? And why that particular article? There was no doubt that the candle and the base had been in Oliver's possession before he died—I had seen it in the barn. The sheriff must not have thought to separate the candle from the base when he searched Oliver's belongings.

I was quite sure Jesse had provided Oliver with the candle and the base.

Had Jesse put the scrap of newspaper there, or had it belonged to Oliver? I could think of no other possibilities. If it had been Jesse, why would he have done such a thing?

And was it a coincidence that Abel Smith and Oliver had both been in possession of the same article?

Of all the articles Abel could have read aloud that evening in the tavern, this was the story he had chosen. He had scanned the newspaper before choosing that article to read aloud. After that, he had engaged in a conversation about the death which had taken place on our property. And, I realized with a start, it was only a few hours before that, just a day after I had discovered

Oliver's body, that Abel had appeared at the inn looking for a room.

And there had to be something special or noteworthy about the article for it to be hidden in such a way among Oliver's belongings.

Was it possible Abel and Oliver were somehow connected?

Somehow the very thought was chilling. Abel was such a pleasant person—how could he have any connection with such a sinister fellow? It was impossible.

The questions swirling around inside my brain were making my head hurt. I needed to talk to Jesse, but I needed some time to think about this first.

I tucked the paper into my pocket and busied myself with work the rest of the day. Jesse helped Father in the tavern long after it closed that night, so I did not have an opportunity to talk to him about the paper.

I had the nightmare about finding Oliver's body again that night.

THE NEXT DAY brought good news: Father and the boys declared the harvest completed for the season. The oats were in, the rye was in, the wheat was in, and now the remaining work to prepare the harvest for storage was for the women in the family.

That night there was a light mood in the tavern, as most of our neighbors had also finished bringing in their crops, and everyone was jovial. Even Thomas came to partake in the revelry and enjoyed a measure of rum.

There was music that night, for Thaddeus Marshall had again brought his fiddle. The men clapped along to the tunes, and several of them sang the words, too. I glanced at Jesse, who watched them with a wistful smile. I knew he wanted to be singing, at least, and perhaps even playing, too. It would be such fun to watch him play for the men's enjoyment, and I knew he would have loved it.

After drinking another measure of rum, Thomas left rather early and I noticed he seemed to be favoring his lame leg even more than usual. He had brought back the candle he had borrowed the last time he visited the tavern, but we insisted that he use it again to get back to his cabin.

Abel Smith arrived some time later and he smiled and laughed along with our neighbors and the other men in the tavern. They seemed to have accepted him as a friend, much to Mother's disapproval. They all wanted to know when he would be visiting their homes, for their wives knew a peddler was in the neighborhood and were eager to see his wares. I sometimes wondered why he had not tried to sell anything to Mother, but when I saw the way Mother looked at him, with such disdain, it was clear to me why he had declined to talk to her about his goods.

Even Isaac was feeling strong enough to join the men in the tavern for drink and conversation. He didn't stay long, though, because he tired easily and wished to return to his room. I noticed, however, that his cheeks were regaining their pink tint and his smile told me he enjoyed the camaraderie of the men in the tavern.

It was quite late when Thaddeus put away his fiddle and everyone went home. I needed to speak to Jesse about the article, so I lingered in the tavern after my work was done. Luckily, the rest of the family retired and I had a few moments before Mother came looking for us.

"Jesse, I found something yesterday. I want to show it to you." I spoke quickly and in a low voice.

"What is it?"

"A piece of newspaper, folded into quarters and hidden under the candle in the wooden candlestick you gave Oliver. It is the same story Abel Smith told everyone in the tavern. You remember—the one about the young man who had been killed in Boston."

Jesse's eyes widened. "Do you—"

"Wait. Before you say anything, tell me. Did you put the paper in there?"

"No. I swear I didn't. Do you suppose it is a coincidence that Oliver and Abel were interested in the same story?"

I barely heard the question, so relieved was I to hear that Jesse hadn't secreted the paper in the candlestick. "What did you say?"

"I asked if you think it's a coincidence that Oliver and Abel were both interested in the same news story."

"Of all the newspapers and all the articles that are written, these two men, both virtual strangers to us, take special note of a particular item? It seems too unlikely to be coincidence."

"I agree." Jesse's voice was grim.

I took the opportunity to blurt out the other issue which had weighed heavily on my mind since the previous day. "Jesse, I have to tell you something."

"What is it?"

I took a deep breath. "Mother suspects you."

"Of what?"

"Of wanting to take up arms."

Jesse made a scoffing sound. "I have made no decision yet. Mother need not worry that I am going to destroy her Quaker reputation any time in the very near future."

"And Father and Sylvanus suspect you of harboring sympathy for the British."

His brow furrowed. "I suppose I cannot keep it a secret forever."

CHAPTER 22

*M*other awoke the next morning with a yen for peaches in her porridge. Though we usually kept the peaches for the wintertime, I had to admit the thought of summer fruit mixed into the porridge sounded delightful. I hurried to the storehouse to fetch a jar of the beautiful, sweet yellow-gold fruit.

The peaches were on a bottom shelf in a dark corner of the storehouse. We kept most of the preserved fruits and vegetables where daylight could not easily reach, because light seemed to rob them of their sweetness and delicate flavors when the time came to eat them.

There were jars upon jars of summer fruits, and the peaches were toward the back of one of the lower shelves. I crouched low to the ground and stretched my arm as far as it would go to the back of the shelf, trying not to dislodge any jars in front lest I break a jar and its contents be ruined.

I was startled when my fingers brushed against a hard wooden object, not the smooth glass I had been expecting. I drew my hand back for just a moment, then gingerly stretched it back again toward the jars of peaches. When I touched the strange object again, I closed my fingers around it, trying to figure out what it was. I had no idea. The only thing I knew was that it did not belong there.

Looking over my shoulder to make sure no one was coming, I hurriedly took the rows of jars off the bottom shelf, setting them on the ground beside me. Eventually I simply pushed the remaining jars aside and grasped the object with my hand. It was about the length of my forearm, from what I could determine. I lifted it and pulled it toward me.

There was enough daylight in the storehouse for my shocked eyes to see that the object I now held in my hand was a holster pistol. I dropped it as if it were aflame.

What was a pistol doing in our storehouse? Father owned guns, of course, but they were rifles used only for hunting. Those rifles were seldom used, and they were certainly not stored in among the peaches.

The moment I knew what I had unearthed, another question crowded its way into my mind: whose pistol was this? I suspected it had been Oliver's. I had seen pistols like this during soldiers' Court Day demonstrations. This was a military pistol. I wondered briefly if this was perhaps one of the munitions that had been moved from hiding places around the county after the list of hiding places for the munitions had been stolen.

But that seemed unlikely. If munitions were needed, they would have to be readily accessible; this one, buried behind rows of glass jars, would not easily be found or retrieved. No, this one had been hidden for a different reason.

And I intended to find out what it was.

I put the pistol back where I had found it, replaced all the jars where they belonged, and hurried back to the kitchen with the jar of peaches for Mother.

That evening after supper I grabbed Jesse's arm as he walked out of the dining room toward the front of the inn. "I have to talk to you," I hissed.

"What is it?"

"Lower your voice. I don't want anyone to hear."

"All right. But we can't talk in the foyer. Meet me by the storehouse after you're done cleaning up from supper."

I hurried through my evening chores and sent Prissy over to the tavern, telling her I needed to look in on Isaac, who had suffered a setback from being in the tavern the night the harvest was completed. The poor man was exhausted and could barely catch his breath. When she left I did, in fact, check on Isaac, but he was already asleep. I went straight to the storehouse to wait for Jesse. Luck was with me, as I did not have to wait long.

"What is so important?" he asked.

"Did Oliver carry a pistol with him?"

"I do not know. Why?"

"Because I found a pistol hidden in the storehouse." I waved my hand at the small building mere inches away. "Do you know how much damage he could have wrought with that weapon? When I think..." I broke off, too overcome by sudden relief over Oliver's death. I could not bear to imagine what he could have done to Prissy if he had brandished a weapon when he was with her.

"Etta, you have to stay calm. Oliver is no longer a concern." He took a deep breath. "That pistol belongs to me."

I could only stare at my brother, my favorite brother, who was becoming more of a stranger to me by the day.

"Yours?" I fear I spoke a bit too loudly, because Jesse whipped around to look behind him.

"Shh! Yes, it's mine. I hid it there because I didn't think anyone would be using the fruit until winter."

"Mother wanted peaches this morning."

"Naturally." Jesse smirked and shook his head.

"What are you doing with a pistol? How did you get it? Why do you need one?"

"If you'll only slow down and stop asking questions, I will be happy to explain everything."

"All right. But please hurry. I am supposed to be in the tavern." I crossed my arms over my chest and waited for him to explain.

"Gabriel Tillotson gave it to me."

Gabriel Tillotson again.

"Why?"

"In the event I decide to join the military."

My arms flailed out, almost of their own volition. "Jesse, do you know what will happen if Mother or Father finds that pistol?"

"Yes, I do know. I will have to find a new place to hide it. Will you help me?"

"No."

"Etta, please?"

"No."

"Now that fall is here, Father will be spending more time in the barn, doing things that were neglected throughout the spring and summer, so that is not a good hiding place. Obviously the storehouse is not a good hiding place because you found it."

"Have you thought of returning the hideous thing to Gabriel?"

"I will not return it. What if I need it?"

"If you do not join the British forces, you will have no need of it."

Now it was Jesse's turn to cross his arms over his chest. He gave me a severe look. "Etta, I have not made my decision yet. If I decide to go, I will need the pistol. You do not want to hasten my decision by nagging, do you?" I stared at him balefully until he smiled. "Of course I say that in jest. But I need to make the decision that is best for me. I hope you understand that."

"I do."

"You will be the first one I tell, I promise."

"Very well."

Jesse opened his mouth to say something, then closed it again.

"What is it?" I asked.

He hesitated, then puffed out his cheeks and exhaled sharply. "Please hide the pistol for me. I would not ask you to do it, but I cannot think of a place to put it where no one will find it. Someone is always around everywhere I think to put it."

I never wanted to touch the thing again, but I could not say *no*. I felt the pain of Jesse's indecision. I prayed fervently that he would stay in Stites Point, but suppose someone found the pistol? Even if Jesse decided not to join the British in the war for independence, Father would not allow him to live in our home any longer if he knew Jesse had tried to hide a weapon in our midst.

"Very well. I'll put it somewhere tomorrow. I've been gone from the tavern too long already to do it tonight."

"Thank you."

Jesse turned to walk away, but I called after him. "Jesse?"

"Yes?"

"Have you fired it? The pistol?"

"No. I swear to you, I have not."

THE NEXT MORNING I hastened to the storehouse and knelt where the jars hid the pistol from view. I felt around for the weapon and once my fingers closed around it, I lifted it above the jars, being careful not to clink the metal or the wood against any glass. When I held it in front of me, I shuddered at the thought of someone using it. I hid it as best I could in the folds of my skirt and returned to the kitchen, where I had left Prissy to prepare the porridge for the morning meal.

When she went into the dining room to make sure there were sufficient bowls and utensils, I hurriedly placed the pistol under a large basket in the corner of the kitchen. I would return to that spot later, once Prissy had left to do her other chores for the morning, and find a better place to hide it.

But I was delayed after the meal, talking to one of the inn guests who needed to know when the ferry between Stites Point and Somers Point might be arriving and leaving again. While I wrote down the time for him, Prissy began cleaning up the kitchen and dining room.

And that was how I came to find her in the kitchen, holding the pistol with trembling hands.

I dared not shout to her, for fear she would startle and drop the weapon. What if she did that and it fired on its own? I did not know if it held ammunition. I cursed under my breath for not asking Jesse. Prissy had not seen me come into the room, as she was staring rapt at the pistol. I stepped very softly backward out of the room and made a small noise in the hallway, one I knew Prissy would hear, so her concentration might break and she would put the pistol down.

It worked. When I moved again into the kitchen doorway, Prissy was standing near the basket, staring at the floor, her hands at her sides. If she was trying to look unobtrusive, she was failing. The pistol was nowhere to be seen, and I suspected that Prissy had instinctively realized it did not belong in the open where people might see it.

When her eyes met mine, I could see the questions that swam behind the blue brightness.

"You found it." I was speaking in a low voice which I hoped sounded gentle. My mind was racing, trying to think of something to tell her, a plausible reason for a pistol to be in our kitchen. But I was unsuccessful.

She nodded.

I had lied to Prissy so often of late, I could not do it again. "I hid it there to protect Jesse. No one must know it is there." I stared at her, waiting for her to respond in some way.

She wrinkled her brow without nodding.

"A friend of Jesse's gave it to him. Jesse has never fired it. But he asked me to safeguard it for him." It was all true. It was not the entire truth, but I had not lied to her.

"Prissy, can you keep this a secret? You know Jesse will be in grave trouble if Mother or Father knows of this pistol."

She nodded. But was she nodding because she would keep it a secret or because she agreed that Mother and Father must not know about it?

"You'll keep this a secret?"

Prissy nodded after an agonizing moment.

I did not know if telling her where I had decided to hide the pistol was a good idea, but I forged ahead. "I will not keep it here in the kitchen. I will put it in our room, behind the chest of drawers. Neither Father nor Mother ever goes in there, so it will be safe."

Prissy nodded, more convincingly this time.

"This is a dangerous weapon. Only Jesse should ever touch it. You'll not touch it, correct?"

Prissy nodded again.

"Very well. Thank you. As soon as Mother goes out-of-doors, I will put it in our room. Then let us not think of it again." I smiled at her, and she smiled back. I let out a long breath of relief. I knew I could trust her.

CHAPTER 23

$\mathcal{I}$saac Taylor came downstairs late that morning. He held tightly to the banister, his face a mask of consternation.

"How are you feeling, Isaac?" I asked. I had just come into the foyer from the parlor.

"I heartily enjoyed the company of others in the tavern, but I fear it delayed my recovery. I came down here because I was hoping for a mug of cider or a bit of food. I asked your good mother earlier, but it seems she has forgotten."

I looked at him in surprise. I had not seen Mother go upstairs earlier in the day, but I had been busy with my own responsibilities. It was possible she had gone upstairs, though I was the only person who ever answered his summonses.

"Of course I will be happy to bring you both food and cider," I said. "Do you need help getting back to your room?"

"No, my dear. I think I shall get back upstairs without assistance."

"Very well, if you're sure. I will bring your meal upstairs straightaway."

I did not know Mother had been listening to our conversation from within the dining room, and now she strode into the foyer, a fire blazing in her eyes.

"I will thank you not to make accusations against one who is not present to defend oneself. I am not feeble-minded, as your words suggest. I simply have not yet had the time to bring your meal upstairs."

"I did not mean to offend, of course, my dear lady," Isaac said with a slight bow. "I apologize if my words were unconsidered and untrue. I would never say you are feeble-minded."

I looked at Mother, who stared at me and Isaac with her mouth in a straight white line. She turned on her heel and went into the parlor.

There was nothing more to be said. Isaac gave me a solemn nod, thanked me for bringing food to him, and began the slow process of returning to his room. I went to the kitchen and prepared his meal, poured a large measure of cider, and set everything on a large tray to take to him. By the time I reached his room, he was back in bed, breathing heavily from the exertion of going down and up the stairs and his confrontation with Mother. We said nothing of it and I left the tray with him, promising to return for it in the afternoon.

I went into the parlor a short time later and found Mother in there with her sewing. She gave me a look of suspicion.

"I suppose you think our ungrateful guest had the right to make such an accusation against me," she said acidly.

"I had not given the matter any more thought, Mother," I said.

"If we do not coddle the man and cater to his every whim, perhaps he will find himself healed and begone."

I disagreed that Isaac was a malingerer, as Mother seemed to be suggesting. I highly doubted the man was capable of such deceit. He seemed a decent sort who would not take advantage of another's helpfulness. In my humble opinion, Mother had reacted to Isaac's earlier words with unnecessary anger. She could have merely admitted that she had forgotten his food, or ignored his comment altogether.

"I took a tray to him," I said.

"Hmm."

She returned to her needlework, and thus I was effectively dismissed from her presence.

Later that afternoon I was sweeping in the front hall when I heard Mother's voice coming from the family parlor. I put my ear to the door and heard her telling Father what had transpired that morning between her and Isaac.

"Nathaniel, I can no longer abide that man in my house. He is insufferable."

"Davinia, he is a paying guest. And he is paying handsomely, I might add, for the services provided by us, and especially Antoinetta."

"Antoinetta has other things to be doing in addition to waiting on that man hand and foot."

I thought with a twinge of bitterness that Mother simply wanted Isaac out of the inn. I knew the reason: she viewed anything or anyone who took me away from my housework as an impediment to her own leisure time. If I were to spend too much time away from my chores and Prissy could not keep up with the extra work, Mother would have no choice but to take on the additional chores herself.

"He is quite harmless, my dear. And as long as Etta is the one heeding his summonses, you are at liberty to ignore him."

"Humph. If it comes to pass that Etta is too busy waiting on him and not tending to her regular chores, it will be time for him to leave the premises."

"That is fair. Please keep me apprised."

The conversation was at an end, so I stepped away from the door and resumed my sweeping. A moment later Mother came into the foyer and reached into the cupboard where the candlesticks were kept. She put them on the desk and took a rag from her apron pocket. Before she began to buff the candlesticks, however, she counted them.

"One of the candlesticks is missing again," she said in a beleaguered voice. "Etta, do you know where it is?"

"No, Mother."

"This is the final straw." Mother was holding a candlestick and she thumped it heavily onto the desk, closing her eyes and hanging her head as she did so. "The last time a candlestick went missing, it was an omen of death." Her voice was becoming tight and strained. "I cannot abide the thought of another dead person in our midst."

I set the broom against the wall. "Mother, I will find the candlestick. You should rest. Come with me into our parlor and I will bring you something soothing to drink."

"Etta, you were the one to find the candlestick the last time one went missing, and you were the unlucky one to stumble upon that abhorrent man's body. I think you should let Jesse or Sylvanus search for the candlestick this time."

I did not dare show my surprise at my mother's words. I would have thought that as long as she was not the one to look for the candlestick, she would not care who did it. It was kind of her, in a way, though I disagreed that the missing candlestick was an omen of death.

"I will tell Jesse and Sylvanus about it, Mother. Do not fret. Here, lie down and I will bring you cider."

Mother did as I bade her and I hurried to the kitchen for the drink. When I returned, I set the cider next to her on a low table and left to finish my cleaning.

That evening at supper we had just said a prayer over our food when Mother's head snapped up.

"Antoinetta, didn't you give Thomas the candlestick when he went back to his cabin in the dark two nights ago?"

"Yes, Mother. I had completely forgotten. I will get it tomorrow."

"That's fine. Thank you."

She did not gripe or complain about my forgetfulness or sloth in attempting to find the missing item, but instead finished her meal with a look of relief on her face. The candlesticks were expensive, I knew, so it was small wonder that she was relieved. It would not do to continue losing them. And besides that, Mother seemed to have rethought the association between missing items and death, so that brought relief to me.

The next day Mother pulled out the candlesticks from their cupboard again. Because she had rested the previous afternoon, I had put them back into the cupboard without buffing them. I was busy cleaning the windows in the dining room and guest parlor when Mother appeared in the doorway.

"I'm going to Thomas's cabin to get the candlestick. I shall be back soon."

"I can go, Mother, as soon as I finish these windows."

"I would like to clean the candlesticks as soon as possible because I have other things to do, so I will get it. You finish the windows, please." And with that, she was gone. She didn't seem to be afraid of going outside by herself. I was amazed at her bravery.

When she returned bearing the missing candlestick, Prissy and I were in a frenzy of work. I had knocked over the bucket I used to clean the windows and there was water all over the guest parlor floor. Prissy was using rags to clean it up while I spoke to two travelers who had come inside looking for lodging. I explained that we only had one available room and told them how to find the next inn closest to us.

I had just ushered the two men to the front door and they were taking their leave when Mother called to me. I bade the men safe travels and returned to the foyer. Mother wore a worried look.

"Etta, I—"

Mother was cut off by shouting coming from outside. I ran

to the front porch and saw Jesse and Sylvanus running toward
the inn and waving their arms.

After a hurried discussion, it became clear that the pigs had
escaped from their pen. Mother and Prissy and I dashed after
the boys and spent a good deal of time attempting to corral all
the pigs back into their enclosure. It was filthy work and we
were all rank with mud and muck when we finally managed to
lock their gate behind us.

"I'm sorry," Jesse panted. "I must not have latched the gate
properly."

"See that it doesn't happen again." Mother grimaced. "We all
need to bathe. Let's get back to the house."

Prissy and I filled the tub with water and waited indoors for
the boys to bathe, then we changed the water and it was Mother's turn, then my turn, then finally Prissy's turn. The entire
ordeal had taken all afternoon and supper was going to be
served late on account of it.

That evening Mother didn't go into the tavern, but stayed in
the house to write a letter to Aunt Margaret while Father and
Prissy and I tended to the guests in the tavern. Sylvanus was
arranging shelves in the cidery. Jesse felt unwell, he said, and
was in the privy.

Mother came into the tavern for only a moment looking for
Father while he was refilling ale in the back room. She said she
would come back later to talk to him.

It was a short while before Father returned to the front
room of the tavern.

"Father, Mother was in here looking for you."

"Thank you, Etta. I shall go see what she needs."

Father left. Presently Sylvanus returned from the cidery, and
just a moment later Jesse came in from the privy.

"Are you feeling any improved?" I asked Jesse.

He nodded and opened his mouth to speak, but the tavern
door burst open and Father stumbled into the room, his face

drained of its normal ivory-pink hue. He made a small noise and the men closest to the door stood up to help him. I threw down my rag and ran toward him, followed closely by Jesse and Sylvanus.

"Nathaniel, what is the matter?" Choruses of men joined in when they noticed Father struggling. It took only a moment for them to surround him.

Father's eyes settled on mine amid the small crowd. "Etta, call for the doctor. I fear your mother has died."

CHAPTER 24

"*D*ied?" I cried. "How? Where is she? When did this happen?" I was in a daze and could think of nothing else to say.

Sylvanus and Jesse were at my side and heard what Father said. They both broke into a run, reaching the tavern door simultaneously. Sylvanus wrenched the door open and dashed outside. Jesse called to the man standing nearest him. "You there! Go fetch Doctor Wheeler!" Then he was gone.

I followed closely on my brothers' heels while Prissy stayed in the tavern to tend to Father. I yanked open the front door of the inn and immediately came upon Sylvanus kneeling next to Mother on the floor at the base of the staircase. Her eyes were closed and her face was pale and ashen. I knelt next to Sylvanus and looked anxiously into his face.

"Is she all right? Is it true what Father said?"

"I have tried, but I cannot feel her pulse. You try." Sylvanus moved out of the way and I placed my fingers on Mother's thin wrist. I tried not to notice the odd way her neck was bent, but I couldn't banish the image from my mind of another neck, bent in a similar fashion, which I had seen not long ago. Oliver's neck had been broken, too.

I knew then that I would feel no pulse under Mother's skin. Nonetheless, I tried. I felt one of her wrists, then the other. I placed my hand on her neck to feel for a pulse there. I bent down and placed my ear on her chest, but there was no breath. No pulse. No lifeblood.

I sat back on my heels and bowed my head. Sylvanus, who had stood next to me while I tried ministering to Mother, turned abruptly and left the hall. He strode into our private family quarters and closed the door behind him. Jesse stood mutely beside me.

Father and Prissy came just a few moments later. Father gave me an expectant look, one filled simultaneously with hope and anguish, and I shook my head. Father closed his eyes and leaned against the desk for support. Prissy clutched his arm.

Jesse leaned down, grasped my hand, and helped me stand up. The four of us stood in the hallway, in a disbelieving silence, until Father was able to utter the words, "What happened?"

A figure appeared at the top of the stairs. It was Isaac, looking as if he had dressed hurriedly. He made his way down the stairs slowly, taking in the scene before him. His face was white. "I heard a commotion from my room. I was already in my nightclothes. It sounded like someone fell down the stairs."

A fall down the stairs would indeed explain the strange angle of Mother's neck. I thanked God her eyes were closed in death. I had seen the dull sheen of Oliver's lifeless eyes, and the sight would haunt me the rest of my days.

We had to move Mother's body to a place where prying eyes could not see her. I whispered my thoughts to Jesse. He nodded and looked around, perhaps noticing for the first time that Sylvanus was not present.

"He's in there," I said, nodding toward our family parlor.

Jesse disappeared and came back a moment later with Sylvanus in tow. Sylvanus still wore a face of shock. His eyes were dry, but red and pained. Isaac, as if sensing his presence was unwanted, returned to his room. I was a little surprised, but relieved, that no other guests came downstairs to investigate the commotion Isaac had heard.

The two boys tried clumsily to move Mother so they could lift her and take her to our parlor, but they could not seem to coordinate their efforts. I had an idea. "Wait here," I instructed them. I ran to my room, stripped the bed of the bedclothes, and hurried back to my brothers.

"Here. Use this." I thrust one of the sheets at them and they quickly realized I meant for them to fashion a hammock to carry Mother's body.

How shocking it was to think of her as merely a body.

While Jesse tried to shift Mother, Sylvanus made an awkward attempt to slide the sheet under her so Jesse could roll her to her original position. When it did not work, I exclaimed loudly.

"Let me do it!" My own voice startled me, and I realized how hushed the house was. I pushed Sylvanus aside and spread the sheet quickly and smoothly under Mother. Jesse rolled her again and gathered the edges of one end of the sheet. I stood back and Sylvanus stepped up to take the edges of the other end. Very carefully and slowly, they lifted the sheet and carried Mother into the parlor.

Father had not opened his eyes while the boys struggled with Mother's body. I knew he was praying for Mother's soul and for the strength to get through the upcoming days and months without her. When he opened his eyes again, he stood up and kissed Prissy's head gently. He followed the boys into the parlor and closed the door. After a moment both boys came into the hallway. They looked exhausted, as if they had aged ten years apiece in the past half hour.

Jesse finally sighed and went back into the tavern. With nothing else to do, I followed him, then Prissy and Sylvanus joined our somber troupe. Back in the tavern, all the men were quiet. They talked in small groups and faced us with questioning eyes when we entered.

"Is she...?" one man asked.

Jesse nodded. "Yes. Mother is gone."

Men removed their hats and bowed their heads in silence. In groups of two and three they slowly departed, expressing their condolences as they went forth. Jesse, Sylvanus, Prissy, and I accepted their words with nods of thanks, and I was glad when the four of us were alone in the room. We sat at a round table, the silence heavy in the room. I don't know what the others were thinking, but I was thinking about Father. I couldn't imagine his pain. Finally I could not sit there any longer. I had to do something.

"I'll clean the tables and counter," I offered. "Prissy, can you help me?"

She followed me, head bent, and we went about our tasks. Within a few minutes Jesse and Sylvanus stood, too, and eventually completed their nightly tavern chores.

I had forgotten that someone had left earlier to fetch the doctor, so I turned from my tasks with a start when the man came into the tavern with the doctor following closely behind him.

"Thank you for coming, Doctor Wheeler," Sylvanus said, stepping forward. "Father is in the parlor with, um, with Mother. I fear it was already too late when we sent for you. I hope we did not rouse you from sleep."

"It is no trouble at all." Doctor Wheeler glanced at each of us in turn and nodded gravely. "May I see your mother now?"

"Of course." Sylvanus ushered the doctor out of the tavern and into the house while Jesse and Prissy and I continued cleaning and preparing the tavern for the next time we would receive patrons. I did not know when that might be; I presumed the tavern would remain closed for several evenings.

We worked in silence that hung over us like a wet dress until the doctor returned with Sylvanus quite a long time later. Doctor Wheeler, like the men who had left the tavern earlier, removed his hat upon entering.

"It appears your mother has died from a fall down the stairs. Judging from the angle of her neck, she was killed immediately and did not suffer. I thought you would be comforted to hear that." He paused, then continued. "I am very sorry for the loss of your good mother. I have spoken to your father and offered him my sincere condolences. Now, if you will excuse me, I must notify the coroner."

He left and as soon as our chores were done the four of us returned to the house. Father was still in the parlor, his head resting in his hands. He didn't even look up when we filed quietly past him. I wanted to reach out and give him words of comfort, but I could think of nothing that might lessen his pain. A pall lay over our private rooms.

I climbed into bed. I had not shed a tear, and the guilt weighed on my chest like a rock. I wanted to cry, but found it impossible. Prissy glanced at me now and then, her eyes visible in the lamplight in our bedroom, and I knew she had not cried, either. I thought I should say something to her about Mother, but I could not find the appropriate words. What to say about a person who was the crux of our family, but who had lived in a constant state of peevishness and vexation with my sister and me? I dared not admit aloud that I would not miss Mother's daily beratements and scoldings, and the shame of feeling little sadness continued to thrash my thoughts until I finally fell into a fitful sleep just two hours before dawn.

When I awoke, it was to find Prissy staring at me. I gasped in surprise as she recoiled. "I'm sorry, Prissy. You startled me. Are you all right?"

She nodded almost absently. "Have you cried?" I asked.

She shook her head, looking down.

"I haven't either. Do you feel as guilty as I do?"

Prissy nodded, her eyes wide. I wondered if she, as Father likely had done, had prayed for Mother's soul last night. I had. I had even prayed God to fill me with remorse and sadness, but that prayer remained unanswered at the break of day.

The coroner was at the house before the sun rose, accompanied by the sheriff's deputy. The boys were still asleep, but Father had remained awake, sitting with Mother in the parlor. He looked as if he had been wrestling with the very Devil. His clothes and hair and beard were disheveled, crumpled, and dirty. His eyes were vacant and red-rimmed. I felt a stab of sorrow for the heartache he must have been feeling.

The coroner examined Mother's body briefly and then, with the help of the deputy, wrapped her in a large cloth. The two men carried her to the coroner's wagon while Father looked on, his face contorted with grief. After the men left, Father went to his bedroom.

Staying busy was the best way to avoid sinking into an abyss of despair, so we went about our morning tasks in morose silence.

When Father appeared in the kitchen doorway a short while later, I hurried to pull a stool close to where he stood. He remained standing.

"Father, please sit down. Let me get you something to drink."

He didn't answer, and a minute later I pressed a mug of steaming coffee into his cold hands. He blinked as if he had forgotten what he was doing. "We'll bring your breakfast straightaway, Father," I said. Prissy was bustling around the kitchen, trying to prepare Father's breakfast. When she set a tray before him, he ate nothing.

Father moved as if in a fog that day, while Prissy and I received the first of the mourners who would come to our home over the next several days. Women brought baskets of food, while their children solemnly handed Prissy and me bouquets of fall wildflowers they had picked for our family. People came from as far away as Romney Marsh, all in shock over hearing of Mother's death.

Isaac came downstairs long before the noon meal and spent a good deal of time with the family. He seemed distraught over Mother's death, much more so than I would have expected, given the bitterness of their most recent exchange. Perhaps, I thought, he felt a strong remorse for the last words he and Mother had spoken together.

Thomas came to pay his respects shortly before dinner. "I won't disrupt your privacy by staying. But I did want to tell you I am sorry about your mother. And you, sir," he said, nodding toward Father, "I know you will miss your wife."

"Thank you, Thomas. I will miss her."

Thomas murmured a few words to each of the boys, then left.

Abel Smith had left the inn early in the morning, but he returned from his workday shortly after the noon meal in order to express how sorry he was about Mother's death. "I confess I did not know your mother well, but she seemed to me a regal woman of high ideals."

I knew the meaning behind his words. He had known of Mother's disapproval of him. Her "high ideals" were the ones that had considered him beneath her family.

As Abel went upstairs to his room and Father retired to our family parlor looking worn and dejected, I was disheartened to see the sheriff walking toward the inn. I held the door open for him.

"Father is in the family parlor," I said. I gestured toward the parlor door and the sheriff knocked.

"Come in," Father said.

"I would like to speak to all of you," the sheriff said to me. I called Prissy and the boys, who followed me into the parlor a few moments later. The sheriff stood in the middle of the room.

"I fear I have bad news," the sheriff said.

CHAPTER 25

$\mathcal{W}$e all looked at him expectantly.

"We have reason to believe your mother did not fall down the stairs accidentally."

There was a collective gasp in the parlor. Prissy's face drained of color, while Father slumped back into his chair. He suddenly looked very small.

Jesse leapt to his feet. "What? Are you sure? How is that possible?" Sylvanus's face showed disbelief as he stared at the sheriff.

I could only sit, mouth agape, wondering what could have happened to make the sheriff think Mother had not fallen down the stairs by sheer accident.

"Doctor Wheeler and the coroner have taken a look at Mrs. Rutledge. There is a large bruise on her forearm. It is unmistakably in the shape of a hand. The bruise is fresh. We believe someone may have grabbed her very hard by the arm and pushed her down the stairs. Were you aware of any such mark?" He directed the question to Father.

"No. None at all." Father spoke in a hoarse voice. The sheriff looked at each of us in turn, and we all shook our heads in answer to his unspoken question. None of us knew of any bruise on Mother's arm.

"I am going to have to speak to each of you," the sheriff said. "Nathaniel, I'll start with you."

"Surely you don't think I pushed my own wife down the stairs." Father closed his eyes as if he could not believe what was happening.

"Of course not. But I do have questions that only you can answer about Mrs. Rutledge's person." His face reddened and Prissy and the boys and I hastened out of the room.

The sheriff talked to Father for a long time, then called for each of us in turn. Of course he could not ask Prissy questions that required a verbal answer, but as I found out when I asked her later, he asked her questions which required only a nod or a shake of the head in response.

When he called me into the dining room, the sheriff wore a grave expression. "I am sorry to put you through this, Antoinetta, but I need information about your mother's dealings with people who came to the house. You are in the best position to help me find the answers to my questions.

"Was there anyone your mother particularly disliked, someone who would come to the inn, perhaps?"

My thoughts immediately swung to Abel Smith, the peddler. I did not know if he had tried to sell Mother any of his wares, but if he had, I imagined her response would be swift and negative.

"Antoinetta?" the sheriff prodded.

"Abel Smith is a guest here. He is a peddler and my mother has expressed disdain for peddlers in his presence. I do not think he has ever tried to sell Mother any of his goods."

The sheriff nodded and waited for me to continue. I did not know what to say, but I felt the need to continue speaking to fill the silence that enveloped me when I stopped talking.

"I think he is a nice man, but Mother seemed not to like him.

He has always been cheerful, though, and I cannot imagine he would ever have harmed Mother."

The sheriff grunted. "Anything else you want to tell me about this peddler? How long has he been staying here?"

"I would have to check the ledger. Will you excuse me?"

"Just a minute, Etta. I have a couple other questions before you do that. Is he still staying here? If so, where is he now? And do you know where he came from?"

"He is still staying here, but I do not know where he is right now. He told me he came here from Boston."

"Anyone else besides Abel Smith?"

"Well, Mother was not fond of another guest, Isaac Taylor. He has been ill since arriving and she did not want the responsibility of caring for him."

"Is he still here?"

"Yes. He has not yet recovered sufficiently to travel. But surely Isaac didn't push her down the stairs. The man barely has enough strength to sustain himself."

The sheriff opened his mouth to say something when I blurted out the thought that had been uppermost in my mind. "Sheriff, do you think the same person who killed Oliver pushed Mother down the stairs?"

He regarded me with a grave look. "There is no way to know that right now. I must say, however, it is highly unusual for two unnatural deaths to occur at the same place so close to each other in time. My deputy and I are working on finding Oliver's killer. My hope is that when we find that person, we will also find your mother's assailant."

"I hope so, too."

When the sheriff had finished asking questions, he followed me to the front hall where I looked in the ledger to find the dates Abel and Isaac had arrived.

Father did not join us for dinner that day, saying that he preferred to stay in the parlor. After dinner Jesse and Sylvanus went to talk to him while Prissy and I cleaned up from the meal. As soon as we finished, I took a tray of food into the parlor in the hope that Father would eat something. Prissy followed me.

The mood in the parlor was dark and melancholy, despite the brightness of the afternoon outside. Father shook his head sadly when I offered him the food, but I set it next to him in case he changed his mind.

Prissy and I and the boys looked at each other. I wish I had something to say to ease Father's pain, but anything I could think of seemed inadequate.

After an awkward moment, Father gestured Prissy and me to be seated. His gaze, which had been focused on something far away which the rest of us could not see, shifted and he looked at each of us in turn.

"Your mother made a valiant attempt to be an innkeeper's wife." Father's words, usually so guarded, took us by surprise. Jesse and Sylvanus were watching him intently and Prissy and I leaned forward.

"She never should have married an innkeeper," Father continued. "And I do not believe she had the constitution to be a mother to four children. I know there were many times when she seemed harsh and unfeeling, but she loved all of you." He looked around at all of us, his expression unreadable.

"She grew up in Philadelphia, the daughter of a successful merchant. She had everything anyone could ever ask for. Did you know she was not born a Quaker?"

The last words were shocking. From things our parents had said in the past, I had suspected Mother had known luxury and wealth as a young woman, but it had not occurred to me that she might not always have been a Quaker. How was that possible?

Father smiled at the surprise on our faces. "It is true. She joined the Society of Friends in order to marry me, a simple

Quaker, despite her family's protests and severe disapproval."
He smiled slightly, as if remembering something.

"How did you meet her?" I asked.

"I was at an annual Quaker meeting in Philadelphia many
years ago and she was riding past in her family's carriage. Her
horse was frightened by something. He reared several times,
tilting the carriage dangerously. He ran amok when next his
hooves hit the ground, but by then I had yanked the carriage
door open and pulled your mother out. She was furious at me."
Father chuckled at the memory, then his eyes dimmed with
unshed tears.

He coughed a bit and cleared his throat. "But when she saw
that I had very likely saved her life by pulling her from the
runaway carriage, she was very grateful. She asked my name
and the place where I was staying, and later sent a footman with
payment for my clothes, which had become torn and dirty when
I pulled her to safety. I refused the money and she came to see
me herself, insisting that I take it."

"And did you take it?"

"Of course not. I was merely helping a fellow child of God in
a perilous situation and I told her I would not accept the
payment. She was exasperated, but she left and I noticed over
the next three days that she found reasons to come calling in the
neighborhood where the Quaker meetings were taking place.
We picnicked and walked along the river. We met like that many
times before I asked for her hand. With the exception of her
sister, Margaret, her family hated me. In fact, her father refused
our union, but Davinia left her family and her home behind,
married me, and we settled here."

The boys and Prissy and I had never heard this story. Somehow, hearing it made me sadder than I had been at any time since
Mother died. If I had known that part of her, the part that loved
my father so much that she would defy her own parents by

changing her faith and marrying beneath her station, would I have felt more tenderly toward her? Would I have understood her frustration at the housework and the chores and the constant toil that accompanied the life of an innkeeper's wife? I would never have the chance to find out, and that knowledge caused me great pain.

"When you all were born and Davinia was raising four children without any help and with an inn to run and a tavern to oversee and a husband who worked in the fields from dawn to dusk, I felt terrible, but what was I to do? Farming and keeping the inn and tavern were the only ways I knew to support the family, and she was my wife. I could not give her the things she had grown up accustomed to. But I think she did not miss living in luxury in Philadelphia and all the trappings and responsibilities that went along with it."

I disagreed, but I did not say anything. I felt a twist of guilt for thinking ill of my mother, but why else would she have continued to talk about the differences between her upbringing and her circumstances on our farm if she did not resent her life in New Jersey? It was finally clear to me why she always seemed dissatisfied with her situation. I thought of the letters we had received from Aunt Margaret over the years, including the most recent one. It was obvious she lived among wealth, and I wondered if Mother had ever read those letters through a lens of jealousy.

And yet ... she had married Father and lived by his side for many years after she left her home in Philadelphia, so she must have felt a great love for him.

I knew what happened to Quakers who chose to leave the faith to marry. They were punished by not being permitted to attend Quaker meetings any longer. They were seldom welcome back into the homes where they grew up and where their families lived. I wondered whether other religions had similar rules. I pondered the strength of the bond between

Mother and Father that she would have left her family and her faith behind willingly and deliberately.

It was exactly that sort of banishment that I feared would happen to Jesse if he left the Society of Friends and joined the British in the fighting against the colonists who wished for independence.

Father stood up and ran his fingers through his beard. "I am going for a walk. I will be back later." His slow footsteps on the wooden floor echoed in the silence left in his wake.

Prissy and the boys and I were quiet for a long time. I think each of us was turning over everything Father had told us. I was also fretting about Jesse, and I wondered if his thoughts were about what would happen if he left behind his Quaker faith.

Sylvanus was the first one to speak. "Jesse, I think we should find Thomas to see if he needs any help. He's been by himself and must be getting behind in the work."

Jesse nodded and followed Sylvanus out the door. Prissy picked up the tray with Father's untouched meal and I held the parlor door for her.

"Prissy, I need to go speak with Isaac. I should probably tell him the sheriff may be coming to ask him some questions." Prissy nodded and went to the kitchen.

I climbed the stairs, wondering how I was going to tell Isaac that the sheriff would probably need to talk to him about Mother. I heaved a sigh. I had no choice but to tell him the truth outright.

I knocked on his door and heard him call for me to enter. He was seated at the desk under the window, perusing a large book.

"How are you feeling this afternoon, Isaac?"

"I am feeling a bit stronger than yesterday. Thank you for asking. How can I help you, Etta?" He slid a small piece of paper into the book to mark his place and turned to me with a sad smile. "How is your family faring, my dear girl?"

"Father is struggling, but we are trying to help him the best we can." I paused. "I came up because I have to tell you something."

Isaac's eyebrows went up expectantly.

"I gave the sheriff your name because he was asking about inn guests with whom Mother conversed. I wanted you to know that he may be coming to speak to you about her."

Isaac sat back in his chair and removed his spectacles. "Thank you for telling me, Etta. If and when the sheriff comes to talk, I will certainly tell him everything I know."

"Very well. I will not keep you from your reading."

"While you are here, I would like to ask you a question."

"Yes?" I waited for him to speak.

"I have been wondering about the peddler who is staying here. His name is Abel Smith, is it not?"

"Yes, that is correct."

"And I believe you told me he is from Boston?"

"Yes."

Isaac rubbed his chin and beard thoughtfully. "I do not remember meeting an Abel Smith in Boston, but I seem to recall his name being mentioned there before I traveled to Cape May."

"I fear I cannot tell you anything else about him, for I know very little."

"That is fine, Etta. I was merely trying to jog my memory of the name. Thank you for indulging me."

I nodded and left. I felt better now that Isaac would not be taken by surprise if the sheriff came asking him questions.

CHAPTER 26

e had not yet finished the morning meal on the day of Mother's funeral when I heard boots clumping on the floor of the front hall. Thinking it was a traveler, I excused myself from the table. I suppressed a groan when I saw who was there.

"Good morning, Sheriff. Can I get you something to eat? It's quite early in the day."

"I have eaten, thank you. Antoinetta, I'm here on behalf of the magistrate, Mister Webber. He has asked that you, your brothers, your Father, and Abel Smith present yourselves at Romney Marsh tomorrow to answer questions about your mother's, er, fall down the stairs. The magistrate will come here to speak to Isaac Taylor, since he is convalescing."

"I will inform everyone, Sheriff. Today is Mother's funeral, as I am sure you are aware. Will you be attending?"

"I am planning to attend, yes."

We knew most of the people in Stites Point would congregate at the inn before Mother's funeral, so Prissy and I hurried around all morning preparing food for them and making sure the parlors were clean for our guests. Thomas came by shortly after breakfast to tell us he did not think he could walk the entire distance of Mother's funeral procession because of his leg, so we thanked him and sent him back to his cabin with enough food for the next couple days.

Because we and our nearby Quaker brothers and sisters did not have a proper meetinghouse nearby, one of our neighbors opened his home to provide space for Mother's service. The funeral procession began at the inn and moved south to our neighbor's home. Father and the boys, as well as several other neighbors, helped carry Mother's simple pine coffin. Father had barely eaten since Mother's death and I wondered how he mustered the strength to assist carrying her coffin. Prissy and I walked behind them, followed by everyone who had gathered at our home before the funeral.

It was a quiet affair, with only one person standing to eulogize Mother. Father wiped his eyes several times during the service, and my heart ached for him. I noticed the sheriff in attendance, as well as Doctor Wheeler and Abel Smith. All of them wore stony faces. After the funeral, everyone in attendance accompanied our family to the closest Quaker burial ground. The boys and Father, with the assistance of several neighbors, carried Mother's coffin. Mother was interred next to a woman who had passed of a sudden fever during the summer. Kind neighbors had dug the hole for the coffin before our arrival, so the interment took place quickly.

I held Prissy's hand when we returned to the inn following the interment to share a meal with everyone who had attended the funeral. Her hand trembled in mine, but she did not cry. Nor did I. In fact, I did not notice either Jesse or Sylvanus crying, either. Again, the familiar feeling of wracking guilt wormed its way around my insides, reminding me that I should feel sadder because of Mother's loss. I wondered if Prissy's hand was trembling for the same reason. I squeezed her hand in mine and some of her tension seemed to ebb away.

CHAPTER 27

ather, Sylvanus, Jesse, Prissy, and I left early in the morning for Romney Marsh. Abel Smith had left an hour before we did. We did not know how long we might have to wait to see the Magistrate.

Romney Marsh was a bustling village compared to small, quiet Stites Point. There were several dusty streets, all converging near the courthouse. The five of us waited outside the courthouse and presently the sheriff came out, followed closely by Abel, who left immediately. The sheriff took Father inside first, and my brothers and sister and I waited for him for what seemed like hours. Finally Father emerged from the courthouse looking drawn and tired. He had looked that way since Mother's death. I felt a twist of pity for him.

Sylvanus spoke to the magistrate next, then when he came out some time later, it was Jesse's turn to go inside. I went next, and Prissy was last.

The magistrate asked me so many questions that I lost track of time. He wanted to know about the guests at the inn, travelers and diners who may have met Mother and then left shortly afterward, and specifically about Isaac and Abel. I told him everything I knew, which was of little help, I was sure. He wanted to know about Father's treatment of Mother and of Mother's physical constitution. I assured him that she had been strong and healthy and that Father never raised his hand to her.

When I left the magistrate, I was exhausted. It was well past the dinner hour by the time Prissy came outside, so Father bought some bread and cheese from a woman near the courthouse and we all, except for Father, shared it. Then Jesse and Sylvanus accompanied him on an errand to the blacksmith's barn while Prissy and I waited under a tree nearby.

I heard a commotion just up the street and I turned to see who was talking so loudly. It was a small group of young men, all wearing smiles and smart hats and frocks. I noticed Elijah in the group. He pulled one compatriot aside and spoke to him solemnly, then the man turned and left. For just a moment, Elijah glanced beyond the man's shoulder and stared directly at me. I nodded out of politeness, but he only stared for a moment longer and turned away from me. I felt as if I had been physically slapped, so great was my embarrassment.

Prissy put her hand on my arm and raised her eyebrows in a question.

"That Elijah Webber is the rudest young man I know. To turn away like that, when he knows we have just buried Mother. Honestly, Prissy, one wonders if he has any manners at all."

Prissy smiled and turned away. Her smile infuriated me more.

I strode over to the Romney Marsh general store in, I fear, a very unladylike manner, and sat down on a bench by myself. My scowl must have convinced Prissy to stay away from me while we waited for Father and the boys to complete their business.

I looked up as a woman came out of the general store. She shifted the basket on her arm and glanced at me. She looked away, but then looked quickly back.

"Are you Davinia Rutledge's daughter?" she asked.

"Yes." I did not wish to talk about Mother.

"I was very sorry to hear of her passing. We could not attend the funeral because three of our children are sick and we were needed at home."

"Thank you for your kind words."

"May I sit down?"

I moved to one end of the bench so the woman could sit. Her clothes were plain, like mine and Prissy's, and I was sure she was a Friend. I softened toward her a bit, not wanting her to form a poor opinion of me as another Quaker woman.

"Davinia used to buy buttons from me," the woman said. I thought of the frocks my mother had made for me and Prissy when we were younger. As plain as they were, Mother had always sewn several buttons on each sleeve cuff. It seemed extravagant at the time, but as I had learned in the past several days, Mother must have had beautiful clothes when she was young. She must have missed those dresses and wanted me and Prissy to have something beautiful, too. I was struck with another pang of sorrow for not having known Mother better before she died.

The woman continued. "I was always grateful to her for buying the buttons, since peddlers often come to the area with cheaper buttons. Many women prefer the cheaper ones. And, of course, we don't put buttons on our clothes, so your mother was risking a reprimand by doing so." She gestured lightly toward me when she used the word 'we' and I knew she was referring to our Quaker traditions. But she smiled, and I knew she did not hold it against Mother that she put small embellishments on our clothes.

"In fact, Davinia told us recently of a peddler staying at your inn," the woman said. I saw her looking at me out of the corner of my eye.

"That is correct. There is a peddler staying there," I said.

The woman lowered her voice. "She told me the man was

untrustworthy and that I and the other women in Romney Marsh should not purchase his wares if he visited our homes."

I could only nod. That sounded like something Mother would say. I grimaced inwardly, not wanting to hear of her gossip about Abel. I found the man kind and helpful, as I know Father did, and I disagreed with Mother's assessment of him.

But what if Father and I were wrong and Mother was right?

How much did I really know about Abel Smith?

Maybe Mother knew more about him than she told us, and maybe her advice to this woman and to other women in Romney Marsh was not gossip, but good, solid counsel that would keep them from wasting their money.

And if Mother had been correct and Abel were a charlatan, could we trust him? Could we believe that his presence at our inn was verily to sell wares? Should we be keeping a much closer watch on his comings and goings?

I forced such thoughts from my mind and faced the woman. "I know very little of Abel besides what he has told me, that he is a seller of items that people need and desire. I have no reason to disbelieve him, but Mother may have known much more than I. I am sorry that I can neither confirm what Mother said, nor deny it."

The woman nodded politely and repeated her sorrow over Mother's passing, then rose and walked away. I noticed Prissy watching me from the tree where I had left her. I joined her and apologized for leaving her. I did not wish to discuss Elijah, so I simply did not mention his name. If she wanted me to talk about him, I would simply ignore her.

"That woman just told me that Mother advised her and other women in Romney Marsh not to buy anything from Abel."

Prissy's eyes widened.

"She told the women that he is untrustworthy."

Prissy lowered her eyes and shook her head slightly.

"I agree. Mother should not have spoken like that, but it *is* possible that she knew something about Abel that we do not know. Perhaps there is something Mother knew about him that she had not shared with anyone else. I know Father likes him, so obviously she never shared whatever it is with him. Just be careful around him, please."

She nodded again and I saw Father and the boys approaching from the blacksmith's shop. "Time to go home, Pris." We all climbed into the wagon for the ride back to the inn.

A surprise awaited us when we arrived home.

CHAPTER 28

I stopped short when I saw a woman sitting on a chair in the front hall of the inn. She wore a long silk gown trimmed with lace and shoes with small, dainty heels. She was holding a lovely sheer handkerchief. It, too, was trimmed with lace and there were letters embroidered on it, though I could not read them from where I stood.

"Good day, Friend. How may I be of service?" I asked her.

Before she could answer, though, Father stepped forward, his eyes wide. "Margaret?" he asked tentatively.

She smiled and nodded, rose, and held her hands out to Father. "Nathaniel, it's been a very long time."

Prissy and the boys and I could only stare at the spectacle, our mouths agape. This *couldn't* be the only Margaret I had ever heard of—Mother's sister.

Father turned to us. "Margaret, I would like you to meet Sylvanus, Jesse, Antoinetta, and Priscilla." He pointed to each of us in turn. Then he spoke to us. "This is your mother's sister, your Aunt Margaret."

The boys were the first to recover. They bowed to her and told her they were pleased to meet her. Prissy and I walked up to her next and welcomed her. I told her to please call us Etta and Prissy. Aunt Margaret inclined her head toward us and smiled.

Turning to Father, she said, "They all look like both you and Davinia." Then she looked at us again. "I am very pleased to finally meet all of you, though I am sorry it took such a tragic event to cause our meeting." She turned to Father again. "Nathaniel, your grief must be unbearable. I left Philadelphia as soon as I received your letter with the terrible news." She used her beautiful handkerchief to dab the corners of her eyes which, I noticed for the first time, looked puffy and red.

"I will miss your mother dearly," she said to us. "Though I have not seen her in a very long time—many, many years—we have corresponded frequently since she left Philadelphia. I feel as though I know all of you." Her smile was genuine and pretty.

"Aunt Margaret, I will make sure there is a room ready for you upstairs," I offered.

"No, Etta," Father said. "The boys can sleep upstairs. Margaret can have their room while she is staying with us."

"Of course." Jesse and Sylvanus spoke in unison.

I excused myself and beckoned Prissy to follow me upstairs, where we set about getting a room ready for the boys. It took only a few minutes because the empty room had already been cleaned. Then we decided that as long as Jesse and Sylvanus had to be relocated to the second story, and as long as there was one other empty guest room, we should clean it, too, so they could each have a room. That was a luxury none of us could recall experiencing.

As soon as we had finished, Jesse and Sylvanus took their few personal possessions, mostly clothing, up to the rooms. Prissy and I then cleaned their room downstairs so it would be suitable for Aunt Margaret. While we were busy doing that, Father and Aunt Margaret sat in the parlor talking. I heard Mother's name mentioned several times and wished I could hear what they were saying. I knew Father missed her terribly, and it was comforting to know that he had someone with whom to reminisce about Mother's younger, less careworn days.

When Prissy and I had finished, Father took Aunt Margaret's traveling cases to her room. I was shocked at the volume of things she had brought with her. It seemed she planned to stay for years. I flushed, knowing Father would be displeased if he knew I could hardly wait to see the gowns and frocks Aunt Margaret had no doubt brought to wear during her stay. She was not a Quaker and therefore not required to dress simply. Even the traveling dress she wore was magnificent and I suspected there were many more lovely things packed away.

I turned to Aunt Margaret as soon as Father had deposited all her luggage in her room. "Aunt Margaret, perhaps you would like to take some refreshment and rest from your trip."

"Thank you, Etta. I would like that. Perhaps some tea and a warm cloth to wash the grime from my face?"

I hesitated, wondering if we had any tea, then remembered one of our neighbors had brought some in the days following Mother's death. I nodded and told Aunt Margaret I would return soon.

"Please call me 'Auntie,'" she said.

I left and Prissy followed me into the kitchen.

"Now, where did we put that tea?" I put my hands on my hips and slowly turned in a circle in the kitchen, searching the shelves on the walls for the tea.

Prissy reached for a small wooden box on one of the lower shelves and handed it to me with a smile. I opened it and breathed in the lovely, earthy aroma of the tea leaves.

"Thank you. I'll pour the tea if you can find a clean cloth to soak in hot water. I'll put everything on a tray and take it to Auntie." It felt strange to be referring to our aunt in such a familiar way.

A few minutes later Prissy presented me with a tightly wrapped cloth that was still steaming from its dunking in the hot water over the fire. I arranged the tray and took it to Auntie's room.

Auntie was standing at the window, looking outside, when I knocked on the open bedroom door. She turned gracefully to look at me. "Thank you, Etta. Just leave it anywhere."

Not knowing what to say next, I pointed to the rolled cloth on the tray. "Your hot cloth is right there."

"Thank you, dear."

I excused myself with an exhortation to call for me if she needed anything, then I left the room hurriedly. I found Prissy still in the kitchen, beginning dinner preparations.

"Auntie seems nice. I wonder what life is like in the large Philadelphia homes," I mused aloud. "This must be very different from what she is accustomed to." Prissy nodded. "I would like to see the clothes she has brought with her," I said, half to myself. Prissy smiled at me and nodded. "Don't tell Father," I said in a whisper, and we both giggled.

It was almost time for dinner when Auntie appeared in the doorway to the kitchen. She took in the room with a glance and asked, "Is there something I should do to help? What would your mother be doing right now?"

Father would have been mortified if we gave Auntie a chore to do, and I smiled at the thought of it. "There is no need for you to do anything. We'll bring dinner into the dining room soon."

Prissy and I carried the stew into the dining room while the men and guests assembled. Aunt Margaret sat across from Father at our table and smiled graciously at the people who were seated nearby. It was noisy in the crowded dining room. Prissy and I bustled about, serving drink and bread to everyone. Auntie offered to help, but Father insisted she not do anything but eat. I was pleased to see Father eating, though he ate very little. I suspected he was only taking bites of food to be polite while Aunt Margaret was there.

Because the dining room was crowded, Father invited Isaac to join our family's table for dinner. He accepted and seated himself in the only empty chair, next to Aunt Margaret. I saw him steal glances at her now and then, but he didn't say anything to her other than to exchange pleasantries about her trip.

I was surprised when I saw them in the guest parlor later in the afternoon. I had gone in to clean the floor and found them discussing mutual acquaintances from Philadelphia. Presently Aunt Margaret retired to her own occupations for the afternoon and Isaac returned to his room. I was pleased the two of them had found friends in common.

I was in the kitchen when I heard Aunt Margaret addressing someone. A quick glance told me she was talking to Abel.

"I understand you sell things as a trade?" Auntie asked.

"Yes, madam."

"And what sorts of things do you sell?"

"I sell most things that a wife needs to run a household smoothly," he said.

"Such as?"

"Pieces of crockery, combs, cloth, candlesticks, things of that nature."

"Did you sell anything to my sister?"

"No. I gathered she was not interested in seeing my wares."

"Hmm. Do I understand correctly that you and she were not friendly acquaintances?"

"I think she would have agreed with that, yes."

"And did you dislike her?"

Abel hesitated. "Madam, I formed no opinion of her. I believe, however, she was not fond of me."

Why was Auntie questioning the man? Was she suspicious of him? Did she think he was the one who had pushed Mother down the stairs? We did not even know if Abel was in his room that night. I hoped she didn't believe that of him. Abel seemed to me a nice man, plying his trade without harm to anyone. I could not understand why Mother had disliked him so, and now it seemed Auntie harbored a similar feeling toward him.

That night Auntie joined us in the tavern. She tried helping, though Father told her not to. She was a guest, he said, and did not need to do chores.

"I insist upon making myself useful, Nathaniel," she declared, her hands on her hips.

Father shook his head and smiled. "Very well. You can help serve the customers."

Isaac had joined the guests in the tavern that evening. I watched from behind the counter as he slowly drank one mug of cider while talking to the other men about the latest news from Philadelphia. I saw him sneak several glances toward Auntie, who was standing beside me.

Isaac left before many of the other men. He looked wan and I thought perhaps it would have been better if he had stayed in his room that evening to rest. But he smiled as he left, bowing slightly in Auntie's direction. She acknowledged him by dipping her chin slightly.

Auntie seemed happy to have something to keep her busy, but she was terrible at serving. She got the ale and cider confused, knocked over a jug of ale, and became peevish when someone spilled a mug of cider on her beautiful frock.

I was relieved when she retired early to our parlor.

It was strange to hear Jesse and Sylvanus go upstairs that night, to the rooms they would use until Auntie returned to Philadelphia. As Prissy slid under the covers and I readied myself for bed, I could hear Auntie and Father talking in low voices in the parlor outside our bedroom door.

"I agree with Jesse and Sylvanus, Nathaniel. From what I

have seen, the peddler—I believe Mister Smith is his name, if that is to be believed—"

"You do not believe the man is who he says he is?" Father asked. I could hear a smile in his voice. "You are more like Davinia than I realized. She did not approve of him staying here, either."

"Nor do I. And nor do your sons, from what I have gathered."

"Sylvanus and Jesse do not approve of him?"

"I have gathered as much. I heard them talking about the peddler today."

"What did they say?"

"They are unsure of why he has stayed for so long. The man says he has visited homes in Stites Point to sell his goods, but they know of no one he has visited. They think he might have something to do with the death of the man whose body was found here on the property. And I must confess, there is something about the man which I find untrustworthy."

I peeked out the bedroom door, which was just slightly ajar. I saw Father shake his head before he responded to Auntie Margaret. "The man is a harmless peddler. He is staying here in Stites Point for a particular reason, which is that he has likely found willing purchasers for his wares in Upper Precinct and there is no reason he should leave until he has exhausted their welcome and their wallets. If he has not yet visited our neighbors, I am sure he will before long."

Auntie scoffed in a most unladylike manner. "I hope you are not making a grave mistake in allowing him to stay here," she said in a warning tone.

"Thank you for your concern, Margaret, but I know my guests and Abel Smith is not one to fret over. Now, the smitten Isaac Taylor, on the other hand ..." His voice trailed off.

"Nathaniel!" Auntie's voice was shocked. "Surely you do not believe...Well, I do not know what to say. I am a widow!"

"I am aware of that, Margaret. And Isaac appears to be unwed. He barely took his eyes off you all evening." Father chuckled for the first time since Mother's death. "I daresay you have an ardent admirer."

Auntie spluttered for a long moment and Father continued. "You could do worse than Isaac. He has an intelligent bearing and a thoughtful demeanor."

And I had thought Father neither knew nor cared much about the guests of the inn.

CHAPTER 29

*T*hat night I found it hard to go to sleep. I tossed and turned for what seemed like hours, until I finally rose from the bed in the wee hours of the morning and, trying not to wake my blissfully sleeping sister, crept out of the room. I thought I might make myself useful by dusting the guests' parlor, so I lit a candle and left our family's living quarters.

I closed our parlor door behind me and moved silently into the guest parlor. I was about to set the candle on the small table near the hearth when I sensed, rather than saw, movement. I froze in place. I caught the merest flicker of motion outside the inn. My breath caught in my throat, so afraid was I that Oliver's killer had returned. I blew out the candle flame and stole to the window in the darkness.

But it wasn't a lone figure I saw out there.

Under the light of the moon, several men were slowly making their way into the woods from the clearing in front of the house. They were pushing something very large in front of them. Obviously, I was not looking at Oliver's killer.

I had to know what was happening. I could not make out the features of the individuals out there, but now that I knew it wasn't a murderer, I suspected at least one of the group was my father or one of my brothers. Perhaps even all three, though I doubted it.

I slipped out the front door of the inn, closing it quietly behind me. Once out-of-doors, I could hear the quiet sounds the men made as they walked: their shuffling footfalls on the pine needles, their labored breath as they exhaled, a creaking sound that came from whatever they were pushing.

It would not do to allow any of them to see me, so I waited until they were almost under the cover of the trees to follow them. I stayed a safe distance behind them but kept them in view until they stopped and stood together, whispering.

I stepped behind a large tree. They were unlikely to see me because of the darkness, but I did not want to take a chance. I strained my ears to hear what they were saying.

Alas, as hard as I tried, I could not make out any words. What I could determine, however, was the presence of Father, Sylvanus, and Elijah among the group. Though their voices were low, I recognized them immediately. Knowing the three men were present, I judged it unlikely Jesse was there. It was even unlikely that Jesse knew of whatever was transpiring. I wondered if this nighttime excursion had something to do with the Committee of Safety.

I watched as the men took dead branches from the ground and placed them over and around the object they had been pushing. I was intrigued, but dared not leave my hiding spot.

Rather suddenly, the men completed their task and made their way back toward the clearing in front of the inn. They walked single file, without speaking and without looking around. I could tell they did not suspect I was hidden very close to where they walked.

Once they were out of my sight, I was seized with a malevolent fear of being in the woods in the middle of the night and alone. Memories of Oliver's face, of Mother's body lying on the floor of the front hall, flooded my mind. The sounds of breaking twigs and the rustling of dry leaves chilled me as no north wind could have done. So as much as I wanted to inspect the thing the men had hidden under branches, I slid out from behind the tree and sped as quickly as I dared in the same direction the men had gone. I stopped at the edge of the woods, noting that most of them were already departing on foot from our house. Only two people remained: Father and Sylvanus. I hung back, listening for any conversation between them, but I heard nothing. They went into the house and closed the front door; I heard the click of the lock echo through the stillness. I was alone.

The same fear gripped me again and I was rooted to the spot for a moment. I could feel beads of perspiration sliding down the back of my nightdress. My breath came faster—I had to get out of the woods as quickly as possible. It was that fear which finally spurred me the rest of the way home. Because the front door was locked, I had no choice but to make my way around the inn to the kitchen door, where I knew I could get inside. There was a key hidden in the storehouse and I only needed to retrieve it and let myself in.

I stole around the tree line to the back of the inn, then ran across the yard in the dim light from the moon. I hoped and prayed no one was about, watching me, but by that time I was not only afraid, but cold, too. I had to get inside and I had to do it quickly.

I reached the storehouse, opened the door, floundered for the key which we kept under an upturned jar, and hurried to the kitchen door. I slipped the key inside the lock, turned it, and gasped as I stepped inside.

A candle flame danced near the floor, where a figure was bent over rummaging through the contents of a shelf. At my gasp, the figure whirled around.

Jesse.

I let out a shaky breath of relief. "What are you doing in here?" I asked in a whisper.

"I might ask the same of you."

"I couldn't sleep, so I went outside for a walk."

"In the darkness? Alone? Come now, Etta, I know you better than that. Especially with all that's happened to Mother and to Oliver, the last place you would be is outside by yourself. Tell me the truth."

Suddenly I did not know what to say. Should I tell Jesse about the group of men in the woods? Should I let him think I really had gone outside for a walk so I could fall asleep? I decided on the latter, foolish though it sounded.

"I am telling the truth, Jesse. I mistakenly locked myself out when I left through the front door, so I had to get the kitchen door key to get back inside."

"You were not following Father and Sylvanus?"

He knows, I thought.

I could not bring myself to admit I knew. "Father and Sylvanus were out there?"

"Yes, though I know not why."

He may know they were out there, but he is ignorant as to the reason. Something was preventing me from telling Jesse what I had seen. Did I feel embarrassment for him at being left out of Father's nighttime activity? Perhaps. Did I have a sudden sense that it might be better if Jesse didn't know what was out there? Perhaps. Instead of answering his query, I asked one of my own.

"You never answered my question. I asked what you are doing in the kitchen," I said in a hiss.

"Neither did you answer my question. No matter, I already know the answer."

"What are you looking for?"

"Something to eat."

"You are lying, Jesse."

"If you can be outside for a walk, I can be in the kitchen looking for something to eat."

"Very well. I will fix you something," I offered.

He stood up with a snort. "Do not bother yourself. I will get myself a piece of bread, then I'm going back to bed." He stalked to the box where we left bread overnight, grabbed a hunk of it, and took the candle with him as he left the room, leaving me in complete darkness.

I was exasperated with him for lying to me, but I had lied to him, too. I could not in fairness be angry. Besides that, I knew the truth of what he had been doing.

He had been looking for the pistol which was hidden in my bedroom.

Once I heard him ascend to the second floor, I returned to my bed. Though I feared the events of the past hour would keep me up the rest of the night, I fell into a deep, dreamless slumber, very likely because I had been walking about outdoors in the cold. There would be plenty of time to fret about the thing in the woods tomorrow.

The next day brought rain and wind such like I had never seen. Father was feeling unwell, no doubt as a result of being out-of-doors in the middle of the night, so he had returned to his bed. Jesse and Sylvanus rode to Romney Marsh at first light to fetch something the blacksmith had repaired, so it was left to me to let the animals out of the barn and into their pens. Prissy cleaned the kitchen while I went to the barn. I did not relish the thought of being outside by myself, but I had to admit it was less frightening to be alone outside during the daytime, and this would be my opportunity to see what was hidden in the woods.

Despite me telling myself I was safe in the daylight, I ran to the barn as if being hunted. I stood inside the barn door, my chest heaving with exertion, until I calmed down. I let the animals out quickly, all the while looking around me for any sign of another person. I saw no one.

I closed the barn door and took a deep breath, then raced through the woods until I came to the place where the men had left the large object the night before. It stood under the trees, a hulking thing covered with branches. I checked again to be sure I was alone, then I moved quietly and quickly toward the object. Peering under the thick layer of branches, I could see that whatever it was, it was covered with a sturdy cloth.

I circled it, trying to figure out how best to uncover it so I could see what it was. It was on wheels, that much I could see despite the cloth covering and the branches. The dirt where the wheels sat had turned to mud in the downpour, and the thing was sinking slightly into the soft earth.

If I knelt on the ground, I thought, I might be able to discern what it was by looking underneath. That way I would not have to disturb any of the heavy, wet branches.

Kneeling in the mud, which squished around my ankles, my feet, and my shins, I lifted an edge of the cloth. It was dark underneath, but I could see that it was something sitting on the bed of a wagon. I caught a glimpse of a smooth length of metal. I shuffled farther under the cloth, half-standing and reaching up to feel the cold metal with my hands until I came to bulbous section. Here the metal became sharper along the edges. I did not want to cut my hands, so I resumed my kneeling position and felt my way to the other end of the metal. It was rounded, like a circular tube.

I peered out from under the cloth one time, just to make sure no one had followed me, and then ducked back underneath to continue my blind exploration of the thing. There was a large wooden box which I opened, of course. It contained muslin bags full of something soft. I could hear a few branches falling off as I moved clumsily around the object, but I paid them no mind. I would simply have to replace them when I emerged into the rain again.

It wasn't until I felt a small pile of metal balls that I caught my breath and stopped myself from exclaiming aloud.

It was a cannon. Right here on our property. Those small round things were cannonballs. I knew it as surely if I were seeing it in bright daylight. And those soft bags were filled with gunpowder.

CHAPTER 30

$\mathcal{T}$he shock of knowing such a large and dangerous weapon was so close to our home made me tumble back in surprise. My only thought was to get away from it. I scrambled backward to get out from under the cloth, then I hastily replaced the branches that had fallen while I investigated the cannon. I ran as fast as I could through the muck and mud back to the house. I didn't stop until I was in the kitchen. I slammed the door behind me and stood against it, panting. Prissy turned to me with a startled look.

"All is well, Prissy. Don't worry. I was just running to get out of the rain. It's terrible out there!" I needed to make her believe nothing was amiss.

She hurried to fetch linens to wipe the water from my skin and hair. I removed my wet clothes and hung them in front of the fire. They would be warm and dry in no time. Prissy ran to get a cloak for me, and I wore that through the front hall of the inn, into our parlor, and then into the bedroom. There I dried off completely, thinking all the while about the cannon.

After I had changed into a dry frock, I joined Prissy in the kitchen. At dinnertime, the dining room was sparse. Isaac came down from his room and sat alone at a table near the window, but he was the only guest to join us for the meal. He smiled at Auntie Margaret when she came into the room, and she invited him to join us at the family table, saying there was no need to dirty two tables. As I had expected, Father did not join us. We enjoyed a hearty meal, though the conversation was slow. Everyone seemed to be in a bad humor because of the weather. Jesse mentioned seeing Abel Smith in Romney Marsh. The peddler had been on foot and thoroughly sodden from the rain. Jesse had offered him a ride back to the inn on his horse, but Abel declined, telling Jesse that his horse was dry in the village stable. If the weather remained bad, Abel said, he would stay in Romney Marsh overnight and return to the inn on the morrow.

After the meal Isaac bowed to Auntie Margaret, smiled, and left the room. We all looked at Auntie as if for an explanation, but she merely looked down, taking a sudden rapt interest in her food. She gave no indication that she was aware of our inquisitive glances, but I am sure she knew we were curious.

It was still raining when Prissy and I finished our chores later that afternoon. I went to the parlor to work on my stitching. Though I loved to sew, Mother had discouraged me from pursuing it, saying my stitches were not proper or telling me I was placing my fingers in the wrong positions. I tried to fend off the pangs of guilt I felt when I realized I could sew as often as I liked now that Mother was not there to find more chores for me to do. Auntie was sitting nearby, making her tiny, perfect stitches by the window. She looked at me and smiled.

"Etta, your stitches are so smooth and straight. You must practice endless hours on your stitchery."

I confess I swelled with pride. "Thank you. I would love to be able to help the Women's Relief Society with stitching projects."

"And you should. You would be a welcome addition to their membership, I am sure."

"Mother was a member, but she did not feel Prissy and I were ready for membership."

"It looks to me like you are ready for membership. I am a member of the Women's Relief Society in Philadelphia and there are always projects for young women. I am sure the Committee here has similar projects."

We lapsed into silence. I continued working on my stitches for a short while, but presently the clouds darkened the room so much that it was impossible to stitch, even with lamplight.

"I am going to rest for a while," Auntie said.

I smiled at her and she went to her room. I set my sewing aside and wondered what I could do to occupy myself.

An idea came to me as I stared out the window at the worsening weather. Jesse had said Abel would not return to the inn if the rain continued, and it had not abated. It was, therefore, highly likely that he would spend the night in Romney Marsh.

This was my opportunity to go into his room and, under the pretense of cleaning, look around a bit. I confess that the words of my mother, auntie, and even my brothers had begun to unsettle my own thoughts about Abel.

I left the parlor and looked around to make sure no one was about before going quietly upstairs.

I slipped into Abel's room without a sound, then closed the door behind me and gazed around the sparsely furnished room, taking in at a glance Abel's belongings and the evidence of his untidy nature. I smiled wryly, wondering if he had a wife at home who was often cleaning up after him.

I put my ear near the door to be sure there was no sound in the hallway. Hearing no one, I walked over to the table under the window. It was a small table, and on it were piled several newspapers. I picked up the top sheet with interest. I noted the date, earlier in September, and read through some of the notices quickly. I set that on the bed and picked up the next sheet, and my eyes were immediately drawn to a short paragraph which someone had circled in black charcoal. Peering closer, I was surprised to see that it was the article Abel had read aloud the night in the tavern, the one about the patriot in Boston who had been killed. I quickly glanced through the rest of the newspapers and noticed they all had dates around the time of the one Abel had read aloud.

It was interesting, but I needed to continue my investigation of his room.

A small case stuck out from under the bed, and I knelt to examine it. I opened it gingerly and found several things inside that a peddler would be expected to have in his possession: several combs, hair pins, thimbles, and other small household items. Under those were a short stack of pamphlets. I picked them up and read through them quickly. They were clearly written by someone who opposed the British. I noted the printer's address, in Boston.

I returned them to the bottom of the case and slid it back under the bed, being careful to keep part of it visible, as I had found it. As I bent down to situate the case exactly as it had been when I came into the room, I noticed another case under the bed. This one was thin and longer than the first. I pulled it toward me. It was black and had a hinged cover. I lifted the cover slowly and saw first the rich red velvet inside. Then I gasped as I lifted the lid further and saw two pistols nestled inside the velvet. I did not need to ponder these. They were dueling pistols. There was black residue around the barrel of one of the pistols.

"Miss Rutledge? May I be of assistance?"

I gasped and dropped the lid of the box as if it were on fire, whirling around to see Abel standing in the doorway. He was thoroughly drenched in rainwater. His hair stuck to the sides of his head and water dripped from his beard onto the floor.

I had been so intent upon looking at the pistols that I had not heard him coming into the room. I jumped to my feet, stammering. "Abel, hello. I came in—I came in to clean your room in your absence."

"Those are already clean." He nodded toward the box I had let clatter to the floor. But they were not clean—or at least, not both of them. One was filthy with gunpowder.

"Yes. I dislodged the box from under the bed accidentally and the lid opened as I was replacing it."

He gave me a hard stare. "Thank you for your concern for the cleanliness of my surroundings, Miss Rutledge. I see you have found the pistols I use for protection on my travels."

"I...I..." My mind forsook me and I could think of nothing to say.

"I must ask you to excuse me while I change into dry clothes."

I hurried past him and rushed down the stairs, my heart pounding with embarrassment and shame. He had not believed one word I had said to him, that much was evident from the look on his face. I brushed past Prissy in the kitchen and set to work vigorously slicing salted meat that we would put into the pottage for the evening meal. Prissy was eyeing me suspiciously, but I could not admit to her what I had been caught doing.

I nearly fainted when Abel appeared in the kitchen doorway. I stared at him for several seconds before recovering my power of speech.

"Can I help you?"

"Yes. I would like to have these clothes dried." He held up his sodden trousers and a shirt. I stood still, as if frozen in place, and Prissy hurried to take the clothes from him.

If I were going to confess my devious reasons for being in his room, now was my opportunity to do so. I had only gone in there to assure myself that what the boys and Aunt Margaret and Mother had been saying was untrue, but how could I tell him that? I could not bring myself to explain what I had been doing in there, particularly in light of the knowledge that Abel possessed a weapon that appeared to have been used recently. Was it possible that I had misjudged him and that everyone else had been correct about him? On the other hand, he had told me the pistols were for his protection as he traveled, and that certainly seemed sensible.

I should have been afraid of him, knowing as I did now that he kept pistols in his room. But still I wasn't afraid. I could not bring myself to think of him as an unsavory person. And I could not very well hold his anger at me against him—I deserved his anger for what I had done.

As I watched him hand the clothes to Prissy, he looked at me and opened his mouth as if to speak, but he must have changed his mind because he said nothing and turned around to leave. A moment later I heard his tread on the steps going to the second floor.

Prissy gave me a questioning look before hanging up Abel's clothes. She wanted to know what had held me in a state of paralysis—that much was obvious. But I did not divulge what I had done. It would not be fair to burden Prissy with the information I had when she had no ability to ask questions or discuss it with me.

That evening as the guests partook of supper in the dining room, I noticed Abel watching me with a bemused look. I knew my own face was reddening with mortification, so I avoided returning his gaze. I could not imagine what he must be thinking. I was seized with horror when it occurred to me that he might leave the inn and find a new place to lodge because of my behavior. No doubt he would tell Father what precipitated his decision to leave our inn, and I could not bring myself to think of Father's shame if that happened.

CHAPTER 31

*I*t was my good fortune to have to work hard in the
tavern that evening, to keep from fretting very much
about Abel and my unfortunate mischief in his room. There
were a good many people in there, so I was kept running from
the moment I entered until the moment Father closed the door
behind the last man to leave. Aunt Margaret supervised the
cleaning and scrubbing of the large room, which was wholly
unnecessary as we had been doing it for years and knew exactly
what had to be done, but I suppose it was better than any "help"
she could provide. I enjoyed her presence, despite her inability
to help with chores around the house.

It was gray and misty when I awoke the next morning. The
rain had stopped during the night and in the feeble dawn light I
could make out a low mist hovering just above the ground all
around the inn. I was in the kitchen, stirring the embers into a
roaring fire, when I noticed the bucket, which was normally
filled with water for coffee, was empty.

I grimaced. "I'll get the water," I said aloud with a sigh. It was
generally Sylvanus's job to get the water from the well in the
evening, but he had obviously forgotten. I bundled my cloak

around my shoulders, took up the bucket, and ventured outside. I hurried, not only because it was cold, but because even though the sun was rising, I did not like being outside alone. My escapade of finding the cannon the previous day had supplied my nerves with all the anxiety I could tolerate.

I had almost reached the well when a noise startled me. It was not a loud noise, but it had clearly come from somewhere in the bay. It sounded out of place along the shoreline so early in the day. It was the sound of heavy metal scraping against heavy metal.

I stiffened at the sound. It was not the sound of a fisherman, as fishermen usually went much farther into the bay early in the morning. I knew it was not a hunter because the hunters in the area knew where our land was and took care to stay away from it.

No, this sound was different and it did not belong here. If I had not been so sure the noise came from somewhere in the water, I would have been terrified that Oliver's killer had returned. But I was quite sure the killer would not approach our property from the water because the risk of being seen would have been too great.

I stopped walking and listened. When I heard the sound again, I turned around and stepped toward it as quietly as I could.

It was a flash of red that caught my eye first. It was closer than I had expected. My immediate instinct was to crouch down low to the ground to hide from whatever—or whomever —was there. I set the bucket down and crept closer to the shoreline on a bed of soft pine needles that muffled my footfalls. I was thankful to be wearing my drab brown frock and cloak, because they helped make me invisible among the trees. I stood up a little straighter when I came to a thick knot of trees growing very close to the water's edge. I parted several branches quietly, just enough so I could see what was out there.

What I saw chilled me.

A boat was making its way from the east. There were at least a dozen men on the boat, all dressed in the red-accented uniform of the British army. Four of the men were straining with the labor of rowing the boat while the others kept a keen watch on all sides of them. I realized now that the sound I had heard was the oars scraping in their crutches.

I watched in horror as the boat moved closer to the shoreline where Prissy and I washed the clothing and linens each week. The soldiers were coming toward our property! I was momentarily rooted to the spot where I stood, but I had to do something to stop this. Who knew what nefarious deeds they intended once they alit on shore? They could pillage all of us, or take the animals, or rob the inn of whatever provisions and goods they could find. Why, they could even kill us!

It was that thought, that the soldiers could kill my family as they lay asleep in their beds, which finally spurred me to action. I had to be quiet so I would not alert the British men to my presence in the woods, but I ran as swiftly and as light of foot as I could.

I knew the men would be ashore before I could wake anyone in the house, and yelling for everyone to wake up would surely give me away.

So I did not go to the house. Without pausing to think, I ran straight toward the cannon in the woods. I felt an ironic relief at having the huge weapon so close, and I yanked off its heavy cloth covering as quickly as I could.

The thought that I, Antoinetta Rutledge, might ever fire a cannon was as foreign to me as the thought that I might lead the Continental Army. But here I was, and I had to act quickly. There would be time later for introspection and repentance. I did not intend to kill any soldiers, but merely scare them away. However, I knew there was danger with such a lethal weapon that some of the soldiers might not survive.

That is, if I could work it properly.

I was not completely unfamiliar with the workings of a cannon. I had seen the displays of men with cannons in Romney Marsh on Court Days—soldiers practiced there with weaponry that Quakers would not generally touch. But I thought I had watched enough times to be able to fire the cannon myself.

I had not considered, however, how arduous and grueling the work would be to fire such a huge weapon.

The muzzle of the cannon faced the water, though there were many trees between it and the shore. I could not afford to worry about that now. I would have to hope and pray the cannonball crashed through the trees and over the water far enough to send the soldiers back where they had come from.

I plunged my hand into the wooden box containing the gunpowder and hurriedly opened the bag on top, fumbling with the strings in my clumsy haste. I poured the contents of the bag into the muzzle, as I had seen the soldiers do, then grabbed a rammer from the floor of the wagon on which the cannon sat. I was grateful to have the implements I needed close at hand.

If I recalled correctly, I needed to use the rammer to push all the gunpowder to the front of the muzzle. I did that, trying to do it as quietly as I could. Next I searched the floor of the wagon for a wad, which I would need to make sure the cannonball flew out the front end of the menacing machine. I found a large burlap sack filled with rags, which I knew had been intended for use as wad material. I pushed several rags into the muzzle behind the gunpowder, then used the rammer again to push the wad tightly into the bore.

Finally it was time to pick up one of the cannonballs and load it into the long tube. When I reflected later upon my actions that morning, only then did I recall how heavy the ball was. I could still hear the soldiers approaching and I had to make haste. I remembered from the cannon demonstrations that it took some time for the fuse to shorten enough for the fire to reach the gunpowder in the cannon. Looking around frantically, I spied a sharp piece of iron on the floor of the wagon. I picked it up and sawed through the fuse as quickly as I could to shorten it. I had seen a piece of flint in the box with the rags. I scrabbled for it and grabbed a rag, too, and threw it to the ground. Seizing a small piece of metal on the floor of the wagon, I knelt next to the rag and on its surface, I struck the flint with the piece of metal over and over again until I was able to create a spark. The spark leapt to the rag, lighting it afire. I tumbled back in surprise, but recovered my wits in an instant. Jumping to my feet, I threw the rag onto the fuse and watched in morbid fascination as the fuse lit and burned steadily until it disappeared into the metal of the cannon.

There was nothing to do but wait, and I knew it would be mere moments before the metal ball flew into the air—if I had loaded it properly. I fervently hoped it would fly over the heads of the British soldiers in the water, scaring them away.

Seconds later I saw a flash of light and heard a terrific *BOOM.*

As I heard the horrible noise, I felt an unbearable pain in my upper body. I slumped to the ground. And as I faded into blackness, I heard voices yelling, yelling in the distance ...

I awoke to a faint awareness of bustle and noise. I tried turning my head, but found myself immobilized by pain. I opened my eyes just enough to see Prissy kneeling on the ground next to me, crying. Her face was a mask of anguish and pain. I wondered if I had died.

But when I felt a sudden agonizing flame shoot through my shoulder and down my arm, I knew I was still alive. I opened my eyes again, and this time noticed Aunt Margaret standing behind Prissy, tears streaking down her cheeks. She was twisting a handkerchief in her hands. I let my gaze wander until it came to rest on Thomas. He had taken the cloth that had covered the cannon and was arranging it on the ground in a smooth rectangle. His limp was more pronounced than usual—he must have strained his bad leg rushing to get to me. He grimaced in pain with each step. Out of the corner of my eye I saw a bewildered Isaac Taylor lurching toward us, his physical limits being put to the test. He leaned against a tree to rest, his hand on his heart.

I tried to talk, but no sound would come out. By now my eyes were fully open. Thomas said something to Aunt Margaret and she hurried over to his side and listened while he spoke. He made motions with his hands and she nodded.

A few seconds later I could feel myself being half dragged, half lifted onto the cloth lying on the ground. I must have cried out in pain, because Aunt Margaret's tears fell faster and Prissy's eyes widened in fear. I tried pointing toward the water, but Auntie shushed me.

"We saw them. They're gone, Etta. You scared them off. You may have saved all our lives."

Isaac came forward. "What happened? I got here as soon as I could manage."

"She repelled a British party out in the bay using a cannon." Auntie wiped her eyes and sniffled.

"My word! You did that by yourself?" Isaac asked, turning to me.

I closed my eyes and opened them again in lieu of a nod and Isaac grinned at me. "What an incredible feat!" He picked up one corner of the cloth, down by my feet, and Aunt Margaret picked up the other corner. Thomas gathered up both corners by my head. Prissy came over to him and shyly put her hands out. Thomas helped her place her hands under the cloth to provide more support for my head. I worried that Isaac would not possess the strength necessary to assist the others and would either die from exertion or drop me. But he surprised me by keeping pace with everyone, albeit with a great deal of perspiration and a pained expression on his face.

Our ragged band moved slowly through the woods toward the inn. The jostling and bumping along was fraying my nerves on top of the pain and the shock, and I still did not know how I had been hurt.

Thomas nodded to Prissy to open the front door of the inn as we made our way toward the porch. She ran a little way ahead, opened the door, and stepped back so I could be maneuvered inside. When I had been carefully deposited on my bed, Aunt Margaret hurried to the kitchen for water and a soft cloth. She returned and knelt on the floor next to me while I submitted to her ministrations. Isaac, who had aided the others until I was in my bedroom, said he was feeling infirm and returned to his room upstairs. Thomas also departed, saying he would fetch a doctor.

Several minutes passed, during which Auntie gently cleaned my hands and arms. Prissy's job was to fetch clean warm water whenever Auntie's cloth became too soiled to use.

"Hullo?" came a raised voice from the front hall. Aunt Margaret handed the warm cloth to Prissy, who continued Auntie's work, cleaning my neck and face. Auntie went into the front hall to take care of the person who had called out.

When she returned, she wore a grimace. "It was that peddler. He wanted to know what was going on. He heard the terrible noise outdoors, but he was bathing and could not run out to see what was the matter."

"What did you tell him?" I asked in a hoarse voice.

"I told him you had set off a cannon to repel British soldiers in the bay. He seemed quite shocked and amused by it."

I closed my eyes, not wanting to know what Abel found so amusing. My injuries hadn't so addled me that I had forgotten the embarrassment of being found in his room with a pistol in my hands.

Finally, when the dirt and soot and dried blood had been

cleaned from my visible skin, Prissy went back to her work in the kitchen while Auntie and I remained in my bedroom.

"What happened?" I asked her.

"Thomas explained it very briefly while you were unconscious. He told me that when a cannon is fired, it leaps backward as the ammunition leaves the weapon. He says you were hurt when the cannon leapt back and struck you."

I had forgotten the part of the cannon demonstrations where the soldier loading the weapon leapt back and away from the area of danger.

"I think you were unconscious for quite some time. It took us a long while to find you once we ran to the water's edge and saw the soldiers retreating quickly. Even Thomas managed to come running to the house when he heard the cannon. The poor man's leg is going to be very sore."

"Are you sure the British soldiers are gone?"

Auntie's face broke into a very pretty smile. It was small wonder Isaac found her arresting. "They were still frantically paddling away from shore when we arrived at the spot where you lay on the ground. I knew you must have fired that cannon all by yourself for a very good reason, and all we had to do was look in the direction the muzzle was pointing to see the cause of it." Auntie laughed as she spoke. "Oh, Etta, if you had seen them rowing away! They were crouching down like the cowards they are, looking over their shoulders in terror." Her laughter came out in peals. "I wish you could have seen it!"

I wanted to laugh, but it hurt too much. *I* had turned back a boatload of British soldiers! The injuries and bruises were of no concern to me when compared with the excitement of doing something to help the cause of the patriots.

CHAPTER 32

It was not long before the doctor arrived. Shortly afterward, I heard Father and Sylvanus rushing into the house. The doctor was examining me to see if I had broken any bones and would not allow them to come into my bedroom, but as soon as he left, having pronounced me cut and badly bruised but otherwise unhurt, Father and Sylvanus rushed in to see me for themselves.

"Etta!" Father cried. "Aunt Margaret told us everything while we waited for Doctor Wheeler to leave. Are you hurt?"

"How did you know about the cannon?" Sylvanus asked in bewilderment.

I answered Father first. "I am not hurt badly."

"I should be angry about what you did, daughter. You should not have fired any weapon, and in particular a deadly weapon like that cannon. But I am so grateful that you're safe and relatively unharmed that I cannot find the anger within myself. I could not bear it if one of you children were hurt, or worse." He closed his eyes and shook his head.

"Thank you, Father."

"Tell us how you knew about the cannon," Sylvanus repeated.

I am sure my face reddened as I admitted my slyness. "I was awake the night you transported it into the woods. I followed you. I knew it was there."

Father had had time to compose himself. "Etta," he said in a stern voice, "if anything like that happens again, stay in the house where you are safe." He waggled his finger at me. "I do not want you wandering abroad in the dead of night. It is dangerous to go out-of-doors by yourself, particularly at night, given everything that has happened." He gave me a grave look, but his eyes were warm and I knew I had been forgiven for my deceit.

"My dear girl, you need to rest," Father said. "We will leave you now so you can sleep."

I didn't want to sleep because I knew lameness would settle in my bones as soon as I closed my eyes. I wanted to get up and get back to my chores. But Father put his hands on my shoulders and gently pushed me back onto the bed. "At least rest until dinner at noon. You have had quite a fright this morning."

"Very well. I'll rest for a short while."

Father and Sylvanus left and it was several minutes before there was a knock on the bedroom door.

"Come in," I called weakly.

It was Jesse. He came into the room and stared at me in confusion and bafflement.

"Aunt Margaret told me what happened," he said.

"I know. Father and Sylvanus have already been in to see me. I wondered where you were."

"Thanks be to God, Aunt Margaret told me you were all right and I knew Father and Sylvanus were in seeing you, so I went to see the cannon. I knew nothing of a cannon hidden on the property. I was shocked to learn about it."

"I'm sorry I didn't tell you, Jesse."

"Why didn't you?"

Had I made a deliberate decision not to tell him because I knew his sympathies lay with the men who had been in the boat out in the bay? I confess I did not have an answer to his question.

"I don't know."

"Well, no matter. I know about it now, though I daresay it will be moved 'ere long. It seems the entire neighborhood of Stites Point knows about it now."

"How is that?"

"When Thomas found Doctor Wheeler in Romney Marsh, he said he had made several stops to find him. He told others what happened at each place he stopped, and of course some of them had heard the report of the cannon." Jesse grinned. "You manned a cannon by yourself! How did you know what to do? How did you manage it?"

I smiled. "I have seen the soldiers practicing in Romney Marsh. I must have learnt more than I realized. And as to how I managed it, I did not even think about it. Everything happened quickly. There was no time for me to think if I was going to keep that party of British soldiers away from our property." I paused. "Are you angry that I shot a cannon at the army you admire?"

Jesse gave me an affectionate look. "Of course not, Etta. I care about you far more than I care about any anonymous soldiers who were probably intent on foraging for supplies among our livestock and provisions." He put his hand on mine where it lay on the bed. "I am glad you were not hurt worse. I cannot wait to tell everyone I know that my sister is a war heroine!"

I let out a croaking laugh and Jesse left the room.

When I roused myself an hour later to join the other guests in the dining room, I heard urgent whisperings in our family parlor before I opened the bedroom door. I recognized my brothers' voices immediately.

They must have thought I was sound asleep, because though they were whispering, I could easily hear what they were saying.

"She might have been killed. How could you and Father allow the Committee to hide a cannon on the property? You two, who are such good Quakers and won't handle weapons of war?" This was Jesse's voice.

Sylvanus responded, "It was not a decision for Father and me. The decision had been made by the Committee of Safety and you are well aware that we have offered our property for storage of munitions because we do not handle weapons."

"If I were welcome as a member of the Committee, I would have known that myself."

"If you weren't known as a British sympathizer, you would be welcome as a member of the Committee."

"Well, obviously I did not alert anyone that there are weapons stored on the property. British soldiers would not have risked approaching if they had known."

"Are you so sure about that? Maybe they were coming to disable the cannon."

"I'm telling you, I didn't know about it. How could I have told anyone? The cannon wasn't on the list of munitions hidden in the county," Jesse seethed.

"And how do you know what was on the list?"

I heard the triumph in Sylvanus's voice, and Jesse undoubtedly heard it, too. "I saw the list. Yes, of course I saw it. I admit that. But I did not share the contents of that list with anyone."

"We are not going to settle this now. I am going to get dinner."

"Wait, Sylvanus. I'm sure you are aware that those British soldiers were probably quite harmless. They were likely looking for food and had no intention of causing any violence."

"That may be true, yes, but we do not know that and thankfully, because of Etta we will never have to know. Do you even care about her?"

"Of course I care. I do not want anyone to think I had anything to do with that party approaching our property."

I paused with my hand on the doorknob. I did not want my brothers to know I had heard them. I felt oddly relieved that Sylvanus had said something aloud about Jesse's sympathy for the British. I had often wondered if Sylvanus was fully aware of Jesse's beliefs and now I had my answer. I wondered, for a terrible few seconds, if Jesse was telling the truth about his ignorance of the cannon in the woods. Had he known? It was possible, but I recalled his face when he asked me about it. He had seemed genuinely shocked.

I fancied that I knew Jesse better than anyone else, but was that really true? Did I know him as well as I thought I did?

I waited for several minutes after I heard my brothers retreat to the dining room, then I followed. I wanted everyone to think I had been sleeping. The guests were already eating dinner when I sat down at the table with a small amount of food. Several of them came to our table to ask if I was all right and to thank me for my actions and quick thinking. I was glad when everyone left me alone.

"Are you not going to eat more than that? You need to keep up your strength." Auntie looked at me with concern because I was picking at my food. I hadn't supposed Auntie to be a good nurse, but she had proven me wrong this day.

"I am not terribly hungry," I replied.

"I know you are feeling anxious about becoming lame, but you need to rest after your fright and exertion, Antoinetta. I am going to insist that you rest this afternoon. Your sister and I will do your chores for you." She looked at Prissy, who nodded earnestly.

"I don't think—"

"I am aware, my dear. But since your mother is not here to

tell you what you must do, I am taking it upon myself to do it. I want you to rest for the remainder of the day and tonight. Tomorrow morning you may resume your normal chores and activities, if you are feeling able."

I had a strong feeling that Mother would not have asked me to rest all day and evening if she had been there to witness the events of the day thus far, but I felt a strange and not unwelcome warmth at being cared for by Auntie Margaret. "Very well, Auntie," I said. "I'll do as you say."

She nodded once as if to satisfy herself that I had listened and obeyed, then returned to her meal.

I rested all afternoon and by evening I was quite bored. At bedtime I tried to sleep, but I was not tired. Unwelcome thoughts tumbled through my head, keeping me awake: how much Jesse knew about the munitions hidden around the county, whether he would join the British army, what Father would do if that came to fruition, why Abel had said he had visited homes in Stites Point when he had apparently not, and whether the sheriff was any closer to figuring out who had killed Oliver and my mother. It was close to dawn when I finally fell asleep.

When Prissy stirred in the morning, I awoke, too. As I had feared, I was lame and sore. My aches and pains, combined with my lack of sleep, made me cross and short-tempered. Prissy must have sensed my dark mood, because she hurried to dress and left to begin her chores in the kitchen before I could say anything to her.

I hobbled into the kitchen to help her prepare breakfast. Prissy took on the job of setting the tables in the dining room for our guests while I stirred the porridge and sliced thick pieces of bread to cook over the fire. I was startled when I heard an 'ahem' in the kitchen doorway. I whirled around to see the sheriff standing there. His expression was grave.

"Can I help you, Sheriff?" I asked.

"I have come to speak to your father. Is he here?"

It was the tone of his voice, combined with his sober countenance, which caused my mood to darken further. This visit, so early in the morning, promised bad news. Of that I was sure.

"Yes. I'll fetch him for you." I limped past Prissy on my way to our family's rooms and asked her to stir the porridge and continue slicing the bread. I found Father dressing and told him the sheriff was waiting for him.

I led the sheriff to a seat in the dining room to wait for Father and poured him a mug of steaming coffee. It was only a few moments before Father joined him; I took coffee to Father, too, and gave them each a large bowl of porridge. Father accepted the coffee but pushed the porridge away almost immediately. His face was gaunt and pale; I wondered how much more bad news he could tolerate.

The dining room was empty save for Father and the sheriff. I stood inside the door to the kitchen, out of sight of the two men, but able to hear their conversation. Prissy shot me a warning look, which I ignored. I had an overwhelming need to find out what the sheriff was saying and did not have the patience to explain to Prissy why I felt so strongly that he was about to say something important to Father.

"I hope you come with good news this morning, Sheriff." Father said.

"I fear not. Nathaniel, it pains me to be here." The sheriff paused and Father was silent. "I am sure the local murmurings about your younger son being a British sympathizer have not escaped your notice."

Father did not answer right away, but when he did, his voice was pained and tight. "I have heard the rumors, Sheriff."

"Can you confirm those rumors?"

"I think you should discuss the issue with Jesse."

"Do I have your permission to talk to him?"

There was another brief pause before Father answered. "Yes.

But can you tell me why this is important right now? Surely you are busy trying to find out who killed my wife and the unfortunate beggar in our barn. Besides that, does it matter which side Jesse favors in this wretched war? There are other people in Stites Point who may have sympathetic feelings toward the British, too."

"There are certainly such people. But a murder did not occur at the homes of any of the other people who harbor such sympathies."

"Are you suggesting that my son killed that man in our barn?" I could hear the tension rising in Father's voice.

"I am only saying that I would like to speak to Jesse. My investigations have led me to wonder if Oliver shared the munitions list with Jesse before his death. And if so, was he killed so Jesse could take the credit for providing the list to the other supporters of the Crown in the area? Is it even possible that Jesse had the list all along and placed it with Oliver's body to deflect suspicion from himself after Oliver's death?"

A chair scraped the floor. I dared not peek around the corner to see who had stood up, but I had a hunch it was Father.

"Sheriff, you may talk to my son. But I ask that you do not make such allegations without being very sure of yourself and your suspicions. You are all but accusing Jesse of murder. Even if Jesse does feel more strongly for the British side of this terrible war, that does not make him a murderer. I do not believe, and never will believe, that he is capable of committing such a violent and horrible act. Good day."

Heavy footsteps thumped across the dining room floor and several seconds later the front door slammed. I moved as quickly as I could to the table in the kitchen and reached for one of the apples on it, taking up a knife in my hand. Presently the sheriff returned to the kitchen doorway and I looked up at him.

"Yes, Sheriff?"

"I would like to speak to your brother, Jesse. Would you get him for me, please?"

"Yes, sir."

Jesse was not in the house. Sylvanus told me he was already outside, letting the animals out of the barn.

I returned to the front hall where the sheriff was waiting. I explained to him that Jesse would return from the barn soon, in time for breakfast. The sheriff sat in the parlor to wait.

By the time Jesse got back to the inn he had apparently spoken to Father, for he went directly to the parlor before I had a chance to talk to him.

When he and the sheriff emerged, Jesse stalked through the kitchen without saying a word. I looked into the front hall and saw the sheriff leave through the front door. Though I was glad the sheriff had not arrested Jesse, I feared trouble ahead. I heaved a tremulous sigh. "Prissy, I wish I knew what was going to happen."

Jesse did not act like himself in the tavern that night. He did his chores as if in a daze, then left before the rest of us, saying he was going to sleep.

The next morning, he was gone.

CHAPTER 33

$\mathcal{W}$hen Sylvanus reported that Jesse had not let the animals out of the barn, I went upstairs to look for Jesse in his room. His bed appeared to have been unused.

We all wore grim faces at breakfast that morning. Father joined us and I coaxed him to eat a bowl of porridge. Shortly after the meal there was a knock at the front door. I opened it to find the sheriff, grim-faced and stern. Behind him stood a deputy. I gave the men a questioning look as I invited them inside.

"We need to speak to your brother."

I didn't need to ask which brother the sheriff referred to, but I asked anyhow.

"Jesse," came the reply.

And I suddenly knew why no one had been able to find Jesse that morning.

He had left us. Whether to go into hiding or to join the British army, I had no way of knowing.

"Jesse is not here."

"Where is he?"

"No one has seen him this morning."

The sheriff frowned and turned to whisper something to his deputy, who left immediately. He stalked off in the direction of the barn.

He turned back to me. "I hope you are telling me the truth, Miss Rutledge. It will not do for you to lie about your brother's whereabouts."

I squared my shoulders and addressed the sheriff. "I am telling you the truth. When I see Jesse, I will tell him you've come to talk to him."

"If you don't mind, I'll wait here for him to get back." Without waiting for permission, the sheriff walked into the front parlor and sat down on a hard chair.

Sylvanus must have heard the sheriff's voice, for he came into the front hall and stood in the doorway to the parlor. The sheriff repeated his request and Sylvanus shook his head. "I have not seen him this morning. I have also been looking for him."

This did not bode well for Jesse. My stomach clenched and my heart pounded in my chest as though it were trying to escape me. I was afraid for him.

I hurried through our family parlor and knocked on my father's bedroom door. He had returned to his room after breakfast.

"Yes?" he called.

"Father, the sheriff is here. He's looking for Jesse. He is waiting in the parlor."

Father opened his door and stared at me. He was holding a small Bible, with his finger keeping his place. He closed his eyes for a moment and sighed. "Tell the sheriff I'll be out directly."

I relayed the message to the sheriff and went back to the kitchen, where I found Prissy standing at the worktable, her head hanging. She was taking deep breaths. She raised red-rimmed eyes to mine when I said her name softly.

"He'll be back, Pris. He would never leave without a word to either of us. I have faith that he'll return. Did you hear him say anything last night about leaving?" She shook her head.

Auntie came into the kitchen while Father spoke to the sheriff. "What does he want?" she asked in a whisper.

I didn't have a chance to answer her, for Father joined us at that moment. His mouth was set in a thin white line. "The sheriff has come to arrest Jesse for Oliver's murder."

Aunt Margaret gasped and I closed my eyes as Prissy put a hand to her mouth. Father continued. "I have asked the sheriff to wait until tomorrow to arrest Jesse. I would like the opportunity to find him and speak to him first."

"And did the sheriff agree to wait?" Auntie asked.

Father gave a rueful sigh. "He has agreed to wait only if I can find Jesse before he does." His eyes searched ours. "Have you any idea where he might have gone? Perhaps to that friend's home? That friend who is known to sympathize with the British? I forget his name." He raked his fingers through his hair, which looked oily and limp. I wondered if Father had bathed since Mother's funeral. I feared this blow would overwhelm him, coming so soon on the heels of Mother's death.

The friend Father was referring to was Gabriel Tillotson, the one teaching Jesse to play the fiddle. It was possible Jesse had gone there, but I discarded the idea almost as quickly as I had considered it. He would know that Gabriel's home would be one of the first places, other than our property, where people would likely look for him.

No, he had to be somewhere else.

I could no longer ignore the thought that I believe had been in the back of my mind since the morning I found Oliver's body: What if Jesse had actually killed Oliver? What if he could not control his anger upon learning what Oliver had done to Prissy? I was chilled by the realization that Jesse might have had the rage and the strength to kill another human being, but I had to admit to myself that it was not unimaginable. With his talk of leaving the Society of Friends, hadn't Jesse given his tacit support to the use of violence? With his decision to support the British army and his talk of joining them, hadn't he shown his willingness to use force against another human being?

If I had to stay indoors another minute, I thought I would go mad. I had to find Jesse, or at least look for him. I could not wait to let the sheriff find him. I tore off my apron and threw it down on the worktable. "I'm going to look for him," I declared.

"Wait, Etta. I do not want you outside by yourself. It's too dangerous. Where do you think he is? Sylvanus or I will go." Father said.

"I do not know where he is. I don't even know where to begin looking. But I cannot simply stay here and wait for him."

"All right," Father said. "You check the outbuildings on the property. If you see any person who does not belong here, I want you to scream as if your life depends upon it and run back to the house. Do not talk to anyone. I'll check with the closest neighbors to ask if anyone has seen him." He addressed Aunt Margaret. "Margaret, you go to his room upstairs to see if he left any information as to where he might have gone."

Aunt Margaret nodded and left the room. I could hear her feet hurrying up the stairs. Father addressed Prissy next. "Prissy, you stay here. If Jesse returns, do not let him leave again. Communicate to him that I need to talk to him."

Prissy nodded, her lips pressed together tightly.

"Don't worry, my dear. We will do our best to find him."

My heart felt a bit lighter upon hearing Father's words of encouragement. I said a silent prayer that we would find Jesse, safe and unharmed, before anyone else could find him.

I ran to get my cloak from its hook in my bedroom, then dashed out the kitchen door and headlong into the woods toward the barn. I pushed away my fear of being out-of-doors by myself because I had something more important to worry about. I called Jesse's name over and over again, stopping to listen for a reply each time, but there was no response to my calls. Upon reaching the barn, I shoved the door open and burst inside. There was enough daylight to see shapes and forms inside the barn, but though I searched every inch of the large building, there was no sign of Jesse.

I closed the barn door and looked carefully around the back of the building. Again, there was no sign of my brother. I retraced my steps through the woods until I came to the storehouse. There was no place for a person to hide in the storehouse, so a glance inside told me what I needed to know—Jesse was not there. I checked the cidery and again, there was no sign that Jesse had been in there.

I stood in the yard, wondering where he might have gone. I hadn't checked Thomas's cabin yet, so I decided to go there next. I strode off in the direction of the cabin.

I hadn't been on the path very long when I heard someone call my name. I whirled around, fervently hoping it was Jesse. My shoulders slumped when I recognized Abel riding toward me on his horse.

"Are you quite all right?" he called. "I saw you running." He guided his horse toward me.

"I am looking for Jesse. Have you seen him?"

"I have not. May I offer my assistance to look for him?"

I did not want Abel to join me. I feared Jesse would be reluctant to reveal himself to me if I had a companion. "No, thank you. I will look for him. But if you see him on your travels today, will you tell him Father and I are looking for him on an urgent matter?"

"Certainly, Miss Rutledge. Please do not hesitate to ask my help if you change your mind."

I would not change my mind, so I merely nodded my thanks and sped toward Thomas's cabin. I was out of breath by the time I reached the cabin door, so I knocked and bent over to take several deep breaths while I waited for Thomas.

Presently the door opened and Thomas stood before me, a look of bewilderment on his face. "Miss Rutledge! What is the matter?"

"I'm looking for Jesse. Have you seen him?"

Thomas shook his head. "The last time I saw him was last night. I will help you look." He made to reach for a coat, but I stopped him. I did not want to wait for him, since his bad leg would no doubt hinder his speed.

"No, Thomas. You stay here. If he comes here or if you see him nearby, will you tell him that Father and I are looking for him?"

"Yes, Miss. I'll do that."

He closed the door and I fled, hoping Jesse hadn't gotten much further away in the time I had spent talking to Abel and Thomas.

CHAPTER 34

*O*nce on the road to Romney Marsh I stopped, wondering where I should go next. Father was checking with the neighbors, so I would not duplicate his efforts. Was it possible Jesse was hiding in the woods? I thought not, since it had been bitterly cold during the night. It was possible he had slept in his bed, then made it and left the inn well before dawn—there had been nothing to suggest otherwise. All I knew was that his bed had been made in the morning.

I called his name as I walked swiftly down the road. I stopped to listen for a response every few steps, but my efforts were in vain. I heard nothing, sensed no one. After more than an hour of calling out and listening, I turned back toward the inn, thinking he might have gone home in the time I had been looking for him.

As I walked, I recalled my encounter with Abel just a short while ago. He seemed genuine in his offer of help, and I wondered if that meant I had been forgiven for rummaging through his room while I thought he was in Romney Marsh. I hoped that was the case. I liked Abel.

Thinking of Abel reminded me uncomfortably of the

remarks Mother and Aunt Margaret had made about him. Was it possible he had killed Mother in a sudden rage over something she had said to him? Could my goodwill toward him be misplaced? As much as I found him rather pleasant, I had to admit that I knew precious little about him, except that he carried two pistols with him, one of which he had recently used, and that my brothers said he had lied about visiting the people in Stites Point to sell his wares. I shuddered at the thought of hosting a murderer under our roof.

In addition to that, it struck me how soon he had arrived at the inn after Oliver's death—less than forty-eight hours later. Was there any connection between the two men? Could Abel have been the one who killed Oliver? And if so, why had he remained at the inn? Try as I might, I could not think of a reason for him to stay on our property if he had killed a man. Why would he not leave without a trace as quickly as possible?

If he had killed Oliver, what could have been the reason? And if he had, it seemed all the more likely that he possessed the necessary temperament to kill my mother, too, in return for an impolite or inconsidered comment about him or his chosen trade.

But for that matter, Isaac had also appeared at the inn around the time of Oliver's death. If I could suspect Abel of being Oliver's murderer, why should I not also suspect Isaac? Was it possible his illness was a subterfuge, as Mother had suggested on more than one occasion?

I thought it unlikely. I had been close enough to the man to see the sheen of perspiration on his brow, to see how pallid his skin was. The times he had tried to come downstairs, he had appeared to genuinely be struggling with his ebbing physical strength.

No, Isaac had not been lying about being ill. He had been very sick, indeed. But he was stronger by the time Mother died, and she had been rude to him, too. Had she, perhaps, said something regrettable to him when she was upstairs the day she died? Would he have had sufficient strength on that evening to grab her arm and push her down the stairs? It was possible, I supposed.

It seemed no one was spared my suspicions.

I was approaching the inn. I hoped Jesse had come home in my absence, but when I found Prissy, she shook her head sadly before I had a chance to say anything.

"No word from anyone?" My nerves were fraying with every passing minute. Prissy rose and took my hands in hers, squeezing them. I noticed her eyes were still red and tired looking. My heart constricted at the sight of her. It could not be easy for her, wondering where her brother had gone and not in a position to go outside and yell for him like the rest of us could do.

"We're going to keep looking for him, Pris. He cannot have gone too far. At worst, he is less than a day's walk from here. The wagon is in the barn and he did not take the horse, so he must have left on foot. Someone will see him and notify us, I am sure."

I think I was trying to reassure myself, too.

Father returned to the inn, as did Sylvanus, who had been in the fields looking for Jesse. Both reported having no success in locating him. Prissy and I prepared supper with a heavy heart that afternoon. I was nearly frantic with worry.

At supper the inn guests filed into the dining room along with several travelers in need of a meal. Isaac was among the last diners to arrive. When he walked into the dining room, he looked around the room several times. I stood up to greet him.

"Can I get something for you, Isaac?" I asked.

"No, thank you. I was looking for the peddler. Have you seen him?" Isaac spoke in a low voice.

"No, sir. Is something wrong?"

"Do you know, Miss Rutledge, I have just had the most

curious experience. I was sitting in my room, just looking out my window toward the water, and I suddenly realized why Mister Smith is familiar to me."

"That is curious, Isaac. And pray tell, why is he familiar to you?"

"I now remember seeing his name in the newspaper in Boston. Abel Smith, correct?"

I nodded.

"I do not remember the exact nature of the article I read, but I do recall that it was in association with the murder of a young patriot in Boston."

I let out an audible gasp. Isaac took my arm quickly. "Are you all right?"

"Yes, thank you. I was merely surprised by your recollection of Abel. You can recall nothing else about the article mentioning his name?"

Isaac stared over my shoulder for a moment, his brow furrowed in thought, then shook his head with a frown. "I am sorry, but I cannot recall any other details. I only remember the name because of its Biblical connotations. It is a remarkable Christian name to pair with a very common surname."

"So you do not know what his involvement in the case may have been?"

"I do not."

"Do you suppose—" I began, but the question was too horrible to ask. Could Abel Smith have been one of the killers? Was it possible that the residue on his pistol had come from killing a young soldier in Boston?

I needed to give this serious thought before discussing it with anyone else.

Jesse was not home in time for Father to open the tavern that evening, and the mood was somber among our family members. I believe it was out of respect for us that the usual patrons talked in low voices among themselves, but I could hear them speculating as to Jesse's whereabouts.

Aunt Margaret and Father were talking behind the counter, and I joined them after serving cider to one table of men.

"And did someone talk to Thomas? Has he seen Jesse? Does he know where Jesse might have gone?" Auntie asked.

"His name is Thomas. Etta, you spoke to Thomas, did you not?"

"Yes, Father. He had not seen Jesse. He offered to help look, but because of his leg, I declined his offer. I will admit it was only because I did not want him to slow me down." I could feel my face flushing, but Father nodded.

"I understand. I am sure Thomas understands, too. It was important to have people here in case Jesse had returned to the farm or the inn."

A moment later, as if he had heard us talking, Thomas walked into the tavern. He sat down at a table with some of the men from nearby farms and they welcomed him warmly. I took a small mug of rum to him and he thanked me with a smile.

CHAPTER 35

I was bustling around the tables, serving cider and wiping up spills, when Abel came into the tavern. I was a bit surprised to see him, as he had not visited the tavern in some time. He stood in the doorway and looked around the room, and I noticed his gaze stopping and lingering at the table where Thomas sat. Thomas and his companions glanced up to see who had come into the room, then turned back to their conversation. Abel joined another table of men and beckoned me over to him.

"Could you please bring me a mug of cider?"

"Certainly." I poured him a large measure of cider and took it to him. He thanked me with a nod and a smile, then one of the men in the group drew him into a conversation about when he was planning to visit the man's wife. I left the table and stood next to Father, who surveyed the room with a sad countenance.

"I wish we knew where your brother is, Etta. The tavern seems empty without him."

I knew what Father meant. When Jesse was in the tavern, he was always talking to our guests, moving among tables and conversing with every man present. He was well-liked among our patrons and his presence was missed. I returned Father's sad smile. "I'm sure he'll be back. He would not leave without telling us good-bye."

"I hope you're right, Etta."

It seemed everyone had heard the news that Jesse was missing. Every man from Stites Point and beyond was in the tavern, probably hoping to hear something about Jesse. Only Elijah was missing and, I thought with a frown, that was to be expected. Elijah was probably glad Jesse was missing, since he so strongly opposed Jesse's alliance with the British. As the hour grew late, Aunt Margaret went back to the inn to prepare for bed. Alone and in pairs, the men slowly finished their beverages and left the tavern. Prissy and I stayed with Father and Sylvanus to clean up after the last man had left. Thomas had asked for a candle and candleholder to light his way back to his cabin. Though Sylvanus offered to accompany him, Thomas refused, saying he could get back by himself without incident.

Jesse had not returned by morning. I awoke before anyone else and hurried up to his room. I opened the door a small crack, only to find his room unchanged from the day before.

I walked with a heavier step that morning, concentrating on completing each task before beginning a new one. It seemed I could only manage one chore at a time. I missed Jesse dreadfully and, worse, feared for his safety. I hoped that wherever he was, he was warm, dry, and fed.

It was mid-morning when Auntie declared her intention to clean the front hall and the large cupboard where we kept our guest book and certain necessities, such as candles, candleholders, and linens—to keep herself from going mad with worry, she said. She was not used to heavy chores that were common for the rest of us, so such things always took her a long time. I did not mind, though, because it was kind of her to help. I knew Prissy was grateful, too.

One of the duller chores in the front hall was scraping the

tallow from the candleholders that we kept under the desk for the guests' use. I equipped Auntie with the necessary implements to clean the holders and she sat down at the desk to scrape. She had finished four candleholders when she came looking for me in the kitchen.

"Etta, how many candleholders are there?"

"Six."

"I only found five."

"The others must be in the rooms upstairs. Would you like me to check?"

"Yes, dear. Thank you."

I hung my apron on the hook in the kitchen and hurried upstairs. I was unsuccessful in finding the candleholder in any of the unoccupied rooms and Isaac had assured me he did not have a candleholder in his room. I returned to the front hall and told Aunt Margaret I hadn't found it.

"Very well, dear. If you find the other candleholder, bring it to me and I shall do my best to make it look like new."

I returned to the kitchen with the uncomfortable memory of finding the missing candlestick when I stumbled upon Oliver's body. I hoped I could find this candlestick in a much more prosaic manner.

I was slicing salt pork for dinner when I remembered Thomas had taken a candle with him the previous evening when he left the tavern to return to his cabin.

"That's where it is," I said aloud. Prissy gave me a confused look. I laughed at her expression. "I just remembered where the missing candlestick is. I believe Thomas took it with him last night. I'll run over to his cabin and fetch it. If Auntie is willing to clean the tallow from the pewter, I intend to let her do just that."

Prissy grinned and waved me out the back door.

I made haste getting to Thomas's cabin, looking over my shoulder all the while. I saw no one. I knocked on the front door and waited for him to answer, but there was no response. I thought he might be in the small storehouse behind the cabin, so I looked there next. I smiled when I saw the door to the storehouse open and heard shuffling inside. I approached the doorway and was about to announce myself when I heard Thomas utter an oath. Not wanting to embarrass him by interrupting him in an angry moment, I waited for him to come out.

But presently I grew tired of waiting. I stepped into the doorway to announce myself, appearing just in time to see Thomas hold up a length of rope. It was tied into a small circle at one end and I blinked several times as I recognized the shape as a noose. It was short, and through one end of it was threaded an iron bar. As I watched, he hid the bar and noose under a pile of rags.

I recognized that rope.

It was the rope that had been used to strangle Oliver. It had gone missing from the barn following my discovery of Oliver's body, and now I knew where it had disappeared to.

I must have made an involuntary sound, because Thomas whirled around and saw me. With a ferocious roar, he lurched toward me with a speed I would not have thought possible for a man with such a pronounced limp.

"What are you doing in here?" he yelled.

"I—I only came out to—ow, Thomas! That hurts!" He had taken hold of my arm and held it behind my back as if his hand were a vise.

"You saw, didn't you?" he demanded.

I tried pretending I hadn't seen anything. "No, Thomas. I—"

"Don't lie to me!"

"Thomas, I promise, I only came out here to fetch the candleholder you used last night."

He let out a harsh barking sound. "You just could not leave me alone, could you? You had to come sneaking around, where there is nothing that concerns you."

"I'm sorry, Thomas. I'll leave you alone now." He still gripped my arm tightly and I harbored a hope that he would relent and let me go.

"I would have brought the candlestick back to you myself. Now you have forced my hand." His voice was quieter now, and it was the sudden calmness of his tone that terrified me.

His grip lessened a bit, but not enough to allow me to escape. Pushing me in front of him, he grabbed two lengths of rope and forced me toward the back door of the cabin. Though I wasn't sure anyone would be able to hear me, I tried shouting for help when we were halfway between the storehouse and the cabin. But he hit me with the back of his hand so hard I tasted blood in my mouth and one of my teeth appeared to be loose. My jaw felt as if it were broken.

He pushed me through the back porch and into the kitchen, then worked quickly to tie my chest and arms to a chair. One thing was paramount in my mind: Thomas was a killer. I needed to get out of his cabin. I knew I could probably run faster than he could, but that knowledge would do me little good if I could not escape him.

Thomas was pacing back and forth across the kitchen of the small cabin, his bad leg making him list to one side as he walked. It was a square room, with a hearth at the eastern end and a doorway to the bedroom opposite. The front door was along the south-facing wall. The chair where I sat trapped was positioned against the wall opposite the front door, and a wooden table separated me from the door. I watched him in silence as he paced, wondering what he was thinking about and what he planned to do to me. I could not allow myself to think on that subject for very long, lest I be paralyzed with fear. I needed to remain calm so I could try to think of a way to escape him.

And on one of his passes in front of me, I knew with sudden clarity what I needed to do—in fact, I no other option. I bided my time as I waited for him to come close to my chair again in his relentless pacing. When he came within a foot of my chair, I lashed out and kicked his bad leg as hard as I could.

He fell to the ground, howling in pain. I tried standing up, but with my chest and arms bound to the chair, that was a clumsy endeavor. Half pulling the chair along with me, I slid forward toward the center of the room.

But I had misjudged Thomas's strength. He reached out and managed to grab my foot. I fell, hitting my head on the corner of the table and landing on my side.

I saw stars and felt myself falling into blackness ...

CHAPTER 36

I don't know how long I lay on the floor, but when I awoke I could not recall where I was. I blinked several times, trying to get my brain to work, but it wasn't until I caught a glimpse of Thomas sitting at the table nearby that I remembered I was captive in his cabin and that I had fallen. My head hurt and my ears were ringing, but at least I was alive. Luckily, I had made no sound, so Thomas apparently hadn't realized I was awake. Very carefully, I tried moving my feet and it was then I realized they, too, had been bound to the chair.

Stealing another glance at Thomas, I noticed that his head was lolling to one side. I craned my neck to see if I could learn what was causing the unnatural position and glimpsed a mug of something on the table in front of him. I inhaled as quietly as I could, taking in the scent of the room. I recognized the unmistakable odor of rum.

Thomas had taken to drink while I was unconscious. I allowed myself to breathe more easily for a moment before focusing again on my predicament. I had to find a way to get my hands and feet unbound before Thomas became more alert and realized what I was doing. I had never seen Thomas drink to excess, so I did not know what to expect. Having seen drunken men in the tavern—indeed, even Oliver had taken too much drink the first time I saw him—I knew they could be angry, happy, sad, or an odd mixture of the three. I did not wish to find out how Thomas behaved out of drunkenness.

Through the ringing in my ears, I became aware of a faint knocking. I looked toward the door, helpless to answer it and too afraid to call out lest I waken Thomas. He stirred in his seat and let out a loud snort. I froze, paralyzed with fear, until I realized he was sleeping. Even so, I did not dare call out to the person at the door. Tears sprang to my eyes. Someone was out there, but I could not tell the person I was a prisoner inside. I had never felt so helpless in my life.

As I lay trying to think of a way to alert the person outside to my presence without waking Thomas, I caught a glimpse of movement at the window.

Looking over, I almost let out a sob of relief when I saw it was Prissy.

She peered in the window and her eyes widened when she caught sight of me on the floor. I watched as she covered her mouth in horror. I tried to signal to her with my eyes, but I blinked in pain and when I opened my eyes again, she was gone.

Had I imagined her?

I was desperate to get free and away from Thomas's cabin. Making as little sound as possible, I moved toward the door, inch by painful inch. I was on my side, so I could only edge forward by moving my shoulders slightly upward and dragging my knees, feet, and the chair after them. I was trying to keep the chair from scraping against the floor and making too much noise, so my progress was exceedingly slow. Splinters from the wooden floorboards lodged in my shoulder and hip and along my entire side, and my head pounded more and more with every slight movement. I feared I would die before reaching the door.

Every few moments I had to cease moving and rest my head. Thomas was beginning to stir, and each time he moved I had to swallow a small shriek of fear.

For a small cabin, the distance between my body and the door seemed endless.

Finally, the door was a mere two feet away. Thomas's body was still leaning to one side. A small cupboard sat next to the door, and I was trying to avoid touching it—I did not want to risk making any more noise. Unfortunately, because of my ungainly movements, a decorative knob on top of the chair hit the cupboard and a small cup fell to the floor with a clatter.

My captor suddenly shook himself awake, sitting upright as best he could with a body full of rum. I immediately lay my head down on the floor and closed my eyes, pretending to be unconscious. I had little hope he would believe my ruse.

"What are you doing?" he cried, his voice thick. I made no movement, but tensed my body in anticipation of anything Thomas might do.

His barrage of vicious kicks came only a few seconds later. He kicked my side, my legs, and my arms while I begged for him to stop. The hot tears coursing down my face stung my eyes as I screamed in agony.

"Why did you have to come here?" he shouted. He steadied himself by placing his hand on the cupboard as he continued his assault on me.

When the door flew open a moment later, I believe Thomas and I were equally shocked. To my immense relief, Father and Sylvanus rushed into the room, out of breath and eyes blazing with anger and hatred. Prissy followed on their heels.

It took a moment for me to realize Sylvanus was carrying the pistol I had hidden in my bedroom. Prissy must have shown him and Father where it was hidden! Waves of relief cascaded over me and I wept openly as Prissy ran over to me and untied my hands first, then my feet. She knelt on the floor beside me, holding me in her arms, rocking me back and forth as if I were a child.

In the meantime, Father had made quick work of grabbing Thomas's arms while Sylvanus trained the pistol on him. It was not until later that I thought of the incongruity of witnessing a Quaker man pointing a lethal weapon at another man, but at that moment I could only feel a blessed solace at having been rescued.

Father glanced around and his eyes lit on the rope Prissy had unbound from my hands and feet. "Prissy, give me those ropes," he ordered. She obeyed immediately and he quickly bound Thomas's arms. Sylvanus's eyes never left Thomas and the pistol, trained on Thomas's chest, never wavered.

We made a sorry band as we trudged back to the inn, with Thomas and Father in the lead. Father held Thomas's arm in a strong grip. Sylvanus followed directly behind them, his weapon held against Thomas's back. Prissy's arms were around my shoulders every step, helping me as I gingerly made my way across the cold ground.

Auntie Margaret met us at the kitchen door. She flung it open and gasped, calling for someone inside the house. Seconds later she was helping Prissy by supporting me on the other side while Elijah ran out the back door of the house to join Father in escorting Thomas into the guest parlor. The moment Thomas was seated in a straight-backed chair, Father ran to the store-house for more rope. He returned quickly and he and Elijah tied Thomas's arms and legs to the chair, binding him so tightly there was no chance of him escaping. Sylvanus never let his eyes falter from Thomas, never lowered the pistol.

After Father and Elijah had made sure Thomas was bound tightly to the chair, Elijah took up a post on one side of Thomas. Father gently took Sylvanus's arm. "My son, let go of the pistol. I need you to go fetch the sheriff and Doctor Wheeler right now." Sylvanus blinked and shifted his eyes toward Father without relaxing his grip on the weapon. "Sylvanus, you can go now. Thomas is not going anywhere."

Very slowly, Sylvanus loosened his fingers from around the trigger of the pistol. "Keep the pistol trained on this maggot," he growled.

"I will. You go."

Father took Sylvanus's place as Sylvanus turned and fled from the room. Only a minute later, I heard the horse's hooves pounding the ground outside the house as Sylvanus raced away in search of the sheriff and the doctor.

Aunt Margaret had been standing in the parlor doorway with Prissy and me, and now she turned to us. "Etta, how badly are you hurt? We need to get you into bed. Prissy, will you help me?"

This time I did not protest as my sister and my aunt led me to my room and helped me lie back against the pillow. Prissy pulled a chair next to the bed and held my hand while Auntie bustled around, getting cloths and warm water to clean the dirt and blood off my face and hair. Prissy fetched clean clothes for me and helped me into them. My muscles and bones were starting to protest now that the worst of the danger was past. I didn't dare look at myself in the glass, because I was sure my face was black and blue and swollen. I shuddered at how I must look, though my appearance was of least concern to me at that moment.

Aunt Margaret's gentle ministrations, combined with Prissy's warm and unwavering hold on my hand, eventually helped me to relax. Even through the pain, I was grateful to close my eyes and sink into the soft pillow, surrounded by familiar things and loved ones who meant me no harm. But try as I might, I could not stop thinking about the violence I had endured in Thomas's cabin. Images flashed through my mind unbidden and each time I flinched as a frisson of fear coursed through me. Auntie smoothed my hair back from my forehead and murmured pleasant things while Prissy rubbed the skin on the back of my hand softly with her finger.

I had almost begun to doze when I sat up with a start, having realized something. Auntie was gathering the wet cloths and preparing to leave the room; she turned around in surprise. Prissy tightened her grip on my hand.

"What is it, Etta?" Auntie asked.

"Why was Elijah here?"

"Elijah arrived just as I heard your father shout on his way back from Thomas's cabin with you and the others. I did not get a chance to ask him the reason for his visit."

"Will you ask him now?"

"Yes, dear. Please try to rest and I'll return when I have spoken to Elijah."

I closed my eyes and lay back again. Prissy let go of my hand and accompanied Auntie out of the room. Shortly after they left, the doctor arrived. He examined me thoroughly and pronounced me very lucky, indeed. I likely had several broken ribs as well as a broken tooth, a possible cracked jaw, numerous deep cuts, and dark purple bruises, but I was going to recover. Father came into my room as soon as the doctor left.

"Etta, are you awake?" he whispered.

"Yes."

"How are you feeling? I have spoken to the doctor and he tells me that, in time, you are going to be fine."

I nodded and he sat down on the side of my bed. I realized, not for the first time, how tired and wan he looked. Between Mother's death, the sheriff's suspicions about Jesse, Jesse's disappearance, and finally, my vicious encounter with Thomas, Father must have been engulfed in grief and despair.

But there was a glint of hope in his eyes that hadn't been there earlier.

"I must apologize to you, Etta. I trusted Thomas when I should have been more suspicious about his history. I do not

know if I can forgive myself for providing him with a place to
live and a job."

"Father, how were you to know the truth about him?"

Father shook his head. "Let us talk about something else for
now. I've come to tell you why Elijah was here. You will be very
interested in what he had to say, I am sure."

I tried pushing myself to a seated position against the pillow,
but Father held out his hand. "No, no. You stay where you are.

"First I need to tell you what happened after the sheriff
arrived. Sylvanus met him on the road near here, so it did not
take long for them to get here. In fact, he was coming back to
inquire about Jesse. But when he heard what Thomas had done
to you, he made Thomas his priority. He placed Thomas under
arrest and took him away, still bound at the wrists. The deputy
had come with him, so he was able to help ensure Thomas
would not be able to escape. By this time Thomas will be in a
jail cell in Romney Marsh. I am sure you are relieved to hear it."

"I am, yes."

"Do you have any notion why Thomas would have attacked
you the way he did?"

It was then I realized I was the only one who knew Thomas
had been in possession of the rope noose that had gone missing
from the scene of Oliver's murder. I sat up with a painful start.

"Father, he killed Oliver! You have to tell the sheriff right
away!"

"What? Etta, what are you talking about? What makes you
think Thomas killed Oliver?"

"The reason Thomas attacked me—" I stopped to take a deep
breath, for my emotions were quickly beginning to overwhelm
me. "I went to Thomas's cabin to retrieve the candleholder he
had taken back to the cabin with him when he left the tavern
last night. He was not in the cabin, and I found him in his storehouse. He didn't know I was there. I saw him with a rope that
looked exactly like the one that had been on the ground when I

found Oliver's body and which went missing directly afterward. He was hiding it."

"I need to get this information to the sheriff as quickly as possible." Father turned to go.

"Wait! You didn't tell me why Elijah was here."

I could hear the grin in Father's voice. "He was calling on us to say that he knows where Jesse is, and that Jesse is safe."

I did not know whether to laugh or cry with happiness. Jesse was alive and safe! The relief I felt at knowing my brother was safe was even better than the relief I had felt at being rescued from Thomas's clutches.

"I am so happy! But you did not tell the sheriff?"

"Elijah waited until the sheriff left to tell me about Jesse. The sheriff has enough to do right now, and especially now that you've told me it was Thomas who committed the murder the sheriff has accused Jesse of committing."

"But why is Elijah protecting Jesse's whereabouts? I don't understand."

"I do not know the answer to that. He had to leave quickly to return home, but promised to come back tonight to tell me everything."

"I am going to talk to him tonight, too."

"Etta, I don't think—"

I interrupted Father, which was something I almost never dared to do. "I have worried myself sick over Jesse, and I want to hear everything Elijah has to say."

"Very well, my dear. I will come and get you when he arrives. Right now I must go, I must get word to the sheriff of what you saw in Thomas's storehouse."

Father left. And now that I knew Jesse was safe and that the sheriff would investigate Thomas's storehouse to find the rope I had seen, I fell into a deep sleep. When Auntie came to wake me up later that evening to tell me Elijah was with Father, I felt a surge of energy and happiness despite my bodily pain. She helped me out of bed and into a presentable frock and led me to our family parlor. Elijah and Father were seated there, talking in low voices. Elijah stood when I went in. Elijah did not appear shocked by my appearance, likely because he had been present when I returned from Thomas's cabin.

"Antoinetta, are you sure you are able to sit here without pain?"

I tried to smile, but it looked more like a grimace, I am sure. "I am fine. I want to hear all about Jesse. He is safe?"

Elijah sat back in his chair and nodded. "He is safe. He is well hidden on my father's farm right now. Not even my father knows he is there."

"But why?" I could only splutter my question, so confused was I by this turn of events.

Elijah looked at both Father and I as he spoke. "I knew the sheriff was going to arrest Jesse for the murder of the man in your barn. It was Jesse's luck that the sheriff told a number of other people in Romney Marsh, and I happened to be one of those people."

"I don't understand," I said.

"I have never believed Jesse capable of murder. I may not trust him to keep Continental secrets from the British, but neither do I think he would kill a man for any reason other than being in mortal warfare. I felt strongly that the sheriff was about to accuse the wrong man in an attempt to bring the whole matter to a hasty close.

"The night Jesse disappeared, I was waiting outside the tavern for him. Jesse had spoken to the sheriff that morning, so he knew he was under suspicion. I told him the sheriff intended to arrest him and that I believed him to be innocent. I offered to hide him and he accepted my offer without hesitation." Elijah looked from me to Father and back again. "He wanted to tell you that he was leaving, but I implored him to make haste. I also told him you would both be safer for not knowing his whereabouts."

"When will he come home?" I asked.

"Jesse will be home soon. I have advised him to stay hidden at least until Thomas has been arrested for Oliver's murder."

"Thank you, Elijah," Father said. He held out his hand to the young man, who accepted it with a bow of his head and a smile.

"I must get back home now," Elijah said. "I am sure we will meet again 'ere long."

He bowed slightly to me and left the room. Father and I sat in silence for several moments, then Father said, "I am very impressed by that young man. He has shown a wisdom beyond his years."

I, too, was surprised by the warmth I felt for Elijah at that moment. I hoped it signaled a willingness on his part to be more cordial toward me in the future.

Finally Father spoke again. "Etta, I think you need your rest. You should go back to bed now."

I did not hesitate to do as he told me. I barely stirred when Prissy got into bed beside me later that night.

The next morning I went to breakfast and all the talk was of Thomas and his assault on me. I did not wish to listen to it, so I went to the parlor directly after breakfast. It did not help matters that I was in a great deal of pain.

I was shocked when the sheriff's deputy knocked on the door later in the morning.

CHAPTER 37

I heard Auntie greet him and say my name. A moment later she came into the parlor.

"The sheriff's deputy wants to take you to Romney Marsh. Thomas is asking to speak to you."

I frowned. I did not want to lay eyes on Thomas again as long as I lived.

"I need to discuss this with your father," she said.

Father was in the cidery. He came into the house directly when he heard what the sheriff's deputy wanted. He strode into the parlor where the deputy and I sat in silence. The deputy repeated his request to Father.

"I do not think Antoinetta is strong enough to go to Romney Marsh right now. Besides that, I am sure she never wants to see Thomas again."

"She will not see him entirely alone. Either the sheriff or I will be right outside the room, of course, and Thomas will be tightly bound and incapable of coming near her."

"Why does he want to talk to her?" Father asked.

It was getting tiresome listening to the two men talk about me as if I were not in the room.

"He says he wants to say something about Oliver Doolittle, but he will only say it to Miss Rutledge."

"Why is the sheriff giving in to such an outrageous request?" Father scoffed. "To think that Thomas should be allowed to make demands like that ..."

"The sheriff will be listening, of course, Mister Rutledge. He feels Thomas may admit his role in Oliver's death if he is permitted to speak to Miss Rutledge."

Father was shaking his head when I finally spoke up. "I will go."

"Etta, you should stay here," Father said.

"It is true that I never want to see him again. But if he will not talk to anyone but me, how can I refuse? What if the sheriff's suspicions are correct? Suppose Thomas wants to confess to killing Oliver?"

Indecision was evident in Father's eyes. He was silent for a long moment, then he gave one nod. "Very well. I will allow her to go, but I am going, too."

"That is fine," said the deputy. "But you will not be able to go into the room with her. Thomas has requested that she go in alone."

Father frowned. "I'll speak to the sheriff about that when we get to Romney Marsh. Come, Etta. We can leave now if you feel able."

By the time we reached Romney Marsh on horseback, I was exhausted and my body hurt all over. I was nervous about seeing Thomas, but at the same time, I was eager to put the ordeal behind me. Father and I followed the deputy into the jail, where the sheriff was sitting at a small desk. He rose when he saw us.

"Thank you for coming. I know this is difficult for both of you."

"Where is the scoundrel?" Father asked.

The sheriff pointed to a closed door. "He's in there. I want both of you to know something. Normally I would not consider this highly improper request, but Thomas refuses to talk to me or my deputy. If we can get him to confess to killing Oliver Doolittle, things will be much easier for both of you and for your son Jesse, too. When Thomas asked to speak to you, I had no choice but to put the question to you. He is chained to a chair and will not come near you, that I can promise. If you were his representative at law, we would not listen to what he has to say. But since you are not, we will be listening to his every word."

"And I cannot go in with her?" Father asked.

"No, Nathaniel. He has asked to speak to Antoinetta alone."

Father shook his head, his eyes flashing and his lips pinched. I squeezed Father's hand, took a deep breath, and squared my shoulders. I followed the sheriff into the room where Thomas sat on a plain chair, his shoulders stooped, his eyes sunken, his face sallow.

I sat down in the chair that the sheriff had provided for me, well out of Thomas's reach. He left after telling Thomas he would only allow a few minutes' discussion with me. I looked over my shoulder to make sure the door had, indeed, been left ajar.

I stared at Thomas, forcing myself to remain calm. My fingernails dug into my palms until they were sticky with blood.

"Thank you for coming here, Miss."

I did not reply.

"I want to apologize for hurting you. If I had been in my right mind, I would never have raised a hand to you."

I continued to stare at him. He didn't say anything else. Finally I asked, "Is that what you asked me here to say?"

"Yes. Rather, no."

"Which is it? Yes or no?"

Thomas hung his head. I could no longer stand the silence.

"You killed Oliver, didn't you? You strangled him with the rope I saw."

Thomas looked at me, then his gaze flicked behind me. I was sure he noted the open door. "Yes, Miss, I strangled him."

"Then you stabbed him for good measure."

Thomas's eyes clouded. "I did not stab him, Miss."

I scoffed. I had no time for lies. "Why? Why did you kill him?"

The silence between us grew until I feared Thomas would say no more. I was contemplating leaving the room when Thomas spoke.

"He wouldn't leave me be, Miss. He demanded that I give him money. I had finally found work on your father's farm and was making a bit of coin, and Oliver wanted more than half of it."

"How did you even know Oliver?"

"I knew him in Boston, Miss."

"And he found you in Stites Point? I cannot believe that."

"He and I traveled to Cape May together, Miss. I traveled a bit further up to Stites Point and when he could not find work in Cape May, he followed me to your inn."

"So you were friends?"

"I would not say that, Miss."

I sighed. "What *would* you say, then?"

Thomas swallowed hard. "Oliver and I killed a man in Boston, Miss."

With those words, I felt a shock as sure as if lightning had struck me. With those words, small bits of conversations and observations from over the past several weeks began to move themselves into place in my mind, much as puzzle pieces might.

"What man?" I asked.

"The Boston Patriot, Miss. The one from the newspapers."

"You and Oliver were the Boston Patriot murderers?"

He nodded.

"Why did you kill that young man?"

"Oliver and me, we are supporters of the British in this war, Miss. There's nothing wrong with that—plenty of people are. One night we got into an argument with a couple of young fellows in a Boston public house. One of them threatened to do us harm on account of our support of the British. We had taken too much rum that night, I suppose, and when we all four left the public house, the argument continued. Somehow it just happened. Oliver and I killed him. When we realized what we done, we ran. I nearabout got a bullet in me and I fell off my horse and wounded my leg. We had to get out of Boston fast. We traveled roundabout as far as Cape May. It was only when I got a job with your father and Oliver started demanding money that he threatened to tell everyone that I was the Boston Patriot murderer."

"You know, of course, that my father and the sheriff and his deputy are listening to this."

Thomas nodded. "I know, Miss. I'm going to hang for what I done. I know that. But I wanted to tell you that I never meant to hurt you. Or your mother. And I'm sorry for everything I did."

I was struck dumb. My mother? I heard a choking sound from the other side of the door separating me from the sheriff, his deputy, and my father. My heart twisted for my father.

"*You* killed my mother?"

"I did not intend to, Miss. Please believe me."

I stared at him in stony silence.

"When your mother came to my cabin to get the candlestick, I thought she might'a saw the rope. I only wanted to ask her what she saw."

I said nothing, waiting for him to continue.

"I saw her going up the stairs when I came into the inn. I followed her because I thought I could talk to her alone up there. I didn't see her in the first room where I looked, so I went to the next room. But she had been in the first room, probably behind the door or on the other side of the bed, leaning down. So by the time I saw her, she was standing at the top of the stairs. She startled me. I grabbed her arm and when she tried to shake me off, I slipped on account of my bad leg and fell into her. All I had done was grab her arm.

"She fell down the stairs and I was so scared I left. I didn't know she died until later. You have to believe me. I would not ha' killed her on purpose."

"You are degenerate, Thomas."

He hung his head. "I know, Miss. I ain't good for anything. I'm going to hang, like I said. I know that. But I wanted you to know that I never meant to hurt you or your mother. I am very sorry for all I've done."

I was suddenly wearier than I had ever felt. I could believe this man might be sorry, but he had killed three people and very nearly killed me, too.

"Thank you for telling me the truth—or at least most of it." That was all I could manage to say to him. I stood up and walked out with my head held high to face the shocked men on the other side of the door. Tears streaked down Father's face, and when I saw them I started crying, too. I went to him and he held me in a tight embrace for a very long moment. Then we left for home.

The sheriff arrested Thomas for murder that day.

THAT NIGHT the tavern was full. I do not think I had ever seen so many people in the room at one time. Father had asked me to stay in the inn and not bother with helping in the tavern, but I insisted on being with the rest of my family. Everyone wanted to talk about Thomas and about the murders of Oliver, Mother, and the Boston Patriot.

Abel came into the tavern after most of the men had already

arrived. He smiled broadly when Father offered to pour him a mug of cider.

"Yes, good sir, I will have a cider and I will buy a cider for every man in the room!" He was speaking in a booming voice, which I had not heard before. He seemed a different man. I must have been staring at him in bewilderment, because he threw his head back and laughed. "Are you surprised at me, Miss Rutledge?"

I nodded mutely.

"I am here tonight in the spirit of celebration!" By this time all conversation in the tavern had ceased and every eye was upon Abel. He waved his arm around, encompassing the entire assembly. "A toast!" he cried. "To my brother, Henry!"

A chorus went up from the men in the room and Abel turned to my father, who was already pouring ciders for the men who had come up to the counter.

"You are in a jolly mood tonight, sir," Father said with a smile.

"And why not? The scoundrel who killed my brother will never again enjoy the blessing of liberty!"

"And your brother is Henry?" Father asked.

"Indeed, sir. My brother, Henry, the Boston Patriot. Murdered by the sinister hands of two cowardly maggots who had of late found themselves here on your very farm." He raised his glass in a silent toast to Father.

I couldn't stop the astonished cry that escaped my lips. "Your brother is the Boston Patriot?"

"Yes, indeed he was. God rest his soul."

"But ... how did you find them? How did—" I stopped speaking because I could not give voice to all the muddled questions in my mind.

Abel settled himself on a stool and took a long draught of cider. He wiped his mouth with his sleeve and began.

"My brother, Henry, and I are members of Henley's Regiment in Boston, formed to help fight the damnable Redcoats after the reorganization in Boston earlier this year. Henry and I were having an argument with two men one night in a public house. The argument became heated as we stepped out into the street. Both men jumped upon Henry. By the time I reached for my pistol to shoot at them, Henry was already dead. He had hit his head on the cobbles in the street. I knew one of the men to be Oliver Doolittle, a rascal noted in Boston for his support of the English and their system of taxes and laws.

"I did not know the name of the other man, but he was a person known to be a constant associate of Doolittle. His face was imprinted upon my brain that night—I would have recognized him anywhere on Earth until my dying day. I shot at him but missed, and he fell off his horse. I knew he had sustained a serious injury. I left my regiment temporarily and made it my work to find Henry's killers. I traced the men as far as Cape May, then learned they had gone north. It was only by chance that I heard of Oliver's death while in Romney Marsh. I came up to Stites Point to stay here, knowing his associate could not have gone far. I stayed in the area to search for him.

"It was only last night that I saw the man here in your tavern, and a brief investigation revealed he had been working on your farm, no doubt without your knowledge of his dastardly past. I was watching him, biding my time until I could avenge the death of my brother, when he was arrested for a cowardly assault upon you, Miss Rutledge.

"I regret that I will not be the one to punish Oliver Doolittle's associate, but I take comfort in knowing he will be hanged for his crimes."

Abel took another drink.

"You are not a peddler, then?" I asked.

"No, Miss Rutledge. I am a soldier. I took on the portrayal of a peddler so no one would guess my true intent in being in

Stites Point. That is the reason, as you may have figured out by now, I have not visited anyone you know with my wares."

"I am so happy to hear it," I said. "I fear we were beginning to suspect you of underhanded leanings."

Abel laughed. "I am not an underhanded man. And now that I have assured myself of Oliver's death and the capture of his associate, I will return to Boston to continue my work there."

"It was an honor to serve you, Abel," Father said.

Abel nodded. "As it will be an honor to serve you and all the good people of these colonies when I return to Boston."

Many of the men in the tavern had been listening to Abel's tale, and now they swept him into lively conversations about his time in the Continental Army and in Boston. Father kept the tavern open that night long past when he normally would have locked the door, and there were likely many sleepy men in Stites Point the following day.

And on that following day, early in the morning, Isaac, of whom we had grown quite fond, made the announcement that he, too, was healed sufficiently to continue his travels.

"I am going to accompany the esteemed Abel Smith as far as Philadelphia," he said. "I have already arranged it with him."

"We will be sorry to see you leave, sir," Father told him.

"I have important business in Philadelphia," Isaac said. "I will be taking part in negotiations with the British to end this war on terms agreeable to both sides." He winked. "But, of course, that is not the only important business I have in Philadelphia."

I glanced at Aunt Margaret, whose cheeks had flamed to a charming pink. Father smiled and shook Isaac's hand. "My good man, I know this woman to be good of character and strong of constitution. You will be well suited."

"And besides that, she is enchanting," Isaac said. His eyes crinkled with a grin.

Aunt Margaret waved her hand at him to stop, but I suspect she did not mind his words at all.

CHAPTER 38

$\mathcal{I}$t had been a full day since Thomas confessed to killing not only Oliver and the Boston Patriot, but Mother, too. Father had eaten three meals since then and some of his color had returned. His eyes had lost some of their dullness. He missed Mother terribly, and doubtless would continue to miss her for as long as he lived, but it seemed to me that he had finally felt peace. Seeing the serenity on his face, I believe I began to feel a sense of peace, too. I hoped I could eventually forgive myself for not missing Mother as much as he did.

I was surprised to see Doctor Wheeler come in the front door that afternoon. He couldn't be there to see me, I thought. The physical evidence of my ordeal with Thomas still remained and would remain for quite some time, but the bruises and cuts would eventually heal and fade. There had to be some other reason he was there.

"Good day, Doctor. How may I be of service?"

"Good afternoon, Miss Rutledge. Is your father at home?"

"I believe he is. I'll go look for him."

I invited the doctor to sit in our guest parlor while I went in search of Father. I found him in the barn. He nodded when I told him the doctor was waiting for him. I followed Father back into the house. He greeted Doctor Wheeler and invited him into our family parlor.

"With your father's permission, Miss Rutledge, you may wish to hear what I have to say," the doctor said.

I glanced at Father, who looked from me to the doctor and back to me. He nodded after a short hesitation and I followed the men into our parlor.

When we were seated, the doctor folded his hands on his lap. "Nathaniel, I've come because of a discovery I made at the time I was examining the body of the man your daughter found in the barn. I think it's time I mentioned it to you." At the mention of me, Doctor Wheeler inclined his head in my direction.

Father's brow furrowed. "What did you discover?"

"As you know, Oliver Doolittle's cause of death was strangulation."

"Yes. Thomas, the man I hired to help on the farm, has admitted to strangling him."

"That is what I have heard. But there is something else I learned. I did not discuss my finding with the sheriff because I am not sure there is reason to."

Father's brow was now deeply lined with concern.

The doctor took a deep breath. "My examination of the body revealed several deep stab wounds. There was very little blood from the wounds, leading me to conclude the body was attacked after it was already dead."

I had a sudden flash of memory—of the jagged holes in Oliver's clothing where a knife or other sharp-edged object had been plunged into his body. I shivered.

"What does that mean?" Father asked. Confusion was writ in his eyes.

"It means that there is a strong possibility that someone else *meant* to kill the man in your barn, but was too late and perhaps did not realize the man was already dead."

Realization dawned on Father and me at the same moment, I think.

"And why did you decide not to share this information with the sheriff?" Father asked.

"Because the person who stabbed the stranger in the barn could not be guilty of killing him." The doctor shifted uncomfortably on his chair and lowered his voice. "Nathaniel, I have, of course, heard the rumors about your son. You know the rumors of which I speak: his support of the British, his willingness to renounce the Society of Friends ..." His voice trailed off.

Father did not speak for a long moment and I dared not speak before he did. I wanted to feel outrage at the doctor's implication, but what he had said was not untrue. It may have been shocking to hear, but it was necessary for the doctor to be honest with Father. In truth, it had been kind of him to talk to Father before discussing his discovery with the sheriff.

Finally Father spoke. "Aldous, I appreciate you coming directly to me with this information. However, I cannot ask you to keep it from the sheriff if that is what you would normally do in this type of situation."

"I do not believe I have ever been in a situation like this one," the doctor replied.

"Of course I take your meaning. Thank you. I will speak to Jesse about this." I could see the pain in Father's eyes. For myself, I was having difficulty keeping my heartbeat steady and my hands from trembling. What did this mean for Jesse?

"If you should discover that you know well the person who stabbed the victim post-mortem, I do not think this needs to be addressed by the sheriff." The doctor gave Father a knowing look as he left.

Father looked lost and bewildered. He had finally been able to stop worrying about Jesse, and this must have been a terrible blow to him, as it was to me. I was sick, thinking that Jesse might have stabbed a man. A horrible man, to be sure, but another man nonetheless.

"I cannot believe such a thing of Jesse," I said.

"Nor can I." Father shook his head. "Etta, I'm going back to the cidery. If you see Jesse returning, please come get me."

I nodded and returned to my chores.

It was nearly dark outside when I saw Jesse's familiar gait coming toward the inn. My heart started beating a strange, fast rhythm that I suspected was a combination of happiness and trepidation. As much as I wanted to run to greet him, I knew what I had to do instead. I ran to fetch Father, who was still in the cidery.

"He's home, Father."

Father looked up at me with the same mixture of expressions I could feel on my own features. He nodded. "Thank you, Etta."

When I returned to the front hall, Jesse was ascending the porch steps. This time I did not hesitate to run out to greet him. He laughed when he caught me up in his arms, swinging me around in a circle before setting me on the floor and holding me at arm's length.

"Are you really all right? Elijah told me what Thomas did to you. That beast! I cannot believe he is the one who killed Oliver and Mother!"

"I could not believe it myself. I'm so glad the entire ordeal is over." I hugged him again. "Jesse, we've been so worried about you!" I was breathless.

"I knew the sheriff was coming to arrest me and I didn't kill anyone, Etta. You believed that, did you not?"

I had *wanted* to believe it more than anything. I was trying to think of a kind way to say that when I heard Father's voice.

"Good evening, Jesse." Father had walked up behind us.

Jesse turned to him with a tentative smile. "Hello, Father. It is good to be home. Please forgive me for leaving without telling you or anyone else where I had gone. I did not want to place you in an uncomfortable situation if the sheriff came looking for me. I'm so relieved Oliver's killer has been apprehended. To say nothing of Mother." His face clouded. "To think it was Thomas all along."

"It came as a grim surprise, certainly. But there is one thing he did not admit doing, and I must speak to you about that now."

Jesse's face clouded. "What are you talking about? I have done nothing wrong."

"Come. We'll talk in here." Father beckoned Jesse to follow him into the family parlor. I turned to leave, but Father stopped me. "Etta, please join us. I would like you to be there."

I looked from Father to Jesse, then untied my apron and set it on the desk in the front hall. I followed them into the parlor and sat down. It was a strange assemblage. We three sat in chairs in a large triangle in the room, no one touching or speaking.

Sylvanus walked in, then stopped short when he saw us. "Jesse! It is good to see you, brother. What took you so long to come home? Thomas was arrested yesterday."

"I was helping Elijah with some tasks on his father's farm. It was the least I could do to repay him for his kindness."

Jesse smiled at Sylvanus and Sylvanus looked at Father and me, no doubt noticing our somber faces. "Why are you all looking so dour? Jesse has returned and Thomas will hang for Oliver's murder and for Mother's fall down the stairs. We should feel only relief!"

"Sylvanus, please be seated. We have something to discuss with Jesse and I would like you to be present for it, as Etta is. This is a family matter."

"Shall I fetch Prissy?" Sylvanus asked.

"No. There is no need to involve her, since it was an affront to her that started the entire sequence of events that led to Oliver's death and eventually your mother's death. I do not wish Prissy to suffer any further."

Sylvanus sat down and cocked his head in confusion. "What have we to discuss?"

Father took a deep breath and addressed the three of us. "Oliver's body was stabbed after he was strangled. That means that someone else meant to kill him, but failed only because he was already dead. This is something Doctor Wheeler has confirmed." He leveled a stare in Jesse's direction. "Jesse, you may not have killed Oliver, but you tried to kill him, did you not? In my eyes and in the eyes of God, it is the same thing."

Jesse's mouth dropped. "I? Stabbed Oliver? Of course I did not stab Oliver! Surely Thomas, that scoundrel, did it in a fit of anger. Do you not believe me?"

Father did not answer the question. "Thomas confessed to killing Oliver. What reason could he possibly have to refuse to admit to stabbing him once he was dead? He will hang for the murder. It behooves no one for him to lie about the stabbing."

"But—" Jesse said, then clamped his mouth shut. He leaned forward, his hands held out in a pleading gesture. "Father, please believe me. I did not stab Oliver."

I had been watching the exchange between Father and Jesse with rapt attention. When I turned to look at Sylvanus, the color had drained from his face and his hands trembled.

"Sylvanus! Are you ill?" I leapt out of my chair and in two steps was across the room, feeling his forehead with the back of my hand.

All attention diverted away from Jesse, Sylvanus shook his head and swallowed hard.

"Sylvanus, say something if you can," Father directed. "Jesse, Etta, one of you go fetch the doct—"

I already had my hand on the door to the front hall when Sylvanus made a choking sound. I whirled around.

"I did it."

CHAPTER 39

At first I thought I had misheard Sylvanus, but the shocked looks Father and Jesse had turned on him confirmed they had heard the same thing.

"You did what?" Father asked. I loosed my hold on the doorknob.

"I stabbed Oliver." Sylvanus's voice was stronger now and a bit of the color began to return to his cheeks. "I'm so relieved to say it aloud."

I could only stare at him, incredulous. Jesse spoke. "I would never have thought it."

"Nor I," Father said. "Sylvanus, what prompted you to do something so ferocious, so unlike yourself?"

"It was Prissy," Sylvanus said. He stared at the floor, his elbows resting on his knees. I had to strain my ears to hear him. "When I heard what he had done to Prissy, I confronted him immediately. I almost killed him right then, Father."

"What are you talking about? He was in the tavern. He fled and you and Elijah chased him. You did not nearly kill him."

It was then we all realized Father still did not know what Oliver had attempted to do to Prissy in the barn. In quiet tones,

I explained to Father what had happened. He closed his eyes, so full of anguish. "My poor, darling Prissy," he whispered.

After a minute of silence, Sylvanus kept talking. "Oliver begged for his life and promised he had not set himself upon Prissy. I thought it would be wise to step away from the situation, so I did not harm him. But the more I thought about it, the more I thought about Prissy being trapped by him. I was filled with a rage that frightened me. I could not help myself. I was consumed with thoughts of killing him for what he had done." Droplets fell from his eyes onto the floor between his feet.

"I returned to the barn late that night. I thought he was asleep when I stabbed him." Finally he looked up at Father. "I am sorry, Father. I know how disappointed you must be. I thought I had killed him, and you can hardly imagine my relief at hearing that he died by strangulation. But these past weeks, I have been feeling more and more guilty for the thoughts which prompted me to try to kill him. I know such thoughts rail against God and you and the Society of Friends and I am relieved to finally confess what I did."

It was a long time before Father spoke. "Sylvanus, now that I know what happened, I believe I can understand where those thoughts came from. You were trying to protect your sister's honor. But vengeance belongs to God, not to man."

Sylvanus nodded. Jesse and I exchanged worried looks.

"We will not discuss this ever again," Father said. He looked into the eyes of my brothers and me as he spoke. "I believe God has punished you with tortured thoughts and fears since Oliver's death, so I see no need to tell the sheriff about my discussion with Doctor Wheeler."

"Thank you, Father."

"But I cannot condone what you have done, and I must insist that you leave the Society of Friends. You will be welcome in my home and in our family, but not in the church."

Sylvanus stared at his hands. "I understand, Father. I had assumed as much."

Father stood and motioned toward the door. "It is time for supper."

Aunt Margaret was already in the dining room. Father and the boys joined her and I returned to the kitchen to help Prissy serve supper. She gave me a quizzical look when she saw me.

"Everything is going to be all right, Prissy." I told her what Sylvanus had done. Tears slid down her face as she listened, and I lay my hand on her arm. "He will always be our brother, Pris. He simply will not attend services with us."

She wiped her nose on her apron and attempted a smile, but it crumpled into more tears.

"Prissy, dry your tears. It will not do to let Sylvanus see you crying. It will be too much for him to bear."

Sylvanus had always been Prissy's favorite brother, her special protector, and I could only imagine how she was feeling upon learning that he had been angry enough to kill a man over what that man had done to Prissy. She was very likely feeling honored and guilty in equal measures.

She did as I asked, wiping her eyes on her sleeve and giving me a hesitant smile.

"That's a good girl, Prissy. Let's serve supper."

When we sat down at the table with the rest of the family, Father was thanking Aunt Margaret for something. Jesse smiled at me. "There is good news. Aunt Margaret is going to employ Sylvanus at her home in Philadelphia. He is going to be her groom for a time, until he can find other employment."

Sylvanus gave Auntie a tenuous smile and she patted his hand. "I received word last week that my groom is leaving Philadelphia. I will need a new groom as soon as I return to my house. Sylvanus will do an excellent job, I am sure."

Prissy maintained her smile throughout the meal, though later I found her weeping silently in the kitchen.

"Do not worry, Prissy. He will be back to visit and we can perhaps visit him sometime. With some of the roads that have been built in the past several years, travel to and from Philadelphia is not as arduous as it used to be." She straightened up, wiped her eyes and nose, and nodded.

"And we can write to Sylvanus, too. And I will make sure you have companionship whenever you wish. But I'm not going to do your chores!"

Prissy smiled through her tears and I knew she understood why Sylvanus had to leave.

I was hanging up my apron beside the back door when Jesse came into the kitchen. Prissy had gone to help Father in the cidery before he opened the tavern.

"I have decided not to join the British army." His voice was quiet.

I gasped and whirled around, my face beaming. "That's wonderful! How did you reach that decision?"

"Something changed when Sylvanus admitted to stabbing Oliver. I had always thought I would be capable of violence if it ever became necessary, and it would certainly be necessary during the course of a war. But I realized that I never want to know what the willingness to kill feels like. Of course I was angry beyond words when I heard that Oliver had hurt Prissy, but I never felt the urge to kill him. It frightened me to realize how much hate must exist before violence can ensue."

"I'm glad you've come to that decision. Father needs you here, especially now that Sylvanus will be leaving."

"I do not want to leave the inn and the farm. I never did want to leave, but now there will be no leaving. I still do not believe I belong in the Society of Friends and I still want to play the fiddle in the tavern, but those things are for a later time. Our family needs time to restore a semblance of normal life before I can think about making any big decisions."

I smiled at him. I would be sorry to see Sylvanus leave, but it was heartening to know Jesse would be staying at home with us.

That night Elijah came to the tavern. As usual, he asked Prissy for his cider even though I was standing right in front of him. I seethed with anger, embarrassed by my thought, so recently, that Elijah might be more cordial to me now. Jesse came and clapped him on the back and the two men shared a hearty handshake. They spoke in low voices and I saw Jesse glance in my direction.

I could not abide being the subject of their whispered conversation, and I determined to speak to Jesse in no uncertain terms about it later, after the tavern closed. I stalked from the room and waited in the back room until my embarrassment subsided. After several minutes, Prissy came to find me. She beckoned me back into the tavern.

"I do not wish to be in there right now, Pris. Can you get the men their drinks for now? Father and Jesse will help you."

She shook her head and took my hand in hers. I sighed and followed her reluctantly into the tavern. Jesse was standing behind the counter, pouring cider for a patron, and Elijah stood opposite him in front of the counter. As soon as Jesse finished pouring the cider, he went into the back room. Prissy followed him.

I clenched my teeth. How dare they do this to me?

"Etta, I wonder if you might pour me another cider," Elijah said. He held his mug out to me.

I am afraid I snatched it out of his hand a bit too roughly, for he looked taken aback.

"My apologies," I murmured.

"It is quite all right." He waited while I poured.

I handed him the mug, filled to the brim with the cider.

"Um, er …" He sighed. "As I'm sure you know, my mother is in charge of the Women's Relief Society. She thought you might be interested in joining."

I felt an incongruous mixture of feelings. Part of me was thrilled at the prospect of joining the Relief Society. I had wanted to join for so long. But I confess, another part of me was disappointed by Elijah's words. I did not know what I had expected, but that wasn't it.

Just a moment later Jesse came up behind me. "Did you ask her?" he asked Elijah.

Elijah shook his head, his face a flaming red.

"Well, ask her, man!" Jesse laughed.

Elijah took a deep breath. "Etta, my mother really does want you to join the Relief Society. But what I actually meant to say was, there is an autumn party and bonfire to be held in Romney Marsh on Wednesday next, following Court Day. I ... well, I ... I wonder if you would like to go. With me."

I felt an odd warmth at hearing his words, though I was quite surprised. I must have stared a bit too long before answering, because he hastened to add, "Of course, I would understand completely if you wish not to go. With me."

"But why?" I blurted out. It worried me that my mouth could say words before my brain could stop it.

It was as if Elijah had no idea what I was asking. He turned this way and that, looking for something or someone.

Jesse burst into laughter. "Why? Why indeed? Because he talks of no one but you and in order to get him to stop, I had to insist that he ask you to the autumn party."

I looked at Elijah in surprise, and he nodded.

"But why haven't you spoken to me before now?"

"I am afraid I am rather tongue-tied around you." His cheeks flamed pink.

Jesse was beaming and Prissy had joined him beside me at the counter. Even Father appeared behind Prissy, apparently eager to hear what I might say to Elijah.

"Well, then, I think I might like that." I could feel myself blushing under the attention from Elijah and from my family.

"I think I will like it, too." Elijah nodded to me and returned to his seat among our neighbors.

Prissy squeezed my hand and I felt a sudden wish to tell Mother what had happened.

I had been wrong about almost everyone—about Abel, Thomas, and even Isaac and my brothers. And now it seemed I had been wrong about Elijah, too, but in the most pleasing of ways.

AUTHOR'S NOTE

As with *Cape Menace*, the first book in the Cape May Historical Mystery Collection, I have taken some creative liberties with this story. Perhaps the most obvious is the use of language, which in 1777 would have sounded quite formal to our modern ears. For the sake of clarity, I have chosen to use language that is more familiar to a twenty-first century reader.

As I noted in the Preface, as early as 1736 there was an inn or tavern on the site where the Rutledge family lives. Little is known about the original tavern, which was likely established to provide food, drink, and lodging to ferry travelers. I have constructed the inn and tavern in *A Traitor Among Us* to meet the needs of the story.

Much of Stites Point was farmland in the eighteenth century, and most of the details in the story remain consistent with the agricultural economy of the area. I do not know whether the owners of the original hostelry in Stites Point were also farmers, but it is certainly a possibility. Throughout history, it has not been uncommon for rural tavern keepers to supplement their livelihoods by farming.

One of the book's turning points takes place when Etta uses

the cannon on the Rutledge property to repel a party of British soldiers. This scene is based on the legend of Rebecca Stillwell, a young woman who lived in Stites Point at the time of the American Revolution. As the story goes, Rebecca, using a cannon which sat near the shoreline, turned back a party of British marauders making their way across Great Egg Harbor Bay with the intention of raiding the inn. They planned to reclaim property, mostly clothing and food, which had been captured from the British army by Cape May County privateers.

I hope you've enjoyed *A Traitor Among Us: A Cape May Historical Mystery* and I hope you'll consider leaving a review online (any book retailer is a great place to start, but you can also post reviews on Goodreads, BookBub, and many other sites). Reviews are essential for authors because they increase a book's visibility in bookstores and in online marketplaces.

Writing a review is easy—all you need to do is jot down a sentence or two telling others why you enjoyed the book. If you need some ideas to help you get started, consider the following questions:

Which character was your favorite?

What scene did you like the best?

Did you learn anything about the late eighteenth century? The American Revolution? The New Jersey colony?

Who else do you think would enjoy the book?

Remember, the best way to help an author is to leave a review and tell someone about the book!

NEWSLETTER SIGN-UP

Please visit https://www.amymreade.com/join-the-newsletter to receive monthly news, updates, promotions, contests, recipes, and more.

ABOUT THE AUTHOR

Amy M. Reade is the *USA Today* and *Wall Street Journal* bestselling author of cozy, historical, and Gothic mysteries.

A former practicing attorney, Amy discovered a passion for fiction writing and has never looked back. She is the author of three standalone mysteries, the Malice Series of Gothic mysteries, the Juniper Junction Cozy Holiday Mystery Series, the Cape May Historical Mystery Collection, and the Libraries of the World Mystery Series.

In addition to writing, Amy loves to read, cook, and travel. She lives in New Jersey and is a member of Mystery Writers of America and Sisters in Crime.

You can find out more on Amy's website at https://www.amymreade.com.